1853 - LOS ANGELES GANGS

1853 - LOS ANGELES GANGS

By

Steve W. Knight

1stBooks - rev. 6/06/00

About The Book

Three men who want to rape his good-looking date. Rustlers who murder women and children. Ute Indians working with white men to steal cattle and horses. A murdering gang leader with 160 men. Just a few of the dilemmas protagonist Horace Bell (22) must face as a volunteer Los Angeles ranger. Can the rangers protect and serve their neighbors? Or will the criminals overthrow the town's 100-man force?

A notorious criminal, antagonist Juan Flores, eludes the rangers from the beginning.

Based on a true and exciting story you, the reader, are shown a word picture of Southern California life 150 years ago when the pueblo de Los Angeles supported only 1600 people. Horace Bell's sidekick is Roy Bean, a colorful character and later Texas judge. In the middle of the story are two major battles, one genuinely caused by a county official.

Meantime, Horace studies law and educates himself into the "semi-gringo" culture of the Mexican-Americans who dominate the pueblo de Los Angeles. Written with humor and sagacity, the story shows hidden Los Angeles history. Immense ranchos, which today hold 400,000 homes each, are taken away by different means from their owners. We now can learn a timely message from their individual mistakes. We can also discover insight into the way our forefathers handled their criminal problems.

Acknowledgments

Elizabeth B. Knight, my wife, my editor, my proof reader, my mentor, and my partner. Her summa cum laude from the University of Alabama is evident.

Susan Mary Malone, who taught me novel writing 101 as my first professional editor.

Max Hurlbut, a retired LAPD supervisor who exhibited enthusiasm and assistance for the project.

Joe Koenig, my first reader who gave me years of encouragement.

Ray Strait, a professional writer who made good suggestions.

Los Angeles County Sheriff's Relief supervisor Jack Kuner who assisted with rare records. Los Angeles County Sheriff's Museum who keeps a copy of my badge history ready for any researchers. Dawson's Book Store who handles rare books and maps.

Dedication

To the fearless men and women who have ever worn a badge in the Golden State of California. Congratulation, California, on your 150 year anniversary.

Preface

100,000 miners flooded into California from 1848 to 1849. Separate races, diverse languages, different religious and moral beliefs were all represented. Each wanted to strike it rich and leave. Most were lucky enough to barely cover their food expenses. After they left the Northern mining areas they made Los Angeles a popular stopping place on their way home again. Many stayed in Southern California for the climate; many tried to get wealth illegally.

By 1851 San Francisco possessed vigilantes; 6,000 of them who hanged anybody they did not like. Los Angeles, being much smaller in population, chose to commission 100 men from their judges, attorneys, and ex-Texas Rangers, to be their Volunteer Mounted Police Force. These volunteers changed their name to the Los Angeles Rangers in 1853.

This story is about them. Those Brave men who protected the pueblo de Los Angeles and its 1600 citizens. The day after they were appointed, on July 13, 1851, they each took an oath of vigilance. They were then licensed to kill. A power they used from time to time.

Forward

I was born in Los Angeles City, and when I was six years old we moved to a suburb called Santa Fe Springs. My father, and his brother across the street, were Los Angeles motorcycle policemen. My grandfather wore a deputy sheriff's uniform and worked in the San Antonio Superior Courts in Huntington Park. The fifties were a wonder for an adolescent to behold. Orange trees by the thousands were removed to make way for homes. The only rural thing undisturbed was the San Gabriel River which was our get-a-way place to explore.

Fifteen years later I graduated from the Los Angeles Police Academy. Times had indeed changed. By then the recent 1965 Watts Riots showed that society was in flux. The general populous wanted the police to change their methods in the way they approached the public. They demanded it. From then on the citizens desired more power to govern their local Southern California law enforcement agencies.

A few years later I entered the Los Angeles Marshal's Department. Therein I started a lifetime historical study of Southern California. All the Spanish names had always intrigued me. When I attained my first real estate license and found the huge "ranchos" on the early maps I was hooked.

I wondered why so many Hispanic people had not retained ownership of those huge pieces of land. During the following twenty-five years, I earned three business degrees and purchased a number of rare book on Los Angeles. The historical real estate interest then led me into old police stories. I was fascinated by the way the pioneers looked at criminals. Using my background and comparing my grandfather's feelings to my father and his brother's, I visualized a pattern. A subtle one, but it was there, none the less.

Knowing that police work is accomplished by tradition, I was able to think backward in time and write this book. When I discovered why the 100 Los Angeles Mounted Police Volunteers were appointed -- I laughed. As part of this story you will probably smile also. I decided to put down on paper this marvelous story of the Los Angeles beginnings almost ten years ago. This is my humble rendition.

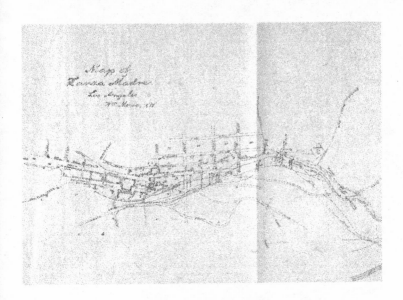

1868 L.A. Pueblo Map

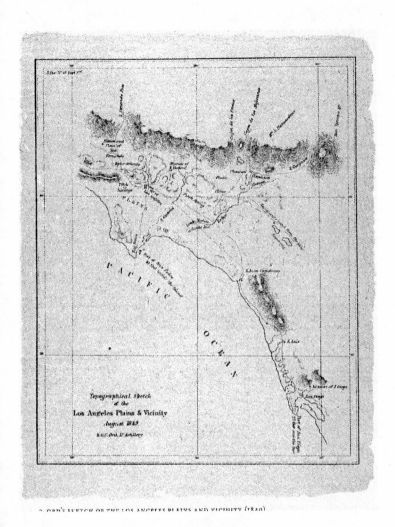

ORD'S SKETCH OF THE LOS ANGELES PLAINS AND VICINITY (1849)

1849 Southern California

Chapter 1

Bong-bong! Bong-bong! Bong-bong! Bong-bong! The alarm from the large brass church bell summoning all on-duty Northern California Rangers to dress and saddle awakened Horace Bell.

The first double-bong roused him, and then he counted two more, knowing that meant general quarters. Sliding on his boots, he cursed his six-foot three-inch frame as he hit the top of the tent pole. Looking out at the darkness, he remarked to the ranger next to him, "Damn, Davis, it must be four in the morning." Only a fool would like police work.

"Sure enough, Horace, and it's about thirty degrees," Davis said as he frowned.

Horace laughed at Davis's hate of the cold.

"Maybe, Horace, this is that damnable Juan Flores that we need to hang."

If so, he'd be dead. Payback time!

Mounting up, Horace noticed a full complement of two ten-man squads ready to ride full saddle under Captain Harry Love. Love had been given permission by the State of California to annihilate as many criminals and gangs as he could with the newly organized California rangers, a volunteer mounted police group in the Northern California mining area. The permission came after-the-fact that the State of California Legislature made into law.

The armed men kicked their horses into a gallop down toward Sutter Creek, where the murders happened hours before. The road was still half-frozen from the nightfall. The hooves crunched into the unmelted water.

Wind side drafts cut into his skin. His ears must be bright red. He threw a dark woolen scarf around his neck. Wow, and he thought the Midwest to be a cold son of a bitch.

He mulled leaving Indiana two years before with Paul, his boyhood friend. At nineteen they escaped farm life for gold and adventure. They spoke of how rich they would become. Sure, right? Now living near aptly named Hangtown, California, his

1

gold diggings' net worth amounted to three hundred dollars after two years in the streams rubbing elbows and sweating with the rot-gut of humanity. Criminals from the four corners of the earth worked the same streams at the same time. Anyway, it was more fun hunting them down than working with them. These rangers were straight guys.

Riding twenty miles with the platoon gave him time to think. His massive horse, Pal, carried his one hundred and eighty pounds as if it were a sack of feathers.

"Corporal Bell I wish Paul were riding with us," a trooper said.

"Yup, I do too," Horace remarked.

"He's gonna miss a good fight."

"Paul loved a good fight almost as much as I do."

A recent offer kept tripping him up. Okay, so he knew he was directionless, but hell, he was only twenty-one. Uncle Alex Bell's letter from small Los Angeles offered him room and board for three years giving him the time to study and pass the Bar as an attorney. He needed to answer the letter soon. Uncle Alex loved a fight too.

Uncle Alex was a ship's captain importing and exporting items to Los Angeles's small harbor. He was very successful, having built one of only three two-story homes in the pueblo. With many rooms, the letter said. As a boy in Indiana, Horace had been home-schooled by his father, who had a Harvard Degree in ministry and law. Horace, being a rebel, decided the gold fields offered more fun than getting behind a plow. California had beckoned like a magnet.

Alex also encouraged Horace to start a newspaper. Horace bit his lower lip. He'd mentioned to his uncle once in passing his desires to be both a lawyer and journalist. Uncle Alex didn't miss a lick.

His wise uncle didn't forget to mention Horace's additional need to study the Spanish culture for his "political good," playing into Horace's proclivity toward outspokenness.

How could he give up the northern California rangers? He loved the excitement and thrill of matching wits and strength in a gunfight. And what about his ranger buddies? The volunteer

2

job fit him like a glove with his mix of humor and courage.

Alex's letter briefly mentioned Los Angeles had the only other group of rangers in the state. With the possibility of working into the Southern California group, Horace decided.

"Yup, Pal, it's off to the Pueblo de Los Angeles when I get back from evening up the score," he said to his horse.

Riding hard, the rangers made Sutter Creek in an hour and a half. The town mayor, James Bentley, dressed in local miner's garb, met them.

"About four hours ago, a small gang of nine no-good Mexicans raided a camp of Chinese miners, kilt three of 'em, wounded two," the mayor said. "One understood English. He pointed south -- toward Jackson City."

"Oh, yeah," the mayor continued, stroking his two-day-old beard stubble. "Apparently the leader rode a big, sixteen-hand black stallion with a saddle full of silver trappings."

Captain Harry Love rubbed his grey-brown beard and said, "Guess we'll know that fellow when we see him, right, men?" They nodded.

"Let's find 'em," Horace said.

"Corporal Bell, you take Jimmy the Tracker. Williams, Davis, and Thompson, go to the camp and track them out so they don't double-back on us."

"Bell makes corporal and we lose rangers," a trooper grumbled.

Horace ignored the remark. He knew he'd saved other lives by his actions.

"Right, sir," Horace answered.

Sergeant Pete Johnson raised up his beefy arm. "Listen up, Bell. If'n ya hear shootin', watch out fer an ambush."

"Sure enough, Sergeant," Horace answered.

"Onward, men!" the captain shouted.

Horace and his four men assisted Jimmy the Tracker. First the men found the Chinese camp. The Chinese miners also pointed toward Jackson City. The Mexican and White miners didn't care much for the Chinese. They pegged the Mongolians as inferior with their pagan religious beliefs. Besides, the Chinese took the Caucasians' part of the gold from the hills.

3

Posses never overexerted themselves capturing criminals when the victims were Chinese. But by God, they'd chase them to Mexico if they killed White settlers.

Horace felt sorry for any victim. He often liked the minorities more than the White mining majority. Even though Mexicans were Caucasians, the White miners considered them inferior. The Mexicans, Chinese, and blacks who worked the mines seemed more humble and gentle than the White miners. The Anglo-Saxons were caustic and bad-tempered. They were just an impatient, angry group.

"Probably just greed and envy," he told Pal, who snorted. White steam came from the horse's flared nostrils. Horace laughed.

Jimmy the Tracker could track anybody over anything except rock and water. The four rangers followed Jimmy out of the Chinese murder scene onto a back trail which led toward the main dirt road to Jackson City. They followed it for about four miles. Then Jimmy jumped off his horse.

"See something, Jimmy?"

"Yup, Corporal. I know something you don't."

"Go ahead, jimmy."

"We thinks they's going that way," he said pointing.

"But, here they did a double-back. Here's where those scallywags jumped off the trail into the light brush." Jimmy's eyes darted back and forth and his voice shook.

"Men, be aware. We might be in the middle of an ambush -- and outnumbered," Horace said. A cold sweat dotted his lineless brow. Were they now the hunted?

Jimmy closely examined every patch of earth, tree, and brush. Horace watched Jimmy getting more reluctant each step. Something must be wrong.

Jimmy to smile after about a quarter mile of tracking off-trail. "Corporal, these men are doing the opposite, tricky bastards. They're going toward Sacramento, not Jackson City!"

Horace thought quickly. He must first follow orders.

"Okay. Will and Thompson, ride and report to the captain as soon as you catch up with him. Davis, Jimmy, and I, we'll go back to Sutter Creek and tell the mayor what we found and that the gang is taking the road to Sacramento. Ride!" Horace said.

"Corporal, ain't this Flores the same scoundrel who got you the stripes?" the tracker asked.

"Yes, Jimmy, I saved the captain and Rogers, but lost my partner Paul with Andrews," Horace said, stroking his day-old stubble.

"Don't worry, Corporal, you'll get another chance," the tracker said, his fists clenched.

His and Jimmy's eyes met. The gang had outsmarted the rangers. Horace needed six more men to pursue them. In Hangtown, Flores' horse had worn silver trappings. His horse made the same track. Yes, This was the same Flores they were tracking. Horace's bullets missed then. Juan Flores would get away again. He didn't like being outnumbered and at the same time have to report per regulations. Frustration filled his soul. He remembered his vow to Paul as he lay dying in his arms.

"I promise you, Paul, I'll kill that damn Flores, I'll get him for you."

Mad both at the outlaws and his situation, pure logic made him respect his enemy.

Chapter 2

As the rangers separated below him, Juan Flores frowned. His beady eyes darted to double-check he could move forward toward Sacramento. Silver trappings lightly jingled on his mounted majestic black horse, a prize possession thanks to highjacked gold. His neck twitched nervously to the right.

"We've saved our asses, amigos. We'd better head south, they got too many damned rangers, and it ain't fun no more," Flores said.

"El Capitan, you're right, those rangers you killed in Hangtown are now haunting us," Francisco Poncho Daniels said, his dark brown eyes glaring back down below.

Flores nodded. Daniels was one true gang member. Flores watched Daniels smile back at him.

"Let's go, they ain't followin' us," Flores said as he led eight men down the steep mountain. The thick short trees made it necessary to follow single file. Flores guided the troupe around the brown, dead ones. Yes, the green ones made it impossible to see eighty feet straight. Decayed yellow-brown pine cones and needles popped and crunched from the horses' hooves. Crisp morning air made the mountain ride refreshing. Flores could see the horses' nostrils blowing out each breath. God how he missed warm southern California.

A cold chill ran through Juan Flores' back. He had to make a change. Four startled deer ran from the nine horsemen crossing their untouched domain. Flores raised his revolver to shoot one for meat, then changed his mind. They would love the meat, but the gunshot might give their position. This was crap always running. Always hungry, and always damn cold. If he saw one pine he saw a thousand. So damn many pines. His neck twitched back to the right. Pine cones, pine needles, pine trees, pine smell, and pine crap.

Juan Flores pulled his big black mare's reins to guide her. His weight was easy for her to handle. Frozen snot formed on his handlebar moustache. He remembered his wife pulling it and teasing him, but that was three years ago. They left Mexico to get rich. Their mining hometown Capala was tapped out, old Capala where his ancestors mined all the way back till sixteen-something. His grandfather taught him about gold. He sure felt the lack of old Papa, his old Papa. His dad ran off at his birth. Guess he didn't love him.

The ride from Mazatlan to northern California had been long and arduous. They'd still had fun. Once in a while he'd been aggravated when she pulled his moustache. Damn it, he wished she could pull it now. Teresa, his dead wife, was the love he missed. He buried her with his unborn son.

He'd flipped and gone crazy afterwards. He wanted to kill everyone. Frustration made his insides feel like a Baja hurricane, everything blowing around inside his head. He lost it all, he had nothing more. The dark side -- revenge -- entertained his soul. He needed to kill back, get even. Who? Who? The Chinese were easy, so easy. The posses gave up quicker when the victims were pagan Mongolians.

So he'd left fifteen dead Chinamen. He'd littered the northern fields with blood revenge. Those two damn rangers. He'd started a gringo ranger war and pissed them off. They had him cornered. He'd just been playing monte at the saloon. There were all them damn rangers in the saloon, and he'd been nailed for card cheating. Ah, all them damn rangers. Must have been six of them. He'd gotten a few, scared a few, and escaped from one.

Chinese gold filled Flores' saddlebags. He would stop in Sacramento and get in a game or two. Plus he could get laid. His scary, dark beady eyes looked forward to the destination. Flores had big plans for his small five-foot eight-inch stature.

Chapter 3

The salt sea spray hit Horace's face. Heading toward Los Angeles, he already missed the rangers but not the cold mountains. With his pouch full of gold, he looked every inch the gallant cowboy trying out a new life.

The Seabird, a fifty-foot steamship, traveled up and down the Pacific Coast. Horace easily made friends on board. Naturally gregarious, without hesitation he assisted Captain Salisbury Haley doing ship chores on the five-day trip down the coast. His friendship with Captain Haley grew by sharing stories and learning about the captain's brother, one of the other four steamer ship's captains. A big stubby fellow with a red face, Captain Haley was full of the gab. He mentioned that it might take a day longer because he wanted to drink "a little" at San Luis Obispo. Horace stopped himself from saying anything. That was a first.

He attentively listened to the passengers talk to one another, having been taught by his mother that listening to others was a wonderful way to learn. His big mouth got him into problems. Being honest simply pissed people off. Nineteen other passengers were on board. Horace made friends with Don Benjamin "Benito" Wilson, the Los Angeles mayor. The mayor seemed to like him. Horace listened as the mayor talked to another man. Wilson mentioned that the rangers in Los Angeles were a cohesive group that fought the criminal element. Horace couldn't understand why he didn't open his big mouth and ask questions. Caution was better than rushing in. He didn't need to screw up his new home.

Passenger Alexander Nelson, with his two Hardy Boys, was talkative. Nelson brought a thoroughbred horse and planned to enter it into a race with Sepulveda's famous big black horse once they reached the Los Angeles Pueblo. Stakes were in the thousands. Seeing the well-groomed, shiny red horse made Horace miss Pal. He became melancholy. He would never sell another horse, ever. Once in the Pueblo de Los Angeles, he would find another Pal.

Horace learned from the mayor about pueblo life. Even the mayor as an American picked up quickly on the pastoral Spanish lifestyle. The culture combined a simple elegance with honor, goodwill, hospitality, and honesty. The mayor had married a Dona, thereby giving him land and title. Now he was a Don, owning a rancho and a pueblo general store. He told Horace the Americans loved the Spanish dances, games, and food. The Spanish possessed a playful heritage against the serious American work ethic. "Horace, my son, the whole damn town is going semi-gringo. It's a hell of a mixture," Don Wilson said.

The travel invigorated Horace, and he watched another steamboat going north. Captain Haley said the ships made up their own schedules. These so-called schedules depended upon where the captains wanted to spend their drinking and gambling nights. Horace also learned many a man fell overboard with fifty pounds of gold, never to be seen again. "The gold took 'em to Davy Jones' locker, ha, ha," Haley chuckled, his barnacled face all cracked. His face showed his darker side; he was glad gold greed got them and not him. Captain Haley wouldn't mind the gold, but he didn't like the drowning.

Poor seamanship or hitting a sandbar sank many a ship. The captain said one went down blowing a newfangled boiler. There were many hazards between San Francisco and the Panama overcrossing. Horace knew the California roads were mere dirt trails. These steamer ships had replaced sailing ships. Horace pondered what would replace the steamers.

Horace and Captain Haley had several things in common, one of which was an interest in law. Captain Haley studied law when he was sober, and on this particular day he was four days sober on their way into the L.A.-San Pedro Harbor. Haley and Horace passed time debating the difference in real estate law between California's community property law and Indiana's title state law.

On the way into San Pedro, a balmy south blowing wind made the day around ninety degrees. Horace found the semi-arid desert climate quite different. Haley put in his anchor and started loading his passengers into the harbor dinghy, an oversized rowboat. The rowboat took ten passengers at a time to the makeshift pier. Wilson pointed out Dead Man's Island where the Los Angelenos had buried the dead Americans in the recent Mexican-American War.

Horace's head still rocked when his legs hit dry land. He wanted to kiss the ground. He now changed his mind regarding sea travel -- the fish could have it, salt spray and all. He remembered an old saying, "After three days in the open air, fish started to really stink."

Once ashore and off the dinghy, all twenty passengers faced a stressful trip by two open-air stages for service into the pueblo. These stages were old army ambulances, hard, flat, and providing no coverings. The backs where the passengers sat were plain, flat boards with ropes to hold onto to keep from being thrown out during the ride. Splinters jutted out from the seats. Attached to each stage, a vicious herd of mules snarled at the passengers. The two drivers looked as though they'd drunk half the ocean. Using every imaginable expletive, both held whiskey quarts and watched who'd be the fastest to guzzle it down. One driver kept pulling up his sailor cap after each swallow. He belched and chided, "You'll not win today, you landlubber son of a bitch!"

The other driver yelled, "Damn you to hell, swaby! Eat my dust!"

Three sweaty Mexicans guided each stage, one at the front and two at the sides. Each front Mexican had a rope on the two lead nasty mules, while the side Mexicans held whips to keep the mules on the twenty-two-mile-plus bumpy race course to the Bella Union Hotel.

"Git aboard, ladies and gents," hollered the stage owner, who introduced himself as Phineas Banning.

A man rode up and saluted Don Benjamin "Benito" Wilson. He wore a badge. "Mayor Don Wilson, caught ourselves four Mexican cutthroats for General Joshua Bean's murder! We'll have our confessions soon. The Vigilance Committee -- they're drillin' 'em night and day. Need your help as soon as you git in." The man turned around and galloped back toward the Pueblo de Los Angeles.

Banning placed on each stage three black bottles containing

11

what he called "refreshment," saying, "Gentlemen, there's no water between here and the pueblo. It gets real hot on the way in."

Horace grabbed the bottle, took a whiff, and said, "Phew! Smells like rotgut, salt water, and homemade whiskey!"

"Just piss 'n shit's all," said one of the drivers, who gave a big-belly drunken-sailor laugh. Horace made a face.

"All ready?" Banning yelled.

"Is there gonna be no bettin'?" grumbled the surly drivers. Horace's driver wore a tattered British naval uniform and a large gold earring, just like a pirate. Maybe he was one? The other driver wore ragged American naval garb. Horace surmised they were fighting the War of 1812 again. They looked that old, too, with their wrinkled sea faces.

Banning laughingly remarked to both sets of passengers the drivers liked to make the ride into town more interesting by betting against one another.

"I'll bet five dollars!" one fellow said.

"I'll see that," another said. "And who'll see me a fifty-dollar gold slug?"

"I'll take that!" Horace said, immediately knowing he'd been suckered. All this trip keeping his mouth shut and now he opened it? Real smart.

Soon all bets were covered. Banning cried out to the drivers, "Watch your helm! Let her drive!"

"Suelto carajo!" screamed the two front Mexican majordomos, and off the mules went.

They were in for the ride of their lives. The passengers held on for dear life while the Mexicans whipped the mules into tremendous bursts of speed. Splinters pierced their hands holding the open-stage sides so they wouldn't be thrown out. The drivers and their Mexican cohorts looked back and smiled in satisfaction at the scared gringos. Horace's hands were white and bare-knuckled as he held tight. Dust-choked, he became apprehensive. His ass had two splinters already. He didn't want to get thrown out. The pueblo was still a twenty-mile walk.

"Get outta my way, you stinkin', ass-smellin' swabby!" cursed one driver to the other. The cussing continued nonstop.

The men on the stage told the two women not to listen to the stage drivers. The women were shocked.

After a few miles, both stages slowed down. The male passengers encouraged the drivers to egg on the lazy mules and speed up again by offering immediate financial gain. Horace shook his head. What a racket. Then the drivers started to put up a real race.

A perfect set of lines marked the mules' rears from the Mexican <u>vaqueros</u>, who struck the same place each time. Horace liked the Mexican horsemanship and balance displayed.

The passengers, like maniacs, gripped the ropes. As bad as the ride was, it was better than walking. More splinters set into Horace's rear as the stage leapt airborne and then dropped hard four feet back down into the ground. Over and over he contemplated his love of thrills when he hated the pain. He was glad he'd relieved himself at the shoreline.

After thirty minutes, Horace knew his gold piece was history and figured the two drivers would split and drink it. Dust-eaten, sweaty, hot, and sick from the so-called refreshment, he decided to be a good sport and accept his loss. Next time he wouldn't be so patriotic. Then two other words crept in -- damn stupid.

From the road Horace first glimpsed the four-foot-high wild mustard grasses. Acres of their yellow tops forged a path to the pueblo.

An hour later, both stages hit L.A. at San Pedro Street. Horace looked behind and saw a pack of twenty stray dogs, some big blacks, some small browns. They looked underfed as they raced after the stages, their ribs showing their hunger. Horace mused if a stray passenger would become dog food.

These dogs pursued them as they lurched onto First Street. The stages made a sharp left turn and almost lost two passengers. They used the ropes to pull themselves back in and regain their precious seats.

Purplish green grape vines grew around the town. Plentiful vineyard stalks contrasted with the pale desert dirt. Horace saw a hundred white-washed adobes dotting the natural drab landscape. He'd come from the frozen north to hell in five days. Where was the water?

Still neck and neck, the stages raced until the one holding Don Wilson turned right onto Main Street. It hit a huge water ditch and lost a passenger in the process. He rolled across the street. Everyone laughed and pointed at him as the dogs jumped and bit at him, his hands flailing back and forth trying to avoid their teeth and jaws.

"Help me! Help me!" he yelled. The stage passengers then laughed even more. These 1853 pueblo pilgrims were cold-hearted.

Horace submitted and gave up the ghost for his fifty bucks. These drivers really were modern-day pirates. The rest of the passengers, mostly drunk by this time, were still laughing at the hapless, dumped, and drunk man fighting off twenty dogs and wallowing in the dirt and dust.

Don Wilson's stage, lighter by one, came first at the Bella Union Hotel. Horace lost. Probably wouldn't be the first money he'd lose there. He laughed.

The passengers, except Horace, with their bumps, bruises, and splinter cuts, went into the bar at the Bella Union to celebrate their survival.

Horace stepped out of the stage just outside the Bella Union, reached back, pulled at a remaining splinter which had not worked its way out, and looked around. The one-story Bella Union Hotel had a dirt floor, ten rooms to let, nine-by-nine feet, and thousands of fleas, just as described by Don "Benito" Wilson -- "The best hotel in Southern California."

The bar was the only thing which looked good to him. He couldn't drink right then. His stomach was green and his head spinning from the stage ride. He needed solid food. A week on the ocean and losing fifty bucks — no way Jose.

The Pueblo de Los Angeles wasn't much to look at with its twelve streets that criss-crossed. Only about fifty white, smooth adobes provided stark contrast to the town's few boardwalks. Only three two-storied adobes were visible downtown. One had to be Uncle Alex's casa. He had to be in the money.

"Cafe Bovierre" read the small sign which beckoned across the street. Horace entered the small, one-story, four-tabled establishment not expecting too much. He looked around quickly at the exceptionally clean, wooden-floored room with its white lace curtains. The cooking aroma knocked his socks off. The restaurant smelled of baked pork, chicken and beef with spices he'd never smelled before -- hot spices, or maybe French spices he'd heard about. He didn't care. Hearty food would calm his rocky legs and stage-sick stomach.

A stunning woman met him at the door. Five-foot-seven, in her middle twenties, she had beautiful light brown hair and a captivating smile. All of a sudden Los Angeles looked pretty. She twisted her long hair with her slender fingers and eyed him up and down. Who was checking out whom? Gosh she was a dish. He almost blubbered all over himself. He had to keep his demeanor, cold like the local pilgrims but gregarious like himself.

"Hi. I'm Horace Bell. Just risked my life to get here." He put his hat on the white linen table cloth. She laughed, causing her green emerald eyes to sparkle.

"Oui -- I know. I watch when people get off the stages. It's little excitement we have close by," she said in a light French accent. "Oh, I'm sorry, my name is Miss Paulette Bovierre, but you can call me Paulette." Three p.m. and the café was empty. Good, real good.

"Okay. Miss Paulette, is it?" he inquired.

"Merci, oui, my little -- what did you call -- Mr. Horace Bell. Oh. I -- perhaps you're related to Captain Alexander Bell?"

"Yes. He's my uncle," he said, sitting down. "So now that's settled, what's on for early -- hearty supper?"

"My specialty is a local favorite called Chili Colorado." She smiled at him.

He frowned. "What's that exactly?"

Again she laughed, and he laughed with her.

"It is large, fresh pieces of beef with a special   Mexican sauce that is delicious. It also comes with my special refried Mexican beans, great rice from chicken broth, and homemade corn tortillas." She stood next to him with her hands on her rounded hips so her slim waist and ample bustline were accentuated. "It will melt in your mouth."

"Serve 'em up, Miss Paulette Bovierre," said Horace.   "I

could eat one of those wet mules out there right now." He smiled and rubbed his brown hair back.

"On its way."

Horace watched her walk into the kitchen. What a handsome body on the young woman. Looked a lot better than those whores at the camps. Wow.

Since they were getting along well, Horace walked back to her kitchen and asked if she could give him a small background of the city. He didn't want to seem too pushy, but...

"Most of the town has grown from the plaza, which was moved twice because of river flooding, each time to find higher ground away from the river," she explained, gesturing rapidly with her delicate, though capable, hands. "Presently sixteen hundred people now call the pueblo home. Only my place and one other restaurant in town have a wood floor. With the desert heat here, we open opposite doors for ventilation."

He hovered over her narrow shoulders to watch her prepare the food. "Are there any big problems here?"

"Oui, like I mentioned, water is our main problem. Citizens have one water ditch called <u>Zanza Madre</u>, or 'Water Mother' in English. The ditch slows to a trickle in the summer. You crossed it just before your right-hand turn onto Main Street."

He nodded and laughed. "Yes, that bump catapulted the passenger to the dogs!"

She laughed as well, tossing her silky hair. He felt at home already. She rolled her eyes at him. He didn't miss that. He might get lucky.

"Oui, every horse, wagon, person, and barefoot Indian crosses the <u>Zanja Madre</u>. I pay a man to go far upstream to gather clean water in a fifty-gallon, empty wine keg."

"How about crime?" Horace asked, using his hand to rub his unruly hair down.

Paulette picked up a plateful of food and motioned him to follow. "Sit down here, please, Mr. Bell," she said.

Horace took a chair and started eating immediately. The beef had a red hot sauce to die for; sweet yet hot and spicy. The delicious rice and corn tortillas complemented the main dish. The tantalizing aromas quickly made Horace a Bovierre Mexican

16

food lover.

"That is problem number two," she frowned. "About a murder a day occurs on Calle De Los Negros, two blocks away. The Americans call it 'Nigger Alley'," she said matter of fact. Then she rolled her emerald eyes at him again. What pretty eyes. He was in love. Maybe not real love. Call it lust. Love later.

"Whoa, a murder a day? Not even two thousand live here. How can ...."

"Oui. Look, Mr. Bell — Horace -- into town every day come recent ex-miners, ne'er-do-wells, and riffraff. They are the one murdered, as you say." She smiled.

He nodded. "Gotcha. The men try to make a killing at the card tables and get killed." What a brain. Maybe she'd fall in love.

She ignored his answer and changed the subject.

"Would you like some hot salsa?"

"What's that?" he answered with a question, realizing she'd missed his brain power.

"A hot-type sauce made with tomatoes and chilies. Quite tasty."

"Good, Yup, please. Just city crime?" The marshal at the harbor could handle that.

She poured salsa over his dish. He bit into it and drank water fast. His mouth was on fire. What the hell did these folks eat?

She shook her head, her sunlit hair brushing from one shoulder to the other. Horace noticed its light red tint.

"Use salt from the shaker. It puts the fire out." Fire hell. His mouth felt like blisters were forming and his whole damn mouth would swell shut.

"No, not just city crime. There are many gangs, Indians, and mean men -- rustlers, murderers... the rangers chase them down," she said.

"Interesting," he said. "Do you know any of these rangers?"

"Oui, they come here for meetings. Would you like to meet them?"

He cleared his throat and rubbed his head. His hair was still

17

a mess, his clothes looked like he'd taken a bath in dirt, and he was on the make? Wonderful.

"Gosh. Could you set that up?"

"Oui, sure, Mr. Horace Bell. Come back tonight around seven p.m., and I will personally introduce you to Mr. Hope, the captain."

"You're as pretty as the small red roses that adorn your tables. I'll be back. And thanks," he said smiling, then flashing his lady-killer eyes at her. He was sure she'd missed the effect.

"Oui, it is nothing for such a large, tall man," she said, flirting back. Maybe not? She was sure pert, and pretty. Gosh, he was in love -- or lust again. He finished and paid.

"Miss Paulette, tonight seven p.m. sharp."

So she was a year or two older, maybe a little more. No matter. He was sure the town didn't have much to offer her in the way of men. Maybe he was the hottest thing going. He doubted it.

Chapter 4

Horace walked out onto the dirt street. The pueblo's streets were full of old, sun-cracked animal bones. Five stray dogs fought over them. A block away an old Indian was carving up a dead horse. Horace walked by and grabbed his nose. Phew! By its putrid stink and the squirming maggots, he could tell the horse had been dead a week. Gosh, eating decomposed horsemeat, worms and all. Horace prayed the Indian would cook it. Sorry life being poor. Just what he needed after an ocean trip.

People walked up and down this main dirt street, Calle Principal, or Main Street. Everything was in Spanish. Everything which looked good was French. The city newspaper at the café was in Spanish. Everyone talked in Spanish on the street. Horace was in semi-gringo culture shock. He had to learn the language. His uncle forgot to mention -- perhaps conveniently left out -- the necessity of learning Spanish. Maybe Uncle Alex wanted Horace to be the son he'd never possessed. That was fine. Besides, the weather in the pueblo was good.

The city reportedly had the best weather in America, with the temperature about seventy degrees all year. That didn't mean it stayed that way every day, his Uncle Alex had written. Rare days it got as low as thirty-five, and few summer days it topped one hundred. But the weather sure beat the freezing cold mountains up north.

His uncle's letter said: "Day in and day out this little city is starting into a dramatic growth cycle," and he'd wanted the younger Bell to grow with the city. Horace grinned. The Los Angeles Pueblo looked like his kind of place. Location, location, location.

As he walked to the Bella Union Hotel to pick up his traveling bag, Miss Paulette's emerald green eyes and her slim waist popped into his mind. Wasn't love grand?

He walked the three quick blocks to his uncle's home. "Casa Bell," a small tile, hand-painted sign read, each letter surrounded by flowers. This would be his home for years. He knocked, and a beautiful lady with her dark hair up in a Spanish bun answered with a tall man behind her. The man looked just like Horace's preacher father.

"Uncle Alex? Aunt Bell?" Horace inquired.

"Haven't seen you in ten years, lad! My, you're even taller than I," his uncle said, hugging him hard and shaking his hand. Good. This was the welcome he wanted.

"This, my dear nephew, is your Aunt, Mrs. Teresa Bell." She was forty-something with black hair, short and petite, with warm brown eyes that welcomed him.

Horace stuck out his hand. "Glad to meet you."

"Come in, mi son. Bring your things. This is your home now," she said with a Spanish accent.

The home, three thousand square feet, had three-foot walls on the outside; two-foot-thick walls in each room, three bedrooms; a dining room; a study; the sala, or great room; the storage area; a kitchen; and outside, a large barn for the horses. Deep orange-, green-, and rust-colored decorations abounded among the dark, sizeable Spanish furniture. The sala contained a heavy Spanish piano, couches and tables, and huge tapestries hanging from the walls. Horace found it quite different than Indiana. The smell had to come from the cattle lard burning in the lamps. All furnishings were imported from Europe. Home looked like heaven compared to the cold, damp, muddy tents which had been his domain.

His uncle told him he'd built the home eight years prior. General Fremont confiscated it as his headquarters during the recent war. After the treaty was signed, Uncle Alex told him to "git the hell out." Horace could see he came from strong character -- the Bell heritage.

His room upstairs came with feather bed and book shelves. Five law books were neatly arranged on one shelf, with four empty shelves for growth, and in the corner was a desk complete with candles and oil lamps. Perfect. The best feature was a balcony with a chair that overlooked the infamous Nigger Alley. Uncle Alex told him to "Git used to the noise!"

He looked down at the Nigger Alley businesses. The vice establishments were flat-topped with overhangs that covered the wooden sidewalk. Twenty-four doors opened into the twelve businesses. Two saloons beckoned customers inside the swinging half-bar doors. The entire Alley with its weather-beaten wood stood in contrast with its white adobe neighbors. The Alley's gambling, drinking, and whoring carried on just two blocks from the tall white steeple of the Catholic Church. Both the Alley and the church were near the same age.

The exciting street sounds were music to Horace's restless soul. Now he possessed a front row, upstairs seat. Soon he'd be ready to walk into those twelve vice dens. Maybe the whores were good-lookin'.

His uncle told him he could borrow any horse he liked. That word "borrow" meant something to him. He'd never been a freeloader. He picked a large brown mare who could handle his weight. He put on a saddle and bridled her, then started a city tour.

He wondered how Nelson was coming with his horse race. Uncle Alex said Judge Sepulveda's black stallion was undefeated. Taking his horse south on Los Angeles Street, he passed over the Madre Zanja, the dirty water ditch. Horace vowed to at least do one thing for the family -- get some clean water upstream, way upstream far and away from the filth.

By Second Street the pueblo was pretty rural. To the south only five homes were visible for miles, a flat land unsettled, beautiful, and quiet. Then he heard loud cheers. A hundred souls converged at the race to his right at Second and Main streets. In one group were maybe thirty well-dressed male and female citizens, in another twenty decked-out gamblers, and thirty worked-out miners in another area. Twenty Mexican and Indian <u>vaqueros</u> yelled and clapped. Some men still were taking bets, probably hedging on their wrong guess to begin with. One fancy gambler yelled out, "Make it ten in a row, ye Old Sepulveda, ye black bastard!"

The Hardy boys' heads hung low and Nelson kept wiping his eyes. Nelson looked worried and said, "Looks like you boys might have to work to git us passage home."

Well, they'd made their bed, and they'd have to sleep in it. Yup, they'd brought in that horse and hadn't even given him a

21

chance to get his sea legs back to the ground. Poor Pal. It broke his heart to have to sell him. Pal's shipping price was ten times his passage. He'd sold Pal for fifty dollars to a fellow who loved the gelding. "Sorry, old Pal," he said looking at his borrowed mare.

Judge Sepulveda's monster black horse outdistanced the red thoroughbred even more. It was well behind the big black. The dark stallion extended his lead by another hundred feet and thundered toward the certain finish.

After nine miles, Nelson's red thoroughbred was four hundred feet behind the native Californio mustang. Horace watched as Old Sepulveda crossed the finish line first. What a champion.

The celebrating winners were screaming, the Don judge was jumping up and down, and Nelson and the Hardys were crying in the dirt. Poor Mr. Nelson. How proud he'd been aboard the ship. Horace wondered how many thousands of dollars were lost betting on the thoroughbred.

To avoid the crowd, Horace returned uptown. A couple blocks from the Bella Union sat a hill structure, a one-story building with a fence around it. That had to be the fort, about half as big as Alex's home. He chuckled. Nothing much was that big in the little pueblo yet.

Nearby, a wooden sign read "Thompson's," a corral and wagon rental place. He dismounted. A fantastic black horse stood tall in a corral. Eyeball to eyeball they made contact. He wondered if this unbelievable sixteen-hand coal-colored stallion was for sale. "Darn thing is as big as Old Sepulveda," Horace said out loud.

"Right you are, son. Old Sepulveda was the black's daddy," said a man, approaching Horace from behind.

"What a beauty!" Horace turned, startled, to see a kind-looking, older gentleman. "What's his price?" He wished he could have kept more of a poker face.

"First things first, young man. I'm James Thompson, the corral master. Who're you?" The man's hands looked like meat hooks as he extended one. His face was aged to forty-year-old leather left in the sun to dry.

22

"I'm sorry, sir. Name's Horace Bell. Alexander Bell's nephew. In from Calaveras County."

"Calaveras County. I rode with a hard man named Captain Love" he said, looking up at Horace, who stood a good six inches taller. Thompson's eyes moved up and down checking him out.

"Captain Love was my superior on the rangers. As a matter of fact, here's a letter he wrote to introduce me to your Los Angeles Ranger Commander." He handed the letter to Mr. Thompson. Horace took off his hat and rubbed his hair back. He didn't want to open his big mouth to change feet.

Mr. Thompson took his time reading the letter word for word. At the end, which seemed like an hour, Mr. Thompson quickly asked, "Are you going to try for a commission as an L.A. Ranger?"

"I'm to meet Captain Hope seven p.m. sharp at Miss Bovierre's Café to see if there's an opening."

"There is, my son. I'm sure they'd be glad to have you on the police force. As for price, Don Tomas Sanchez wanted only a first-class ranger to have the black stallion. I think you qualify. How about only fifty dollars -- special?" What a deal, a perfect trade, Pal for him. Maybe he'd feel better transferring his feelings to a new horse.

Horace slapped a fifty-dollar gold slug into the man's huge palm, rubbed his head with the other hand, and said, "A deal is a deal. Thank you. And Don Sanchez."

"Yup, he's a real winner. His former owner was a city marshal who took a .45 in the chest. Be careful. Oh, by the way, I'm with the rangers too."

Nice old guy. These Los Angelenos were pretty decent people. Too many lawmen were killed. He had to be mighty careful.

Horace took the saddle off his borrowed mare and placed it on the big black. Riding the three blocks back was a snap. He placed the borrowed mare in its stall, put in the night feed, and closed the barn door against the chilly night air.

Quickly remounting his new horse, he said, "I'm naming you Pal. Got a habit of talking to my horse. Never be afraid.

Always be brave, Pal." The horse snorted.

Walking into Miss Bovierre's at six fifty-five p.m., he said hello to Miss Bovierre as she came out of the kitchen with a chair. How timely. The smoke was so thick you could cut it. Everyone smoked a cigar after dinner. A full house, all four tables were taken. Miss Bovierre even had an extra Mexican gal who ran from table to table. Paulette still looked attractive. More like exquisitely fine.

Horace looked closely at the four wooden tables. Four gamblers sat at the first one; four miners at the second; four businessmen in suits at the third; and the furthest away had four Dons, who wore formal black suits with fancy white lace shirts and red sashes. With the Dons sat an older white-headed American. He wore a businesslike black suit and smoked a long cigar. His eyes squinted from the clouds of gray smoke. The smell of a cheap cigar burned the air.

Horace wanted to sit down and get out of the fog. He prayed for fresh air. Miss Bovierre placed the empty chair by the white-haired gentleman and motioned for Horace. He sprang toward it.

In English and Spanish she said, "Gentlemen, I would like to introduce you to Horace Bell, who would like to be a ranger."

"Glad to meet you, Mr. Horace Bell. I'm Tomas Sanchez," the Don said, extending his hand to Horace.

He looked only a couple years older than Horace and was a dapper dresser.

"This is Don Coronel, Don Benito Wilson -- who mentioned your acquaintance -- Don Abel Stearns, and the Captain of the Rangers, Dr. A.W. Hope," Sanchez said.

Wow. All the Dons were dressed to kill. Red sashes and lace shirts. Even the American, Don Wilson, who owned the store that sold them the clothes, was in a nice suit. Horace would have to dress the part.

"Thank you, gentlemen. I'm overwhelmed with your courtesy," Horace answered. "Captain Hope, I have a letter of introduction from Captain Harry Love of Calaveras County up north." He hoped he'd pass muster.

"Why thank you, young man. That's cutting to the game quick, I'd say, huh, gentlemen?" Dr. Hope smiled as he put

24

down his wet, stinky cigar. Horace smiled, realizing who had the cheap cigar.

Quickly reading the letter, Hope passed it around to the three who could read English. Tomas Sanchez translated it to Don Coronel.

In came a five-foot Don who walked with a leader's confidence.

"Horace Bell, please meet Don Andreas Pico, mi general and hero at San Pasqual, the only battle we Californios won!" Tomas said. Pico had even a fancier shirt on. His red sash was fringed to stand out.

"Captain Tomas, the Americans could have used big Horace here at San Pasqual," Don Pico said, laughing.

"Now, General, let's all get along. Those were different times and too long ago to remember," Tomas said.

Horace respected peacemaker Tomas right away.

After some discussion, Tomas Sanchez said, "Gentlemen, we have a quorum here now with five members of nine. I, Tomas Sanchez, hereby make a motion that Horace Bell of Los Angeles County is hereby granted the appointment as a Volunteer Mounted Police Ranger for the City and the County of Los Angeles. All in favor, aye. All against, nay. Your votes, please?"

By unanimous agreement, they voted Horace into the L.A. Rangers. Horace was elated. He tightened his fist and then rubbed his hair back.

"That settles it, Mr. Bell. Report tomorrow to Lieutenant David Brevoort across the street at the two-room adobe next to the Sheriff and Marshal's offices," Tomas A. Sanchez said with a smile. "Mr. Bell, that was a fine letter. We are proud to have you."

"Thank you, gentlemen," Horace said. "Thank you."   He turned to Miss Bovierre. "Thanks for all your help."   She grabbed Horace's arm and walked him to the café door. "You're welcome," she whispered.

Horace looked at her directly. "You've really been a friend since I first came to town. I saw the way you did things tonight." The chair, the timing, her shapely body, all of it.

"I'll get you to make up for it," she said and winked. She loved him! She was coming on!

"How about a Sunday picnic next week?" he asked, almost stammering. Fifty-fifty chance, but what the hell.

"That would be a grand idea," she said. He'd played it right. He was in like a bandit.

"Three o'clock," Horace said, his pulse quickening.

Gosh, he wished he had more experience.

"Oui. I'll pack the lunch, and we can both take our horses," she said with a smile.

He couldn't believe it; a picnic date and an appointment to the southern California rangers! What a great beginning! She was even bringing the food.

The candlelights were still burning at the adjacent barber shop. Standing in front of it, he glanced back into the café to see Miss Bovierre again, but she had already left for the kitchen. He turned.

Wham! The door hit him in the knee, and a striking, young black woman in a satin, low-cut purplish dress and matching hat walked out the door. She didn't linger to acknowledge him or say a word. In her hurry, the heel of her spiked boot stepped into his foot.

"Owe!" Horace said.

She looked at him and smiled. Her bright brown eyes caught him off guard. They were sexy and full of the devil. Great figure. His knee hurt like hell and his foot stung. He needed to sit down and get a haircut.

Inside the barber shop, a stocky, round black man pulled up his pants. Sweat beaded on his broad face, and his shirt was in disarray. A hand-carved sign propped up behind the man's barber chair against the adobe wall read "Peter Biggs, Barber and Proprietor."

"We's closed, young man. My God, must be seven o'clock," Biggs stammered.

"No problem. Who was that little Negro gal that just ran over me?" Horace asked, seeing that Biggs was caught with his pants down.

"Now, that's a diff'rent business. Her name's Lilly Brown,

26

the wildest lil' gal in the pueblo. She do everything to you in abouts an hour for only twenty-five dollars payable here in advance. She got nothing yet for ten 'n eleven. What's your desire, Mr....?"

"Mr. Horace Bell. Nothing right now. Just curious." Horace scanned the shop with its dirt floor, half-dirty shaving knives, filthy and stained water basin, and Biggs himself still buttoning his pants.

As he rubbed his hands with a filthy white towel black from old bear grease, Biggs said, "Well, when yer pecker need a real home, gimme a call here. Usual barber hours." What a character. The place hadn't been cleaned in years.

The prices on the wall quoted one buck for a haircut and half a buck for a shave. With the money for the prostitute, a haircut, and a shave, he could almost buy a horse. What a screw. He laughed at the pun. A haircut should only be a quarter dollar. And Don Wilson had remarked the whores on Nigger Alley only charged two to three bucks. Every couple of screws was a horse with Biggs' prices. He could do twelve whores on Nigger Alley for the price of Lilly. He pondered if she was worth it. Probably.

Chapter 5

That night at home, Horace laid down in a twilight sleep. Crying, yelling, and screaming came from across the street. Nigger Alley was in a row. His curiosity went wild. He dressed, checked that his weapon was loaded, and ran downstairs.

He entered the El Monte Bar. He first thought the bar and floor were painted surreal red. Then he realized he'd been deceived; the color came from bright human blood. His eyes adjusted to the light. He heard men screaming and crying. Men were dying on the floor, six of them. All were cut from ear to ear. The one closest to him gulped and drowned in his own blood. Ranger experience taught him to quickly look around for danger. Across the bar five men rushed a Mexican in a bloodied shirt. The once-white shirt had many lacerations. The five men had their large Bowie knives out as they charged the lone cut-up Mexican.

"Urives, you kilt my friends!" screamed one man.

"Urives, you're dog meat!" another said.

Urives calmly wiped his bloodied hand on his pants, put his knife in its scabbard, and drew a hidden revolver which he fired once, twice, and three more times. He hit one man in the head. Horace ducked as brains and bones splashed him. Luckily the deadly bullet only grazed his hat. Two men grabbed their chests and fell down. Another two gurgled blood while holding their throats. They dropped.

Horace studied Urives and saw him swaying back and forth. Urives was intoxicated and fighting like a demon. God help these men when he was sober. Eleven men were dead within minutes.

"Never insult mi sister -- the Dona -- you stupid American gringos!" Urives screamed as he pulled out another gun in his bloody hand, throwing the empty one at the bartender. The bartender's face showed pure human fright. Then Urives reached down and pulled out his twelve-inch Bowie knife for backup. He was quick. Horace couldn't believe that six more men ran toward this one-man slaughterhouse.

"You murderin' Don bastard! We're gonna get you!"

Bang, he fell. Urives fired four more times. Four fell. He knew the gun was empty and it was time for one- on-one hand-to-hand combat. After five quick slices, in less than three seconds, Urives stood victorious on the attacker's chest. The dead man's head rolled unconnected across the saloon dirt floor.

"Dumb gringos," Urives sneered. "I kilt twelve Sydney Ducks last year. You damn seventeen ain't no big deal!"

Three men stood up and promptly disappeared, running as if the banshee from Hades was behind them. Then two more fools got involved in a backward jump into hell. Horace watched as three bodies stacked up.

Urives picked up his gun, demanded the pistol he threw at the bartender, and wiped his blade on the top dead man's pants. Calmly he put everything in his belt, grabbed a Mexican gal, and headed for the door. He was a real one-man nightmare.

"I'm gittin' patched up and I'll be back," he promised.
God. Don't hurry.

Horace went home, but he couldn't resist the urge to see Urives return. He saw five rangers down at the El Monte trying to keep the peace.

Horace went back to the bar. He wasn't surprised when Urives returned on horseback with a bottle in his unstitched hand.

Urives challenged anyone to fight him one-on-one to the death. No one was interested. How could he still want to fight? Red blood permeated white bandages from his head to his toes. He appeared as the devil incarnate come back to life.

The rangers laughed at the local talent until Urives came up to them and begged them to try to arrest him. The stipulation was first a fight to the death. All took the unadventurous side and humbly said, "Hell no!"

The whole Alley went into hiding. They counted nineteen dead as enough for one night.

Horace, glad he wasn't sworn in yet, rubbed his hair back. The ranger corporal yelled out, "Write the whole damn thing off as an incident report, and let's go home."

"Okay, Corporal Bean," they agreed.

This place was something. Never were the mines this exciting.

The next day at eight o'clock a.m. sharp, Horace walked into the ranger barracks. The sleeping quarters room housed two tiers of bunkbeds, three on the back wall, then three rows in front of them, making a large letter E. A wooden table with seats for eight was in the center. The age-old piece possessed the stains of life. He was told the night shift consisted of twelve men all snoring at the same time until awakened at the next emergency. He hoped he could sleep with the smell of Mexican beans refrying again and snores permeating the room. Just great. He loved being right in the middle.

Horace knocked on the inside door. Lieutenant

David Brevoort, a man of about thirty, answered. Horace introduced himself and produced a note from Captain Hope and the letter from Captain Love. The lieutenant read both papers quickly.

"I see, Bell, that you have previous service."

"Yes, that's right, sir," he said, trained to respond quickly.

"All the men just call me the Luie, which is short for lieutenant. Kinda like my new name -- Luie Brevoort." His hard-crinkled red face broke into laughter. His carrottop hair stood out. His twisted his moustache as he looked up at Horace.

"Raise your right hand, Mr. Bell. Do you swear to uphold the laws of the State of California and of the United States of America, so help you God?"

"I do," Bell answered. The short guys really never liked the tall ones. Had to keep his mouth shut.

"You are now a Los Angeles Volunteer Mounted Police Ranger assigned to one of four full-timer's squads that rotate every five nights. That way nobody gets to have all the fun or gets burned out." Five nights so they weren't farted out. Brevoort talked like a gun spurting out bullets for words.

"I like that," Horace said, trying to smile.

"Also, I hope we can get your corporal rank back. I like having brave men in charge."

Horace's eyes dropped. "Luie, that gun battle cost me my best friend. I learned loss and gain from that damnable Juan

Flores ..." Maybe he was wrong about the Luie.

"Heard about him killing those two rangers --Hangtown. If he shows here, Bell, he's all yours," Brevoort said, looking eye to eye with him. Horace nodded.

The Luie handed him a city white ribbon police badge. He added, "Oh yes. Let's go to Sheriff Barton's office. He's close by in case he needs help. If he's sober, he bothers us to do his dirty work. Anyway, you'll find out about him. Stupid voters..."

James Barton swore in Horace as a deputy sheriff with county-wide authority.

"Yup, two hundred fifty miles east and west by one hundred fifty miles north and south. Damn jurisdiction is 37,500 square miles!" Barton said through his four-day-old stubble and breath that reeked of alcohol.

Horace recoiled. "Gee, that's enormous." An open whiskey bottle sat on the sheriff's desk.

The sheriff told him that of the one hundred rangers, only fifty in overnight squads were sworn in as deputy sheriffs authorized by the Court of Sessions. Barton apologized for not handing him a new Colt revolver and gave him a Spanish lance ten feet long and weighing fifteen pounds. Was this part of the Spanish culture, he wondered?

"We don't use these like English knights in a dual, man-on-man, do we?"

The Sheriff and the Luie laughed until tears came to their eyes. Boy. They had to think he was young.

"No, Bell. Three Spanish judges on the court remembered the last police officers they saw in Spain carried lances for authority. They were too cheap to issue guns," Brevoort said.

"No shit," the sheriff added.

"Gosh. I'm amazed at this heavy thing," Horace said, acting like one of the guys as he laughed at himself while moving the lance around trying to fit in.

Brevoort explained. "The Californios at the Battle of San Pasqual used those things against us pretty good. They caused fifty casualties, killed twenty-two. Like pigs in a skewer. They stuck us with those damn lances and kilt my C.O. Rain soaked our rifles. Couldn't fire. The memories -- I can't touch one of

32

those damn things."

"Any Mexicans wounded or killed?"

"Nope, thank God. General Kearney's prize white horse bolted after Don Sanchez lanced him off, or those Californios would've killed us all. Guns didn't work, swords were too short. The Californios chased the white horse goddess for miles," Brevoort said, his eyes watering, sweat running off his forehead.

Horace nodded. "Heard about that battle last night. General Pico mentioned it to Dr. Hope."

"Yes. Dr. Hope had to care for the fifty men. A gentlemen's ribbing contest."

"Right," the sheriff confirmed. "Bell, you're all sworn in. Have everything? Yes. Here. I almost forgot. Here's your badge."

The thick three-inch six-point blacksmith-made star had "Deputy Sheriff L.A. CO. #14" chiseled into its center. The pin ran horizontally. Horace's chest swelled as Barton pinned it on.

"Horace, you start on shift C next Tuesday night at five p.m. and work until end of shift, four Sunday morning," the Luie said. "And Horace, that shift is still three extra bunks light. Pick your favorite."

Refried bean heaven was on the horizon.

Horace walked to the café for breakfast, anxious to tell Paulette about his day. He wanted to better their friendship. A beautiful, new green dress made her emerald eyes even more vivid. Early breakfast was over. Only one Chinese man sat at a table. Horace asked her to seat him with the Chinese man.

"Name's Horace Bell from Calaveras County," said Bell, holding out his hand.

"Peased to meet your acquaintance," the man replied, bowing at the table. "Name Cho Ling. I do Missy's laundry for business, am friend of Missy's."

"She's my friend too," Horace said with a smile.

"You say Calaveras County. And you wear sheriff's badge here. Miss Bovierre tell me you be ranger up north. My cousins tell me only rangers protect them up north. Nobody else. You must be brave man fighting for Chinese."

"True, but not so brave. Just doing a job that I like."

Miss Bovierre placed a steaming plate before him. "Here you go, ranger, my special, bacon, poached eggs with hollandaise sauce, country biscuits and gravy."

"Wonderful! I feel like a thousand dollars today. And you -- um – you look beautiful."

Her green eyes flashed as she smiled back.

Horace shared experiences with Cho Ling and talked to Miss Bovierre about the day's happenings. She shared her need for a trusted friend in the crime-infested pueblo. Was that a hint? Maybe him?

After finishing his meal, he went to meet some of the rangers who were getting off duty. They'd slept long into the morning after working late the night before. He wanted to get a feel for his new ranger life.

Horace saw a fellow with a flared handlebar moustache cleaning his gun at the barracks communal table. A long cigar hung from his lips. The burned ash was two inches long. Ashes like an Indiana snowfall sprinkled the dark stained wood.

"Name's Bell, Horace Bell."

"Welcome aboard. I'm Corporal Bean -- Roy Bean."

An older ranger stepped forward laughing. "Bell, be careful of Corporal Bean. He's all wine, women, and song!"

"You're just jealous all the senoritas are in love with my good looks, you old fart," Bean said. "Bell, you stick with me and leave the grumpy old salts to their old-fashioned ways. I'll show you the ropes."

"Some senorita's daddy's gonna show you the end of his rope, Bean," the old ranger chimed in.

"Thanks, to both of you," Horace said as a peacemaker.

"Young pups," the old ranger said with a smile.

Seven glum men arrived and walked toward Bean.

"Been eight days. What's the verdict on my brother's murderers?" Roy Bean asked.

"We seven rangers makin' this here Committee of Vigilance have decided..." the leader said.

"Don't be so damn formal," Bean said.

"Okay, Roy. We've been at it for over a week questioning the four Mex, sometimes twenty-four hours a day. Joshua

Bean's murderer will be punished. We'll hang three we've drilled," the leader said.

"Yeah, Roy, put 'em together with four from the jail
log and make it a nice seven Mex hanging," another said.

Horace's mouth fell open and he nervously brushed his hair back. Roy Bean curled his moustache.

"Who in the hell are you lettin' go? You've got four damn Mexes?" Bean asked.

"Yeah," several men said in unison.

The leader cleared his throat. "We decided that Felipe Read, Don Read's oldest son, shouldn't be hung."

"Damn Mexican politics. He's probably the guilty one!" Bean yelled.

The rangers rose as a group and left to act upon the committee's verdict.

One by one they gathered the condemned. The wooden jail log, two feet in diameter with its huge staples and attached chains, secured the four unfed, dirty criminals. Somehow the rangers decided to make it a group hanging to "make a damn statement to these peons." Horace was amazed.

"Three are felons, and the fourth was only a chicken thief!" the jailer complained.

"Look. I'm the sergeant, and the Committee of Vigilance stated all were to be executed," a huge bronze man said as he slammed the jailer's desk with his fists as big as bear paws.

Horace wondered why the hurry to hang. He accompanied the rangers as they gathered the condemned.

"Put up seven ropes on the wagon maker's head post," the sergeant yelled.

The chicken thief cried out in Spanish, "I only took a chicken, just one little chicken! Please, please!"

The other prisoners were quiet while the six nooses were placed over their heads. Most men prayed and looked upward. At the sergeant's command, all seven lives were terminated. Fifteen female spectators wept as the seven limp bodies swung in the mild breeze. The vile body stench permeated the air.

"Bell, this is the way I like it. L.A. Pueblo justice," Bean said with a Cheshire cat smile.

Horace looked up, thought about it, and bit his tongue. He knew something was wrong. He understood the chicken thief's cry for mercy and couldn't understand why they hanged him instead of the Don's son. The logic came to him. Power politics wouldn't allow them to hang a Don's son without serious social repercussions. They could not risk dividing the pueblo. The Mexicans still had the numbers, while the gringo Americans had control. Yes, he smiled, maybe the guilty went free because they had money and position. This was common sense but conflict for his soul. A lesson to learn. He was learning to keep his big mouth shut.

Chapter 6

Juan Flores wiped his wet brow. The hot desert sun made his dark black eyes squint. His horse glistened with sweat and moaned for a break. Flores thought about resting at the upcoming river's Spanish Oak Tree strand. He contemplated his position while watching his horse drink. He'd gotten into an argument in Sacramento, fired his gun, missed, and ran. He was cursed. Everything he did went wrong.

The three-hundred-mile trip from Sacramento was difficult traveling from one dilapidated mission to another. The priests appreciated his gold. The priests also dreamed Flores' dream for bringing back the old Spanish ways. Maybe the old ways were just a romantic fantasy. His body was exhausted and his mind tired.

"Mi amigos, let's take a short siesta." Watching his two partners lying down made him think about his past and his plans for the future.

A few years before, the blood in his mining tent had turned his life upside-down. The mines were backbreaking work and the gold he panned turned into a nightmare. He lost his tender sweet wife to rape, mutilation, and murder. Somebody sick and depraved entered his tent, raped his wife, and stole his gold. His unborn son was cut out of her stomach and laid on the dirt floor, his seed totally spoiled. The perpetrators even mutilated the baby. Both his loved ones were cut in awful places, his wife's breasts cut off, his unborn castrated. Her body was slit from her chin to her legs. Terrible memories. Everything trusted was gone. His eyes watered as his mind did rage somersaults. Sleep came at a hard price.

At the mines they'd camped near the Chinese because the gringo Americans stayed far from the Chinese and didn't revenge them. The Chinese were easy hits. They rarely fought back. They worked hard and buried their gold. He killed Chinese neighbors and took their gold as his own. Their buried sacks popped up easily with Flores' good knife.

Juan grinned. He'd done great. But why did he have to kill

those two damn rangers?

Juan Flores still had hysteria bouts filled with fury over his lost Andrea. He prayed she rested in peace. He wondered if God still heard his prayers. He sinned much. But he needed to strike back and kill to satisfy his grief. He couldn't control his anger. It drove him to a frenzy.

Flores dipped his bright red Mexican headband in the creek. Quickly putting it on, he felt the cold water sharpen his thoughts. His reflection in the water accentuated his moustache and neck twitch. In Sacramento, after the gunfight, he'd split his gang into three groups and told each one to meet him at the San Juan Capistrano Mission. Riding off in separate directions, they'd all headed south. He could trust one leader -- Lieutenant Poncho Daniels. If he could keep the gang together, he'd have big plans.

The shady oak sheltered his thoughts. The babbling brook tranquilized him. A lone bird's song put him to sleep.

After a time Flores woke. He rubbed his eyes. The grass was imprinted where his men laid. Their horses were gone. Now he was alone. But he was used to it and not afraid. They didn't mean a thing compared to his lost wife and son.

His neck twitched nervously to the right. The Santa Barbara Mission was an hour's ride. He saddled his mount, placed the bit, and rode slowly to the mission for a good night's sleep and a hot meal. He promised himself that next time, he'd pick better men. He lit his last thin Mexican cigar. Nicotine comforted his evil, dark soul and relaxed him. His heinous eyes gazed toward the future with a wicked cause.

Chapter 7

Don Tomas Sanchez and Mexican Joe rode from the seven-square-mile Rancho La Cienega O'Paso de La Tijera toward the pueblo. This land went to the Don as the only surviving male. When Tomas was a boy, his father died and his grandfather raised him. Don Vicente Sanchez was the Alcalde of the Los Angeles Pueblo, effectively making him the Mexican judge, jury, mayor, council, and executioner for the city. He taught Tomas to avoid enemies and to be an honest politician. Three years ago, his Alcade grandfather passed away.

Mexican Joe needed supplies, and Tomas had meetings to attend. First on the agenda was his monthly visit. His two sisters, Sophia and Theresa, received the "in town" part of Grandfather Sanchez's estate. Tomas demanded as his first-born male right the La Tijera Rancho ten miles west of the pueblo. His older sisters received the better deal. They preferred the Pueblo de Los Angeles to the distant rancho. They inherited the family two-story adobe on Sanchez Street. In addition, they received all the lucrative rental properties on Nigger Alley. All twelve cash-cows paid on time each month: four gambling places, four bars, and four houses of ill-repute. The whoring business morally bothered both the sisters but not enough for them to refuse the money. Tomas realized their benefit was based on vice. The negative side was seeing human nature at its lowest -- gamblers, drunks, whores, criminals, and drug addicts. The plus side, it was a sure thing. They owned the most secure, money-making properties in the whole pueblo. With the rents at their doorstep the first of each month, who could refuse? The Alley businessmen made high profits. If they didn't pay the rent, they could easily be replaced.

The sisters considered the goings-on at their properties conversationally gruesome -- their twelve properties averaged a homicide a day -- but they shared what they heard and saw with their neighbors. That made for stimulating conversation. Human nature being what it was, they'd think, "Thank God it happened to someone else!" Then they'd gasp and turn red.

Mexican Joe was Tomas Sanchez's majordomo, who managed the <u>vaqueros.</u> Tomas rubbed his well-groomed and short, full-face beard. "Look, Joe, look at the blanket of cattle and horses all the way to the pueblo."

"Si, mi Don, what a beautiful sight."

Out to the horizon an entire full pepper shaker of cattle appeared dumped on a huge table cloth of land. There were thousands of specks for ten miles. Tomas and Mexican Joe rode on a solid green grass sloping mesa. They looked over the wild mustard grasses flooding the untouched basin. The growing pueblo sported a few hundred white-washed adobes. Tomas smiled. Wine, after cattle, was their next biggest export.

Sanchez breathed in the fresh morning air. Soon the day would grow hot and bright once the cool overcast burned away. Yesterday had rained. Southern California smelled like wild herbs and flowers all year long, and even more so after a rain, which fell thirty days a year. Tomas loved his land and was blessed with a rancho home and a large, growing family.

The unending criminals and local Indians who stalked the county proved the only threat to Los Angeles and its surrounding ranchos. In the southern California area, criminal gangs looted at will. Those unsuccessful in the gold fields soon turn toward the dark criminal downside.

"How many head did we lose last month, Joe?"

"About fifty -- the Indians, rustlers, and the northern trail drive."

Sanchez sighed. As Don, he was responsible for his whole rancho, much like the feudal lords that he'd read about in Spanish history. He bought and sold the cattle, horses, and other livestock. As the Chief Democratic Boss of the Los Angeles Pueblo, he managed the Democratic party and helped get out the vote. As one of five councilmen for the Common Council, he governed the city.

As a founder of the Committee of Vigilance, he'd make sure records were kept and that people voted correctly and that decisive action was taken when the pueblo was threatened. For the city to survive, the strong hand of the law must work with quick justice.

Extremely conservative, he believed in states' rights. He wanted to make his town safe. He didn't favor San Francisco with its thousands of vigilantes. My God, they killed everybody up there. He did favor a trained volunteer police force called the rangers. He initiated the idea and pushed it until it was fulfilled. The day after they formed the rangers, they all took a vow of vigilance. Instead of thousands, Los Angeles then possessed a hundred police vigilantes. He tried to avoid the Committee of Vigilance movement. The majority of public opinion overruled him. He decided to join because "It's better than fighting the system." Besides, they saved court costs.

"Don Sanchez, isn't that Sheriff Barton riding down on a woman?" Mexican Joe said, pointing a hundred yards away.

"Jes, you're right, Joe, that's his half-Indian woman. I recognize her long black hair."

"He's pulling her by her hair. What a spiteful man."

"Joe, look. Here comes her brother, Andreas Fontes. He's a scrapper," Tomas said, pointing.

They watched as Fontes leapt from his horse and took Sheriff Barton out of his saddle. Barton let go of Fontes' sister but held on to his whiskey bottle. He swung the bottle at Fontes. Fontes ducked and hit the sheriff with a one-two-three punch. Then he did another. Barton fell to the ground, knocked out.

"Don, will Barton get even when he wakes up?"

"Joe, I hope not, but a man of his morals..."

"At least Andreas saved his sister from losing her hair. Barton kicked his horse..."

"Barton is a fool, living with that woman, not being married," Tomas said.

"The ones in power break the rules, mi Don," Joe said.

"But I see that a higher power like the church makes the rules stand for all."

They watched Fontes' sister hug her brother. Fontes helped her onto Barton's horse and they rode toward the pueblo. She rubbed her head, and Tomas and Joe waved. Her beautiful long black hair blew in the breeze. Tomas shook his head at Barton laid out cold. Tomas smiled with satisfaction knowing how Barton now had a three-mile walk to town.

Riding to his sisters' pueblo adobe where he'd grown up, he remembered his father and grandfather teaching him Spanish values and Mexican politics. His neighbors, General Andreas Pico and Governor Pio Pico, were his great mentors.

His grandfather taught Tomas of the unstable Mexican government and the stable American one. The number-one reason the Mexicans wanted to be part of America was the stability. Mexico accomplished two good things: abolished the land holdings of the missions and freed the Indians from their mission bondage.

These Indians produced inexpensive labor. After 1833 they all ran to the ranchos to become servants. His grandfather taught him that Los Angeles was just like the southern states in America. They each sold one major product -- cotton in the South and cattle in California. Both industries demanded cheap labor -- California Indians, Southern slaves.

He knocked, and both his sisters came to say hello. Sophia and Theresa were content with their latest cost-of-living raise on Nigger Alley rents. Both dressed in the finest Spanish fashions together with the latest San Francisco accessories. He complimented them on their clothes and mentioned he hoped they saved a little for a rainy day; something he wished he'd done, but the rancho needed money. In addition, the American culture kept inventing new material things that the Spanish culture demanded. Materialism -- the desire of America. Since the Spanish culture was one of honor and pride, the Dons and the Donas had to have the latest things. The Spaniards competed to see who was the richest or owned the best.

"So, my dear sisters, how are you?" Tomas asked, sitting in his favorite chair where Grandfather Vicente occupied most of his adult life.

Chico, their large green, yellow-headed Amazon parrot, started his verbal rampage, "Damn you, damn you --you son of a bitch, you son of a bitch -- you two-bit whore, you two-bit whore -- squawk, squawk -- shit face, shit face!"

Tomas couldn't hold a straight face. Sophia and Theresa, dressed in their long Spanish black dresses, blushed bright red. Left in his cage outside, he'd acquired a vocabulary in cuss words from nearby Nigger Alley. The gamblers and drunks walked by and shouted at him. Chico loved to learn horrible English words. He had the perfect Alley vocabulary. His sisters were mortified.

Yes, the bird was quite a character.

"Chico's still quite colorful," Tomas said.

"How are your English lessons, and that pretty Bovierre woman?" Sophia asked, her eyebrows raised.

Bang, Bang! "Si. Mi God — what's that?" Tomas jumped up. It sounded like next door. He pulled out his Colt revolver and headed out the door.

"Be careful, Tomas!" Sophia said.

Tomas ran around Sanchez Block to Nigger Alley. A man with a green gambler's apron held a double-barreled shotgun at his side. Both barrels were still smoking. The apron man watched the man he shot expire. They were in front of El Monte Saloon where the man shot twice in the gut lay in the street.

"Sorry, Don Sanchez, this no-good cheat pulled a gun after I caught him pullin' cards from his sleeve."

A red puddle formed below him. The man, spread- eagled on his stomach, groaned in pain. Alley dust blew from his mouth as his expelled his last breath.

Tomas saw a card fall out from the man's sleeve and shook his head. These police duties aged him. Middle twenties and his black hair was showing light hints of grey. Shit, this was a street of fools. His tall, six-foot frame felt heavy and tired. He rubbed his close-cut black beard with his left hand as he saw Sheriff Barton run up. Barton's right eye carried a big purple and black shiner from the Fontes fight earlier. Tomas smiled. He wondered if the sheriff was sober.

"Sheriff, it's self-defense. The dealer saw him cheating, the cheat drew, the dealer defended himself," Tomas said, pointing at the man's sleeve.

"I'm the coroner. Oh good. The cheat has money for his burial," Sheriff Barton said quickly, finding the deceased man's wallet. Like a crow after dead vermin.

What a legal pickpocket. Barton would buy himself a case of whiskey on those impounded funds. Barton's violet-circled

43

eye looked like it found heaven. Only heaven was in a brown bottle together with beating his unwed woman. Sanchez shook his head and headed for Miss Bovierre's café.

The dear lady had helped him over the years to learn English. Knowing the language really helped him advance in politics and in adapting to the growing American culture. He set all of his meetings at the Café Bovierre as a way of thanking her. English language was important.

He hoped Paulette would find happiness someday, for she seemed like a fish out of water. Her past memories in love and war kept her from it. He loved to talk to her about the rapier, its use, her training, and her fighting in North Africa. Nobody could outdo her with the rapier.

Too bad Mr. Horace Bell wasn't five years older. He had the strength she needed. Bell loved the gusto in life, the thrill of it all, just as she did.

His own marriage to Maria began when he was sixteen and she only thirteen. So precious, so adorable, he thought of her as still the same. They grew together. She could listen for hours, offer consolation, encouragement, and some great suggestions for any frustration or problem. Nothing in the world was like having a perfect wife. Nothing.

Tomas tied his horse at the café. He was meeting with four Democratic workers in regards to the Democratic party in order to double-check the next elections a month away. The day was still warm. Normally October's temperatures dropped ten degrees, but this day was hot. Too damn hot. Already the insects buzzed.

Inside, Sanchez greeted his fellow committee members. They sat comparing notes and details, which Democratic candidates were weak and strong. They counted how many extra Mexicans and Indians they'd have to pay to vote. The Democrats' votes were the county joke. The rich Democratic candidate paid a poor Indian or Mexican to vote several times. They first were taken by wagon and allowed to vote with their true name. Then they got a free drink and a haircut so the registrar of voters wouldn't recognize them when they voted again. Another free drink followed. They switched clothes and

44

they were taken to vote the third time with a third name. Finally they were rewarded with a third drink. The bars loved the game.

Sanchez chose to let the others get involved with the vote plan. He was a few years away from public office. When he failed to refile for Common Council, his backers begged him to stay for another term, but he declined. He would run again. Then he would reconsider the extra votes. Nobody was perfect.

As the meeting broke up, Horace Bell came in for lunch. Sanchez invited him to his table. Though from different backgrounds, they had much in common. They were close to the same height and build and only five years apart in age. One had a large rancho and title. One was looking for land and maybe title. Both were rangers. Both had a friend in Miss Bovierre. Both enjoyed the thrill of a chase. Their lives became exhilarated when they made a capture. Even if they complained, right?

Nothing like a pursuit and capture. Nothing.

"So, Mr. Bell, how do you like the pueblo?" Tomas Sanchez asked.

"Don Sanchez, I feel like it's my home already, and thank you for my horse, and last night."

Tomas shook his head. "Jes, I saw you tie up. You presented a good letter. My wife, Maria, would like to meet you. She heard about you from Don Coronel's wife. She told her you were a tall, dark-haired giant."

Horace laughed as he rubbed his hair back. His lineless face crinkled and his bright blue eyes flashed as he answered. "I'll ride out tomorrow, say about three?"

"No, make it five-thirty, and enjoy a real treat of supper under Old Maria, our cook. We have the best cook in the county."

"That's a deal, Don Sanchez. Gracias."

They shook hands, and the Don departed for his horse. Sanchez had noticed Miss Bovierre serving Horace without him even ordering. Bet she liked the fellow.

Mounting El Capitan, Tomas thought how his wife had made him change the horse's name. After the horse brought him home safe seven years prior, she re-christened him El Capitan. Out of respect to Maria, Tomas kept the name. He turned El Capitan toward the old plaza church.

He liked visiting Padre Lopez, the priest who'd married him and Maria ten years before. The padre didn't like the new Mexican-American culture. Tomas empathized for he didn't like change either. No one did. But he could foresee after a time the Americans becoming more powerful. Politically to resist the culture blend was foolish. He visualized his mission to mix the cultures and protect the Mexican landholders. He sought to keep the Spanish heritage and protect himself.

Yes, these Americans were a strange people. He feared they would wipe out the Spanish heritage. No wonder Padre Lopez had been so downcast. Plus, Nigger Alley businesses proved an exciting magnet for his parishioners. He was losing them to gambling, whiskey, and whores. Tomas reminded him that twenty years before the Americans, a Mexican Don pounded in the sign Calle de Los Negros. The Americans just made Nigger Alley fun and popular.

"One a day killed dead from liquor, whores, and gambling -- no bueno! Go look!" Padre Lopez said.

His visit got him down. Tomas left. All they needed now was a gang back in town. He headed back toward Miss Bovierre's Cafe.

Riding down Main Street, he saw what looked like two Mexican young men talking as friends. As he came closer, the view changed. They were arguing. When he passed them, one man pulled a Bowie knife and stabbed the other in the stomach. Tomas drew his Colt. The man dropped his blade and said, "I've just killed my best friend."

Tomas took the man to the District Court judge. Testimony by Tomas and the guilty man's confession brought an immediate sentence: hang him. The Mexican told the judge when leaving the court, "I wished I didn't kill my best friend over that damn woman." The constable carried the death order and escorted the man to the sheriff's office. Sheriff Barton was ordered to hang him as soon as possible. Tomas shook his head. More death occurred now than during the last war.

El Capitan needed water and feed. Tomas left him at

Thompson's Corral. Then he walked over to Miss Bovierre's for an advanced lesson in English nuances. He'd completed his study with Miss Bovierre but was working on the fine points.

Tomas admired her background. She had finished college in Paris and majored in English. With a medical minor, she enlisted as a nurse in the French Army. After a failed romance, she joined the French Army in Algiers. She'd learned rapier fighting techniques from the same lover -- a French National Champion. He'd taught her well.

The rapier had saved her in Algiers, North Africa. She had often protected herself from being a victim. She'd told Tomas how she once grabbed one of two attackers' swords and skillfully disposed of them both. Tomas knew she was a deadly, yet beautiful, friend. She came to America to avoid love memories in France and to join other French citizens in the pueblo. She came with a mule train full of emotional baggage.

"Ready, Tomas," Paulette said with her lovely smile, "to gamble -- jugar -- and to lose -- perder?"

"Jes, Miss Bovierre."

"In English there are words that can have two meanings depending upon the way they are said," she stated, twisting her light brown mane.

Tomas' mind wandered. "Miss Bovierre, I have invited Mr. Horace Bell out to the rancho for a nice supper tomorrow night. May I be so bold to ask that he escort you?"

"Oui. Oh, Tomas, I'd love it." Her teacher's face changed to a pretty smile. Probably gave her something to do. The dinner might strengthen his friends' relationship.

"I can get my helper to cover supper here," she said. "My friend Tomas, sometimes you even surprise me."

"I'm sure my wife, Maria, and I will enjoy the company. Our old cook Maria makes a tasty meal. You'll enjoy the break."

"Oui. Maria's cooking is known throughout the town."

Just then the city marshal burst in to talk to the Don. His tall frame and nervous eyes jumped as he blurted out, "You need to know what happened this morning, Don Tomas."

"You mean about Ricardo Urives?"

"No, Don Sanchez. I figured you'd have that under control," Billy Reader said in a quick staccato. "This one's about our Sheriff, Barton, and his live-in, half-breed unwed woman, Juanita Fontes, from San Juan Capistrano."

"Jes. I saw him pull her by her hair today. Go ahead."

Miss Bovierre stood all ears next to him, her eyes wide open. She loved gossip.

"Last night around six, Barton drank his favorite whiskey and got drunk. He begins using Juanita Fontes as a human punching bag. She has a temper, but she's no match for Barton's one hundred eighty pounds hitting her in the face, knocking her down, and pulling her by her hair across the dining room to the bedroom.

"So then she kicks him in the balls -- excuse me, Miss -- the groin, and hits him on the head with one of them big Spanish vases," said Billy, pausing to catch his breath.

"Serves him right," Tomas said.

"He is lucky she didn't grab a knife and cut him ear to ear when she knocked him out," Paulette said.

Tomas grabbed his throat. Miss Bovierre, clearly, would serve Barton cut up in pieces to the city dog pack, while Barton's non-married girlfriend just took it until she had enough. His hoped his Maria would act more like Miss Bovierre than Juanita Fontes.

The marshal continued. "When Barton comes to with a large bump on the head and a hangover, he's mad. He guesses she left for her folks' place. So our gallant sheriff goes in pursuit mad as hell. She sees him and runs." Billy excitedly danced up and down.

"Barton sees her, rides up on her, and boots her in the head."

"I saw the end of it," Tomas said.

"So he gets off his horse and grabs her long, black hair, remounts, dragging her behind him on the horse!"

Paulette, hands on her shapely hips, swallowed, "And this drunk is elected to protect us?"

"He gets his, Paulette," Tomas said, ashamed of his sheriff.

"Great, huh?" answered the marshal. "So big brave Barton's towing his one-and-only by the hair when her half-brother,

Andreas Fontes, rides by on his horse."

Tomas frowned. "I saw Fontes put Barton down in six punches."

The marshal nodded frantically. "Yes. Now it gets good. Barton comes out of the knockout. Barton goes to his buddy Judge Burrill, and the Sheriff swears out a warrant for Andreas Fontes."

"For interference, by God?" Tomas asked.

"No. The Sheriff charges Fontes with horse stealing!"

Tomas's eyes dropped and he shook his head. "I suppose that our moral sheriff has already arrested him."

"Right, Andreas Fontes swearing he was framed and that he'd be back to kill and maim Sheriff Barton and his deputies."

"Barton has a problem now. They'll let him out early at San Quentin."

"One more thing," the marshal added. "Two more first-class desperados just came into town, Crooked Nose Smith and Cherokee Bob. I talked to Smith, and he told me the half-dozen men he killed up north were all in self-defense. He promised he wouldn't kill anyone until he leaves for Mexico. He explained that it's important for his image as a killer. He actually smiled at me as he was talking.

"Last year when Cherokee Joe was here, he got into a fight with seven Mexicans from Sonora town. He killed six of them and left the last one half-dead, bleeding on the bar at the El Diablo. He was mighty good with that Bowie knife. He went after seven and got them all in the same fight, seven against one." The marshal paused, his eyes gleaming. "He'll be a problem."

Tomas told the marshal they now had the resources to manage the crime and violence, that if they had to, they would just use the power of the gallows both by court and by committee to control any problem. No matter what, the city had to survive.

"I'm going to stay in town, then, see what happens in Nigger Alley," Tomas said.

"You'd better bring four rangers with you," the marshal warned.

"No. I would rather just change clothes at my sisters' and

49

take a friend with me."

Horace Bell walked in for lunch. Perfect. Horace lived right at the end of Nigger Alley in his uncle's place. Horace could go with him.

"Boy, this is an exciting town. Eighteen killed in less than twenty-four hours. Over one percent now gone, poof!" Horace said.

"Yeah, partner, but fifty newcomers will be here tonight. Good day," the marshal said as he left.

"Specials, gentlemen?" Paulette asked.

"Yes, thank you," they both said.

"Horace, would you accompany me to the Alley tonight?"

"Sure. I'm free."

Paulette served up charbroiled New York steak mixed with Mexican rice, beans, and homemade salsa, and served it with fresh tortillas. She called it carne asada New York barbecue as one of her specials on the menu. Tomas smiled.

"Just smelling this makes you want to marry the woman that can cook this good, huh, Horace?"

"That woman can sure cook," Horace said smiling, though knowing somebody had just set a trap.

Later, Horace and Tomas walked around the block to the top of Nigger Alley. Dark at six p.m., the natives were out in force. They watched the gambling, liquor, vice, whores, and excitement. As they passed a whorehouse, the customary red-glass-covered candles glowed from two small windows. An informal line of about ten men, mostly miners, waited their turn at the sporting action. Tomas whispered, "This place supports eight women full-time. The whoring started over twenty years ago under the Mexicans."

As they passed the bar El Diablo, Tomas said, "It's named right -- the devil." Inside they saw a number of Americans, Spaniards, Indians, and foreigners milled around the tables and the bar.

The sounds and sights of the Alley were different from anything Horace had ever heard or seen before. Mexican music, mixed with the clanging of solid fifty-dollar gold coins and slugs hitting the bars and tables, reached their ears. Painted women aged twenty to forty lingered in doorways.

They passed a gaming house called the El Monte, then another bar, then a gaming house.

At the end of the Alley stood the old Coronel building. The crowd was so thick that no one could leave or get in unless they went around. Inside five bands played primitive music. The men howled out loud. They heard slapping sounds of a fight here and there, and once every half hour or so there was a surprise gunfire blast. Then everything would settle down, only to start over in twenty minutes. To Horace it was like a San Francisco symphony orchestra building to a crescendo with a gunshot and then re-starting.

"Horace, we have more murder here in southern California than in the whole of the United States. Rather a sad commentary on gold," Tomas said.

"True. But everyone feels rich here."

Tomas nodded his well-groomed head. "But not rich in values, morals, and ethics, things that really matter."

"You're right, Don Tomas."

Bang! Horace instinctively drew his Colt .44. Tomas just ducked low. They looked toward the gambling place Ultimo Juego, or Last Game. A man dressed like a professional gambler ran out with blood gushing from his right shoulder, his white shirt marked red. He hurried north on Nigger Alley. A crude-looking, dirty desperado stepped out after him yelling, "Take that!" Bang! "And that!" Bang! "You goddamn cheat, I'll blow your asshole to hell!" Bang! -- each time cocking his Colt and firing after the running man.

"One of our famous gamblers, I guess, decided to terminate his employment with a quick run in harm's way down Nigger Alley," Horace said. Tomas chuckled. Horace too started laughing, to the consternation of the crowd. Many started yelling at them not to laugh. Horace and Tomas laughed even more at the absurdity. Tomas felt like a school kid. Then some in the crowd grabbed their saloon batons.

"This is putting us in harm's way!" Horace said, still giggling. Tears were running down his eyes.

Tomas looked at Horace quickly and bit his tongue. They

51

ran for the Sanchez Town Home. The two sisters stood out front and shook their heads.

Chapter 8

"Horace! Horace! Horace Bell!" a man yelled below Horace's second-floor window. Horace jumped out of bed, trying to gather his wits. "Horace, we need your help. Saddle up and follow us. Injuns just attacked the Lugo Rancho in San Bernardino and took their horses up the Cajon Pass. These Utes may have some Whites helping them. Damn Injuns are well armed. Bring what you got!" Lieutenant David Brevoort shouted nervously, as he stroked his red handlebar moustache.

"I'll follow right along," Horace said.

"Your whole squad is falling in behind. Just catch up," Brevoort yelled, riding away with a group of twelve rangers.

Good, a pursuit. Horace ran downstairs. His Uncle Alex's face was white as snow. The uncle's gravity concerned Horace.

"Be careful, Horace. I've learned that the Utah Indians have been armed by Salt Lake friends. Those Mormon wives need livestock for their kids. Some Mormon men have thirty wives and a hundred children."

Must keep the husbands busy in thirty different rooms. Big homes too. "Thanks for the warning, uncle. I'll use my head when we catch up to them."

Horace double-checked his belongings while his uncle saddled Pal in the barn. Aunt Bell fixed him some trail food and clean underwear.

"The men would wear the same undies for a week if they could," she mumbled.

She packed four pounds of beef jerky, or Carne Seca, four pounds of apples, dry beans, some spices, and a half pound of coffee. She split the weight into two flour bags connected with a two-foot draw rope that would hang evenly over the horse.

"Be careful," she said, kissing his cheek and handing him the food all ready for the chase.

"That's real nice, I will," said Horace, who left and then returned to the kitchen to kiss her on the cheek. She smiled and pulled her graying hair back into a bun with her wrinkled hands.

"Thanks again, Uncle Alex, for getting Pal ready," Horace said. The musket was in the scabbard.

"Get going. You stay with the Marshall boys, Green and Wiley. They're ex-Texas Rangers -- professional Indian fighters!"

"I promise," Horace answered, giving his strong horse a sharp kick. The huge black animal took off like a bat out of hell. His hooves flew over the rocks and sand below. The excitement in a pursuit was overwhelming. Horace felt his heart beat in his throat.

Horace had opened Pal up once prior on the outskirts of the pueblo. Right now he couldn't believe the speed beneath him. No matter that the others had a mile head start, Pal was going to be there. His champion bloodlines pounded the earth below.

Horace flew past the first group of five rangers from Company D. Company A was leading a mile in front. Company C was in the middle. He figured Company B remained in the pueblo in case this was a ruse. Good administration.

Horace caught up with the Marshall brothers, Stanley, Banning, Roy Bean, Marshal Billie Getman, and Cy Lyon near the Mission San Gabriel. The Marshall brothers taught him some Indian tricks to watch for. Horace rode next to Roy Bean as they made tracks toward San Bernardino.

"Horace, did you ever hear 'bout why we formed the rangers?" Bean asked.

"No. Go ahead."

"Back two years ago a gang called the Sydney Ducks offered to spring Don Lugo's boys out of jail for ten grand. They made one mistake and pissed off old man Lugo by ruining his son's rancho at San Bernardino."

"Why were the boys in jail?"

"They killed some Indian and an Irishman who lied to them, causing a family death."

"That doesn't make sense."

"The same boys knocked out the D.A. to protect his wife when the D.A. beat her."

"Politics again. How many Ducks were there, and isn't the Lugo Clan the largest landholders in California?"

"Thirteen Ducks, and you're right."

"So what was the big mistake?"

54

"Oh, sorry. The Ducks tied up Urives at his Cerritos Rancho, raped the Dona, and robbed the place."

"Oh, no, not the Nigger Alley Urives?"

"Yup. He gets loose, all beat up, and goes after the Ducks."

"Single-handed?"

"Nope. He gets the Cahuillas chief to throw in twenty braves, they chase the Ducks into a blind canyon and fill 'em with drugged peyote arrows."

"Wow."

"Then Urives and the braves fall on 'em, cuttin' 'em into little pieces. Shocked the hell out of the pueblo, havin' the Indians forced to do their dirty work!"

"I'll bet in less than a month the citizens formed the Volunteer Rangers to do their bidding."

"Two weeks, next day we took an oath of vigilance to take care of eye-witnessed criminals immediately. Oh, one Duck rolled away scot-free -- Dirty David Boe."

Horace grasped the reason for the rangers. The citizens didn't want the criminals running wild. Yet, like most folks, they didn't want to do the dirty work themselves, nor did they ever want some so-called damn savages doing it. The Indians forced their hand. Bet they'd use the Indians again. And later, the rangers would take the credit. The whole rangers' history made sense.

At San Bernardino they rested their horses and received intelligence on the Ute Indians they were chasing. The local Indian Chief of the Cahuillas, Juan Antonio, was a close friend of the Lugos. His braves reported that fifty Ute braves and four Whites were the culprits. Four Whites' horses left horseshoe prints. Other peaceful Indians had seen the Utes in the Cajon Pass. The Utes had many guns. The Mormon settlement in San Bernardino expressed their sorrow to the ranchos, but the Mormon men were too busy to assist the rangers to even up the odds, which was understandable.

"And pretty damn suspicious!" Green Marshall said.

Horace smiled. The four major ranchos in the area sent their <u>vaqueros</u> to help recover the horses. That added thirty men to complement the thirty-four camped rangers. The Lugos brought in fifty of their best horses to help out. Chief Juan Antonio volunteered twenty-five of his best warriors and five trackers to help.

With the odds two to one in their favor, the mixed ethnic posse rode out on rested horses. This marked the first time a ranger army chased rustlers into the desert.

Lieutenant Brevoort said, in both English and Spanish, "Men, this army, one hundred strong, might have to go all the way to Salt Lake. Our mission is to get the stock back and teach those thieving savages a deadly lesson." He paused for an instant, thin lips forming an even line, then shouted, "Forward ho!"

The trackers reported that they'd counted forty Indians and three horses with shoes. They'd tracked the thieves all the way to the Mojave River in the Black Mountains. From there, the bandits had proceeded toward Salt Lake City to sell off the stolen goods.

The Cahuilla Indian trackers told Commander Brevoort they had added a couple hundred head of cattle to the bounty, and the cattle had come from separate directions. They'd all met at this rendezvous point to be driven north probably through Saint George.

"Oh, we're gonna be real popular chasing these bastards through the land of the Later Day damn Saints," David Brevoort said with a laugh.

They traveled up the El Cajon Pass, a wide area that breached the Pacific Mountain Range. Behind him, Horace saw purple peaks covered solid with snow. He thought of how his mom would make a chocolate cake and cover it with frosting on the top and let it drip down. Traversing the three-thousand-foot El Cajon Pass was easier than climbing over the ten-thousand-foot peaks.

Once on top, they found a flat plateau with a thirty-mile run to the first water -- the Mojave River. This was the high Mojave Desert with one main river, a twenty-five-foot-wide stream they called a river. Some river. They should have seen the mighty Mississippi.

Bean told him the next water was miles inland. He watched

as some <u>vaqueros</u> stored water on supply pack horses. They would have a few creeks, but this was going to be tough. The desert heat was a killer, so hot the men just rode praying for cloud shade, a winter storm, or a cool breeze. Kind of like sitting in a Mexican oven -- turn them over when they were medium rare. Every thirty miles or so, they would pass dead stock.

Horace understood the Ute Indians feeling secure with the Mormons both with them and behind them back at San Bernardino. He first noticed droppings left by the stolen stock. The droppings became fresher.

They stopped at a spring and small fort run by five Mormons. Brevoort told them to stay there at the fort and not warn anybody on fear of death. By then they had traveled two hundred and fifty miles, mostly through desert. And he signed up to be a ranger?

"What is the name of this basin fort?" Horace asked.

"The Meadows, in English; <u>Las Vegas</u>, in Spanish," a grisly old man answered, waving his leathered hand like a big paw.

After another eighty miles, Horace sensed they could easily surprise the rustlers.

"Lieutenant, how about our troop taking front point?"

Horace said.

"No problem, Bell. Troop A is tired being on guard up there, and we're almost to Saint George."

"Like to be in the thick of it, don't ya, Bell?" Green Marshall said.

"I can smell 'em, I can taste 'em, now I want to see 'em, Green."

The Indians' extra cattle slowed their pace. Trackers told Horace ten Indians, with a White, left the group toward the south. Only forty Indians and three Whites drove the stolen stock toward Salt Lake City. Traversing near Saint George, they picked up the pace as the land became much easier to drive the stock.

Horace was the first to see the Indians. "Look, Green, they're sleeping. It's them!"

"Now it's gonna get bloody," Green said.

57

Just short of Saint George, Horace saw the band of Utes. The Cahuilla scouts drew first blood. They shot arrows into five sleeping Utes. Twenty Cahuillas took out another five Utes with a well-placed volley. Horace and his troop mounted a calvary charge headlong into the Ute camp.

Horace got a taste of blood as a gunshot glazed his thigh. He drilled the Ute with his .44. He was scared but loved the excitement. His troop killed ten more and wounded three others.

The three White men escaped toward Bryce Canyon on fresh horses. The culprits were rested from their previous sleep. The posse, on the other hand, had ridden miles without stopping so they could catch their prey.

The White leaders were in a hell of a run and fired their guns left and right. Then the gunfire ceased. Corporal Stanley pointed and yelled, "Bell -- both you Marshall boys -- get 'em!"

Horace gave Pal a big kick. Off he surged. He left the Marshalls in the dust. Horace chose one of the three that was closest. Pal closed the distance down to half, a fourth, then an eighth. He got closer by jumping rocks and gullies. Horace's enemy, now a hundred feet away, turned and shot at Horace. Damn that pissed him off. Again and again. Thank God that gun was empty now. Horace looked at the White guy. He was dirty, wore a full beard, and possessed dark eyes that looked like death. God. Did he have a second gun? Pal narrowed the gap.

Horace bit his tongue to clear his head. The Marshall brothers followed two hundred yards behind. Damn, why did his horse have to be so fast? He'd have to do something quick.

The escaping rider reached behind to grab another gun. Seconds meant the difference between life and death. They were close to one another. Horace grabbed his big Colt .44. It felt like ten pounds. Horace searched for an advantage. Ahead was a five-foot ditch. The adversary would have to jump it before taking a shot. Horace knew Pal would jump it and be hanging in the air. He'd use his head and his legs.

One, two, three, he let go of the reins, tightened his legs around Pal, and brought up the revolver with both hands. Instinctively he cocked back his big single-action Colt. Twenty feet away his adversary started to bring up his revolver. Horace, now airborne on Pal, lined up his front and rear sights and squeezed off a round.

Wham! The half ounce of lead zipped eight hundred feet per second faster than the outlaw's horse. The bullet slammed into the man's neck. Had the criminal been just a tenth of a second faster, Horace could have been killed.

The man's head was almost decapitated. Oxygen- brightened red blood blew back at Horace. Still warm, it landed on his face. Horace would never forget the grey smoke, the horror on his enemy's face, his head flopping on his shoulders, and the taste of real blood.

The bandit's horse slowed. Horace stopped both horses. Only the man's spinal vertebrae kept his head attached as it hung down between his shoulders.

"Too bad you made me do that," he said.

Why were White men giving the Indians guns? And why had they helped the Indians steal the horses and cattle?

Horace examined the dead man's saddlebags. Beside a third latest-model Colt was a Bible and a Book of Mormon. The circumstantial evidence was good enough for him, but not a court of law. Good reason number one to be a lawyer -- to even up the law for the victim. He wanted to change things for good.

Wiley and Green Marshall slapped Horace on the back. "That damn horse could beat Old Sepulveda," Green said in his Texas drawl, then giving Horace a handshake.

Wiley hitched up his pants on his slender frame and added, "Without you, Horace, that scoundrel woulda beat our horses. He mounted a strong mustang there. Good thing Pal was stronger."

"We're gonna report it like that, Horace," Green said. "Where in the hell did ya get such a fine horse?"

"Yeah," Wiley said. "Boy, I couldn't believe that shot, dropping your reins and using both hands. Wow!"

Wiley held both hands up to imitate the shot while he aimed at the dead man.

"Thanks, rangers." Horace dropped his head. Inside he was proud, but he saw no reason to brag about having to kill a man. As much as he loved the excitement, his belly grew sick. Maybe that was why most folks left the outlaw work to the ones who could do it. Yes, it all figured now.

Green and Wiley Marshall reported to Lieutenant Brevoort in accordance with their paramilitary rules. The Luie, in support of his actions, gave Horace an immediate battlefield promotion to corporal.

The lieutenant calculated the total dead, wounded, and escaped, and gave the results to his men.

"Men, I'm proud to ride with all of you. Special thanks to our Indian friends, the Cahuilla, who cornered the camp for us to win this battle. Let's see. We killed a total of twenty-one Indians and one White Mormon. Nineteen Indians and two White men escaped on fresher horses. We saved two hundred and twenty-five head of cattle from four separate ranchos and one hundred and thirty head of Don Lugo's horses. Fifty head died. Best part of all is we got only two minor wounds. One ranger took a friendly arrow in the butt, and one Indian got a bullet in the leg."

"Hey, next time, ranger, keep your ass out of the line of fire!" someone shouted.

"Wanna kiss my boo-boo, wise-ass?" he answered.

"Boys, let's round 'em up and head 'em back," the Luie said. "I'm not too fond of being in Utah Territory right now. We'll rest on the other side of the river and let the stock drink. You Cahuillas under Chief Antonio, we are all proud of you. Chief Antonio, form a rear guard for our drive back home. Forward!"

Bean told Horace all this horse and cattle rustling was over trade. What the hell -- why not open up a trade route with Utah. That gesture alone would cut out the black-market profit potential.

Horace had heard the rangers talking about the Utes and Paiutes, the Mojaves, the San Joaquin, and the Tulare Indians. All were known to poach and rustle cattle and horses. They mostly liked the richer, large ranchos by the coast where they could sneak in and out fast. The ranchos were so big, one to two days passed before the <u>vaquero</u> scouts picked up on their telltale signs and prints.

Horace loved the way Company C fit together like a family:

Phineas Banning, Stanley, the Marshall brothers, Roy Bean, Billie Getman, and three more that were more quiet. They had a camaraderie; though all different personalities, they worked together pretty efficiently. The relaxing time going home was especially fun, even though the stock slowed them down, particularly when they had to wait at the Mojave River to make sure every animal was checked before that last terrible desert crossing. Even in the late winter the desert was ninety degrees.

Chief Antonio told Horace through a translator, "The Indians for miles heard that a mighty army from where the sun sets had come and wiped out all Indians by the great river." The chief remarked, "The local Mojaves will stay fifty miles away."

The legend made Horace smile. Horace had become a celebrity by running down the Mormon. Nobody else caught any Whites. They were safe back at Salt Lake City.

"Rangerin' gets addictive, Bell," Bean said. "For almost a thousand years, all victorious Roman generals got a parade when they got home. But you ain't gittin' one. Anyway, his chariot would lead. Sometimes the general was allowed to have his family on the chariot. Citizens by the thousands lined up to worship and applaud him. They'd throw bright flowers, yellow, red, and purple, at the chariot. A slave ran for miles just behind his chariot. He carried a Roman evergreen victor's wreath above the general's head. The slave would cover his mouth with his right hand and whisper a thousand times into the victorious general's ear, 'Remember. All glory and honor is fleeting, my general!'" Bean laughed.

"I get it," Horace grunted.

"My fightin' friend, we ain't bulletproof," said Bean. "You are one brave son of a bitch, and I'm proud to call you my friend."

Like the Roman generals of old, the rangers were received as conquering heros. The entire staff from each rancho rode out and waved as they passed. Horace felt proud. All along the trail home they received food and wine.

Though Horace would remind himself a thousand times that all glory and honor were fleeting, he could hardly wait to tell Miss Paulette of his adventure. Truly, this was an exciting place.

Chapter 9

Juan Flores nervously twitched his neck as he left the Mission Santa Buenaventura, a day's ride south of Santa Barbara Mission. Ahead the shallow river beckoned him toward the Mission San Fernando and Los Angeles County. The sun was up, and it became hotter as he proceeded inland. Flores wished he'd left earlier. The wine at the mission left him with a headache. The flies and other insects bit his dark brown neck. Mission fleas made his skin itch. He felt terrible.

Juan Flores missed the ocean breeze as he headed east following the Santa Clara River. He felt alone. All alone. He planned what he'd do if no one met him at San Juan Capistrano. He told himself that at least Daniels would be there. Damn, people always disappointed you. Daniels never would, would he?

To humor himself, he planned what he'd do with all his friends at San Juan Capistrano. First he'd have a big fiesta, perhaps attend a fandango and get a woman. He still had a two-day ride to San Fernando Mission, a hot, lonely ride. At least the birds sang.

Then they stopped. Flores saw movement ahead in the brush. Flores twitched his neck. He knew it was trouble. He quickly pulled out his revolver. An Indian jumped him from a tree. He quickly fired. The Indian fell dead. Thank God his weapon was out. Another Indian shot an arrow at him. He fired again. He missed. The Indian stood and aimed at him. Flores aligned his sights and squeezed the trigger. The arrow whizzed two inches from his ear. The second mortally wounded Indian fell. He heard the bushes and river trees sway as two more ran away. Soon he saw two Indians ride over the hill to the south. Whew, that was close. He'd have to be alert. Only the fastest thieves survived. Flores smiled his evil smirk.

A rabbit looked over the river bank. He fired. Dinner was in the bag. He felt better now, things were going his way. He would live from the land for two days and then be in north Los Angeles County.

63

He approached the seventy-something old red-tile roof. San Fernando Mission was the first settlement he had seen for fifty miles. He watered and fed his horse. Then he sat down to eat a fine Mexican dinner. His neck twitched. The next night he'd be at San Gabriel, and soon his final destination. There he'd see how loyal his other six men were.

He left at first light. He stayed away from the Headquarters Bar. The padres mentioned a man named Roy Bean ran it after inheriting it from his murdered brother Joshua. "Roy Bean is a Los Angeles Ranger, and good with the gun," the old lined padre said.

"Gracias," Flores said, twisting his black handlebar moustache.

No drinking that night. Tomorrow he'd celebrate in beautiful San Juan Capistrano.

As Flores went from twilight to deep sleep, he saw the ocean and his wife too many years ago. She was dressed in her finest dress, vivid greens and reds. Her gentle face beckoned him. He followed her over the verdant green meadow filled with mustard grass. He ran after her. He grabbed her but never could hold her. She whispered to him and kissed him good night. Then she slipped away and disappeared behind the murdered Chinese, Indians, and those two damn rangers.

Chapter 10

Horace was almost home. He wanted to be back at the pueblo. He was impatient. Nervous, he rubbed his hair back. He realized he'd missed his first date with Paulette. The Indian adventure had taken three weeks. He'd also missed his dinner invitation at Tomas Sanchez's rancho. He had to make up for both as soon as he got back. Arriving in town early, he cleaned up and reached the café by seven a.m.

"Morning, Miss Bovierre," he said, noticing her red dress with the hint of an ample bustline.

"And a good morning to you," she said. She was glad to see him alive. "Oui. I hear you ran down a Mormon leader?"

"Nothing, Miss Bovierre, but what I had to do. We're alone, so I'll tell you I was scared to death. But confound it all, I still loved it," Horace said with a slight shake of his head.

"I like your honesty, Mr. Bell," she said, flashing her little-girl eyes at him. Horace saw the coquette and played up for another.

"Sorry about our Sunday date," he said nervously.

"You're not getting off that easy. Sunday is two days away, it's going to be warm again, maybe hot, and we are going to relax and enjoy ourselves."

"Great! Then we're still on."

Just then Roy Bean came in and sat down. He turned his chair around and straddled it. He twisted his unruly moustache. Great timing, Roy, just when he was on the make.

"If you turn out okay," she teased Horace, "I might let you take me to Don Tomas's rancho for supper Wednesday." She was one smart little tease.

"Yup," he answered under his breath trying to keep their untried romance still a secret in a small town.

Bean's dark eyes were wide open like saucers.

"Did I miss something?" Roy Bean asked.

Paulette moved hastily into the kitchen. Her hand covered her mouth's laughter.

"No, nothing," said Horace, choking on his words and

grabbing a quick cup of water.

"Well, what can I get you gentlemen?" Paulette asked, returning completely composed. Horace could see she was a good actress. She also had a cute way of walking. He was smitten again.

"Bacon and eggs French style with all those spices," Horace said, trying to keep his cool.

"Make that two. Hear the news?" Bean said.

"What news?" Horace asked.

"The Yorba and Workman ranchos got hit big last night. We got our best trackers workin' the signs."

"What's the word so far? Think it's Indians or rustlers?"

"Luie thinks, from the signs, it's a professional gang. Maybe forty-five to fifty ex-miners tryin' to make a killin'."

"Probably be their own," Horace answered. Was this new development going to blow another Sunday date? Here they were going again off to the chase and away from the café.

"I heard. Another run for glory, oui?" Paulette said. Her eyes fell to the floor. Her sweet mouth turned down. "Get those rustlers, boys. They're no good for our livelihood," she added, then turning her spirits up into a smile. Gosh she responded quickly. Had to be a strong inner drive.

Horace appreciated her support, knowing that someday soon they would be alone and see if they had more in common.

"There's the tracker from Company A now," Bean said. "Let's forget the meal. I've a feelin' we're gonna be in the saddle again." Bean rose and left quickly.

Taking his time, Horace grabbed two biscuits and stuffed three pieces of bacon in his mouth. He blabbered he'd try to be back as soon as he could. She nodded.

The captain announced a major callup. Companies B, C, and D were to be in formation immediately. Already most rangers were saddled for the mission.

At home Horace packed for the campaign. Would he get back and have some time with Miss Bovierre? He felt as if he were playing with a half-grown tiger. She was fun yet dangerously smart. Oh, well, all conquest, glory, and honor were fleeting.

When Horace arrived at the barracks, the three companies were ready. The men left town with their horses at a brisk pace. The news traveled back from the trackers that the Yorba and Workman ranchos had been hit by two separate divisions of one professional gang; the criminals were using Tujunga Canyon as their hideout and gathering point. The rangers split into two groups to approach the canyon at its north and south points. They learned that perhaps two hundred and fifty horses and a hundred head of cattle were hidden away there.

The north group, Company B, galloped off in a faster gait to gain the time needed to cover their longer distance. The other two companies divided into two groups, each under corporals. Horace had Banning, the Marshalls, and Getman. The Luie told him to take the trail furthest to the east when coming into the canyon.

The canyon spread before them, two miles wide at the south opening. Horace knew the rangers' plan was correct. They entered on the easternmost trail, nary a sound from the wildlife. Suspecting ambush, he motioned to the Marshall brothers to get down quick.

Ka-bang! A rifle bullet swished past Horace's head. Feeling like a target riding high above the mustard grass, he jumped down. Bean and Getman went toward the sound of the rifle shot. The Marshall boys followed them but stayed fully bent. Thank God for the mustard grass. Horace said a prayer. In battle everyone was a believer, right? Especially when you were the target.

A shining silver light came from the short cliffs off to the right. The light was two hundred feet away and near his fellow rangers walking in the grass. He grasped his rifle. He'd practiced out to three hundred feet to hit a deer. Reloading the musket would take a minute.

Horace found a good rock to steady his aim, cocked the flintlock rifle, saw the silver glint again in the sun, and squeezed one a couple of inches higher.

Ka-bang, then a quick ka-splat! Horace heard the half-inch slug hit something. Someone groaned. Green and Wiley ran to find the sniper dead with three first-class loaded rifles.

"This guy musta been a pass guard," Green said as Horace walked up. Horace was gratified to stop him before he picked off a couple rangers. Horace gave the three rifles to his friends. They said thank you, not for the rifles, but for saving their asses. Horace had now earned his stripes again.

"The gunshots probably alerted the rustler's camp, men. Our best bet is to hide our horses on the other side of that ridge," Horace said. "Then we'll all stay low and crouch along those cliffs. That way we'll blend in and use the sun against any escaping rustlers."

They nodded, all faces grave, knowing they were dealing with professional outlaws. They climbed and took command of the eastern cliffs.

Soon, just a hundred feet away, came a group of seven rustlers -- five Mexicans and two Americans -- trying to leave the area quietly. With guns drawn and rifles ready, Horace told his men to sight them in and fire at will. All five fired. Five rustlers fell. Shots boomed throughout the canyon. Now only two men crouched below them. Both wayward Mexicans looked at each other and dropped their guns.

Horace appreciated the way his rangers could shoot when it counted. They tied up the two, deposited them by the horses, and went back on duty to cover the cliff. Soon another three Mexicans walked their horses out. They were quiet, very quiet. They put their hands up and put down their guns. Horace heard more gunshots coming from deep in the canyon.

"Let's go help out our brother rangers in there," Horace said as he removed his hat and rubbed his hair back. The morning sun started its daily rise to a hot screamer.

Horace mounted up his men to take their five bound prisoners into Tujunga Canyon to report. They piled up the dead below the cliff for burial later.

They rode into the rustlers' camp, leading the rustlers by a rope as they walked. Two wounded rangers, slowly dying, cried for help. He asked the Green brothers to bring them water. Horace recognized them from the other troops. Sad, sorry day for them. All around lay the signs of rustler professionals: the way they hid the stock, the five phoney branding irons to change the animals' brands; the hidden bushes to block the blind canyons. These felons were masters at their game.

Riding further into the camp, they discovered two large, open graves with just a little dirt hurriedly thrown on them. Men and women lay in those graves, ten naked men with their heads scalped, their penises removed and stuck into their mouths prior to death, their eyes open wide from the ultimate horror they'd witnessed. Horace surmised they must have been forced to watch their women and children being mutilated. Then they were murdered. Horace felt physically ill. Their contorted faces suggested they suffered tremendously prior to dying. Surely these helpless victims saw lusty, vile wickedness from their attackers.

In the second grave lay ten naked women with their breasts cut off and heads scalped. Four of the women were cut right up the middle like butchered steers. They'd probably fought off the advances of these low-life scum while their men watched. The dead women's eyes still screamed. They cried out in desperate and shamed horror. Horace threw up Paulette's bacon and biscuits.

The Rangers hung their heads. Some just retched until only dry heaves came from the pits of their stomachs. They didn't talk. They were speechless.

The women's scalps of bloody blond, red, brown, and black hair were displayed like trophies on a long stick by their graves. The men's scalps hung from another pole by the firepit. By now no one could control the pits of their stomachs. Everyone heaved, dizzy, sick, and weak.

Then far off a ranger found the children's grave, five in it, all less than ten years old, all naked and sexually abused. Each body orifice was bloody, each young child sliced up with the parents watching.

Total disgust fomented into pure rage through the rangers. Their stomach weakness turned into wrath. Thirty of the murdering rustlers were already dead. Horace's five and two others were in custody. Seven Mexicans remained, and the rangers-turned-vigilantes "didn't need no damn signed confessions."

The rangers' command met to regain control. The Luie said that these trash had gone too far. All six corporals seconded Brevoort's suggestion. They decided upon the quiet and deadly rustlers' just reward.

The rangers could not bring out these horrors in a trial. National headlines would condemn Mexicans in general. The dead rustlers numbered fifteen Americans and fifteen Mexicans, but the seven survivors were all Mexicans, none deserving to live a minute longer.

Horace found eight wet slaughtered beef hides left on the ground. The rustlers had eaten the steak parts only. Horace ordered his men to finish the butchering. The Luie commanded the remaining rustlers, already tied up, to be rolled up very tight inside the wet steer hides. Additional outside ropes secured the criminals in place. They could barely breathe. Each man had a handkerchief over his mouth. If a man screamed, he was knocked out, then awakened.

The rangers found the settlers' five wagons in a box canyon off from Tujunga Canyon. They were stripped of supplies and burnt. Poor souls were on the wrong trail and made a shortcut at the wrong time.

The lieutenant left behind four men who promised not to touch the rustlers. All seven rustlers were placed in the middle of the canyon to absorb the rays of the hot sun, a direct, hundred-degree-plus sun.

The slaughtered cattle skins, when dry, shrank to one-third of their size. Anything inside this large ten-by-ten-foot hide also became two-thirds smaller. Compared to a python snake, Horace would prefer death by snake — it was faster. The sun needed five to seven slow, quiet drying hours to do the execution. Each man could then think of his crimes against the women, children, and men as they slowly squeezed into their first hot hell. The second hell would follow.

The cooked, crushed rustlers were not buried. The birds and vermin scavengers would pick their flesh from their bones until they returned back to earth as dust. They would never hear nature's birds or the coyote's wail again. Spring was coming, and they'd never see the flowers again.

Not one of the rangers would mention these obscene men or their crimes, nor would they tell anyone else what they did about it. The rangers swore to silence. The rustlers crossed way over the line and received their just punishment. Beyond that, the point was moot.

The rangers, like all law enforcement officers, transferred personal feelings into humor or substituted it to "happening to someone else," never losing empathy, but never using sympathy. Sympathy was reserved for family only.

Back at the barracks, the Luie explained to his men, "Rangers, imagine if we brought back the dead women, their children, and their men, with just the seven living Mexicans. What would happen in the pueblo, in California, in the United States? This specific incident would cause a major civil bloodbath against the Mexican peoples. Even we couldn't stop a riot that large."

Los Angeles didn't have the jails, courts, or law enforcement to handle the crime. Horace Bell now knew how important it was to be a ranger. He was proud, while he was realistically saddened at dark human nature.

Chapter 11

Horace realized he needed some romance in his life. For dinner, he stopped by the café. Miss Bovierre greeted him with a smile and with her hands on her hips. Horace sat down as she brought him a cup of hot coffee. The steam softened her face against the light.

"Getting to know how much I love coffee, aren't you, Miss Paulette?"

"Oui, Horace, I am." She winked.

"I'm free tonight. How about we go to the bullfight?"

"Okay. I'd love to."

Horace wished there were more sophisticated date opportunities. San Francisco had plays, operas, and orchestras, while the small pueblo sported horse races, bullfights, rodeos, and mountain or ocean picnics. Thank God they were building a new theater by Tomas' sisters' home. A Mexican bullfight provided a chance to talk to Miss Bovierre away from her café. The date would break the formality barrier.

Horace decided to rent a carriage for comfort, have their private riding seat, and be alone at the fight. When he picked her up at the café, her face looked pleased. She wore a yellow dress with matching bonnet. He drove the matched team of horses to the bullfight and stopped at Calle Del Toro. The bullfight was well-attended. Across from their position were four wooden seat stands, all packed. Dons walked around dressed like plantation peacocks and talked so everyone looked. Horace chuckled at the sight. They wore red sashes, white or blue lace shirts, and fancy black suits with quarter-inch white symmetrical Spanish designs sewn into the sleeves. Their black patent-leather boots and black, flat-topped Spanish hats really made for a command performance. All they had to do was scream like the colorful birds.

"What are you so happy about?" Paulette asked, her head turned up inquisitively.

"I was comparing the Dons' fine feathers to peacocks strutting on the plantations."

"Oui, I agree with you, dressed to the hilt and making their noises." She smiled and twisted her long light-brown hair at the end.

"Yes. Now tell me about you, Miss Paulette."

"Born close to Paris, studied English and medicine at the university, moved here with friends relocating, and purchased the café to make a living. How about you?"

"Born in Indiana, raised in religion and law, came for excitement and gold, found cold mud, and became a ranger. Plan to be a lawyer."

"Oui. I can see you panning in the cold." She handed him some warm coffee.

"Thank you. That'll work. What are your plans?"

"Oh, buy as many rentals as I can, live here -- You?"

"Pass the Bar, stay a ranger, start a practice, settle down."

"Oui, you have a good plan. Oh look. There's the first bull."

Okay. So she planned to buy rentals and watch the city grow. Smart young lady. He wondered about her love life.

They watched three bullfights. A champion matador let the last one live. They cheered for each bull charge. The crowd hoped for a matador to get gored. People loved the danger, especially when they could just watch. Paulette cheered for the underdog bull that was allowed to live. She shared with Horace about how many short swords the bulls could take before they were incapacitated. The best part was he felt closer to Miss Bovierre. On their ride back to the café, he realized they were compatible. He wanted to be around her more. He was ready for their picnic.

He hadn't been on a picnic since Indiana. He remembered going to the park on the lake right after church. His dad called it a pond, but to an eight-year-old, the lake was as big as the ocean. The outdoors smelled better, probably because it was fun. He had good childhood memories.

"Daydreaming, Horace?" Paulette asked, startling him as she came into the dining area with a pot of coffee.

"Oh no. Uh -- I was just thinking," said Horace. "Just -- "

"Just thinking it's time to relax, right?"

"No, daydreaming, you were right. I remembered Indiana years ago and those Sunday picnics at the lake that my dad called a pond." He was sad that those times were past.

"Good. I'll pack tonight, be up, oh, six a.m. We'll meet at Alameda and High and ride to the Angeles Mountains. This Miss Bovierre will show Mr. Bell a lake that he can call a pond." She smiled broadly, her face glowing.

"Sure. Think you can trust me?" he asked, just half kidding, thinking lusty thoughts.

"You are a man of high principle, Mr. Bell. We will have fun, most certainly."

Wonderful. She made him feel guilty. He could always just hope, right?

"Be there at six, Alameda and High?" she asked.

"I'll be fifteen minutes early," he said, almost panting at the thought of being alone with her in a quiet lakeside spot.

"Good. Bye now," she said, holding the door for him. He watched her hurry back to her kitchen. Their picnic date would further define their relationship -- stop or go forward, maybe even stay status quo.

Horace could hardly sleep with the rustler memories juxtaposed with the upcoming picnic, but he managed to be up at five raring to go like a young bull stud. He took his coffee, saddled Pal at half-past five, and arrived early.

Soon Paulette arrived and off they went. She appeared stylish in her English riding outfit -- pants -- the latest fashion. She'd probably sent for it from San Francisco. She looked beautiful. Was this love or infatuation? Maybe it was just plain sex, he smiled to himself. But he felt a little odd. He wore nice, clean clothes, but not a gentleman's suit, and he felt more like the pauper and the princess as they rode away. He certainly wasn't Napoleon the Third.

They chatted as they took the main road north. After a few hours, they stopped at a plateau overlooking the pueblo. Paulette told him during the fall, the Indians left the mountains for warmer places; they'd be alone. She told him the picnic area was a few miles inland and that they should rest and water the horses at a nearby spring.

Sitting by the water, she looked beautiful. Her green eyes sparkled.

"Horace, I once heard a wonderful old legend about these mountains and the pueblo."

"Really. I love old legends," Horace said, leaning back on a rock and folding his hands behind his head.

"Back in 1780, three bronzed Spanish dragoons ascended the highest hill above the Los Angeles River.

Sergeant Navarro, the oldest, led them up steep ravines with their mules and horses. His second in command was Corporal Quintero, with a soldier, Bannegas. The corporal and the soldier both wondered why they were working so hard to get to the top. They thought the sergeant had lost his mind."

Paulette paused, smiled, and continued. "Hours later, they climbed to where no man had stepped before -- the summit. They looked down to the basin of the future Los Angeles County. They even saw all the way to Santa Catalina Island across the ocean. They could not believe the undisguised beauty and splendor. They stood there in awe; they were speechless. Then the sergeant went to the mules, pulled out three cups, a bottle of wine, and three cigarritos. Handing the cups out, he filled them and lit the cigarritos. They sipped the wine and smoked, enjoying the view that followed their hard work.

"They saw the San Gabriel Mission now only ten years old with its new red tile roofs. Its white walls seemed foreign to the lush, green landscape around it. The winter green of the hills contained summer robes of light brown. The lakes, rivers, valleys, forests, hills, and mountains formed a perfect panorama. Countless antelope and deer bounded below and all around. They felt like armored knights of old, guarding the Portals of Paradise. Navarro said he felt like a Spanish prince guarding the Holy Grail. They were breathless and full of wonder.

"Some minutes passed when Corporal Quintero asked of his sergeant, 'I wondered and wondered where we were going up this large hill, being down there for ten years. Now I see that you must have made this trip before because it is unbelievably beautiful. It even surpasses our native Granada in Spain!'

"The sergeant answered, 'Oh no, my Corporal, I have not

been here prior. But thirty years ago as a child, I had this dream. I was right here. Yes, Our Blessed Lady, the Queen of Angels, stood right here and told me to build her city down there. Our Lady pointed to the spot, right there beside the Los Angeles River. She promised me that if I started a city there, she would bless it for all time. The city would become a fantastic jewel in the world community. The Queen of Angels' city wealth would exceed anything we saw in Spain! I plan to start that city. Both of you will help me in my endeavor. We shall call our city Nuestra Senora Reina de Los Angeles -- Our Lady Queen of the Angels. With our ten years in service, we shall be given permission and the lands to start our vision together.'

"All agreed right there to ask permission from the Governor Don Felipe de Neve. The governor asked where they would find the workers for their vision. Sergeant Navarro showed him the forty-four brave souls who shared his vision. Their mixed ethnic backgrounds impressed the governor. Permission came, the city was founded.

"The military at the mission all turned out to celebrate on August 1, 1781. The citizens -- Mexican, Indian, Negro, and Spanish -- were fearless. The Negroes were in the majority from three centuries of relentless slaving under the Spanish conquistadores.

"The governor helped the city by finding men and women who had worked the soil before. The Spanish cities made up of soldiers had failed prior because the soldiers gave up when life became hard. The Governor de Neve was a man of foresight, Horace. He wanted a militia of men attached to the soil. He wanted a series of cities up the coast that would protect it from foreign invasion. He did not want these men under the missions. The missions could function under any government. He didn't trust the missions to fight for Spain. Governor de Neve had foresight."

"I like it," said Horace. "Gives Los Angeles a spiritual founding."

"Yes, with hope, growth, and promise for tomorrow," she answered.

"The governor's view, besides religious politics, included

police/military protection from all outside forces," Horace said.

"Good, Horace. A protected city is a growing city."

Maybe that was why she was investing in properties in Los Angeles. She had inside information the city would become one of the world's greatest commercial centers. It did have coastal access, continental location, and border position. He appreciated her insight into the little pueblo, how it started, and where it was going. She was one sharp lady.

Horace complimented her and they talked for another hour until they finally saw the two-mile-long blue lake. She took him down an Indian trail. He was ready with his rifle and revolver in case a bear or lion challenged them. Delicious aromas of pine trees, wild herbs, berries, and wildflowers filled Horace's nostrils. They first took their horses to the start of the lake. A stream flowed fed by springs and winter snow runoff. They found a sheltered and secluded spot to lay out the picnic blanket.

Horace made the animals comfortable giving them the oats and grain he'd brought. She unpacked the lunch, wrapped to stay cold. She brought two canteens, one with a good red wine and one with water.

Horace questioned this second date and how it might turn out. The elevation made the sun appear hotter. The temperature had to be near ninety. He made sure the horses had shade. He bent down and touched the water. Boy, it was cool. If he were alone or with his ranger friends he'd strip down and jump into that refreshing lake.

Paulette had found a flat place, all rock under a fifty-foot, healthy pine tree. The tree afforded shade to their rock table which jutted out over the lake and stood about three feet higher. She set up the tablecloth on the flat rock and set out the cups and utensils.

Paulette started to laugh.

"You sure look happy here laughing and all," Horace said.

"Oh, oui, Horace. It is just the freedom, the quiet, the adventure, the smells, and you --"

"Alone we are, Paulette. Can I pour you a cup of....?"

"Wine, please, Horace. Nothing like Vignes' best to relax in the mountains," she said.

Two doe sipped from the lake fifty feet away. Then a flock of black mudhens landed in the lake. Several squirrels ran up and down the trees around them. Horace felt unstressed.

"The animals are cute, especially after a glass of wine. How about you, Horace?"

"Yes, I'll pour myself one. You're right about our different friends out there. Mind if I remove my boots and vest?"

"Make yourself comfortable. That's what we came for," she said, taking off her hat, her boots and socks too.

"Oh, that's better," he said.

"Oui, Horace, it sure is."

A warm, dry breeze of about eighty degrees blew over the lake. They finished the wine, made some small talk, and then she opened her picnic basket and started serving the food. First she brought out pieces of fried chicken flavored with garlic and spices, then a French coleslaw, honey and biscuits, a dozen cinnamon-sugar cookies, seasoned potato salad, fresh oranges, and Dutch apple pie. Past noon, it was already a cloudless ninety degrees. She told him how she first came with married friends to this spot and how the men went into the forest a few hundred yards so the women could swim. They hadn't seen a soul since starting to climb the mountain. She also mentioned how the women went way over to the other side of the lake. She pointed to the place. Horace got the hint.

"Would you like me to go to the other side so you can take a dip?" he asked.

"Oh no. I had other companions then, two females. It's not smart to split up in a forest," she warned.

"Okay. Then let's roll up our pants and see how the water feels."

"Sure. Help me, Horace. I need to get this food secure from all our newfound friends. Let's pack up and place this basket in the shade by the horses. We'll leave the canteens out with the cups for later."

They went to the lake's edge, the water a warm eighty where the sun heated it from top to bottom. Walking side by side, she suddenly slipped. Horace grabbed her right before her head went under, getting himself all wet. They laughed and went back to the tree.

They stripped to their underwear. The white cotton covered Paulette's whole body and accentuated her hourglass figure. Her chest moved up and down from the exhilaration. Her breasts pushed out with tight nipples. God, she was perfect! His lust grew. She was the best he'd seen in a long time. She sure as hell wasn't one of his three-dollar whores!

Horace's erection was well under way. The noticeable bulge made him extremely embarrassed. He wished he had more control. He tried to change his focus, but he just stared at her inviting body. Her eyes told him she knew he was aroused.

"Hey, look," Horace said. "Our clothes are drying and we're out in the heat. These undies can dry on our bodies in a half hour. How about we dive in and have some fun. Do you swim?"

"Yes."

Horace thought he could see the reflection of the entire lake when he looked into her vivid green eyes. Swimming, they found the further out they went, the water got colder, especially down about three feet. About ninety feet from shore, the water grew even colder, cooling Horace's ardor.

They swam back and sat on a rock shelf and looked at the fish darting around them in the crystal clear lake.

They smiled. She put her head on his chest. He held her face and gently moved around to face her. Her eyes said yes. She closed them. He wrapped his arms around her and kissed her. She kissed him back with passion. After a few minutes of kissing, she said breathlessly, "Oui. Oh Horace, let's take a little break."

"Sure, Paulette. That was nice."

In the sun, and on the rock, she looked devilishly seductive, but he was a gentleman first. Besides, he could find any number of whores in town, plus perhaps even that night a few wild Mexican girls ready to take on a ranger. They loved the uniforms. His relationship with Miss Bovierre might not work out into sex.

Horace politely followed her wishes. They still had

a fine time. But he was rather frustrated. Was she too strong for him? What was it?

Chapter 12

Thirty-year-old Mexican Joe was the current majordomo for the Rancho La Cienega O'Paso de la Tijera, Tomas A. Sanchez's rancho in west Los Angeles. In English, the translation was The Ranch of the Swamp and the Pass of the Pair of Scissors, and its forty-five hundred acres included several hills. Under Mexican Joe's authority were forty <u>vaqueros</u>, or cowboys, and thirty Indians who worked the cattle into its main raw products: meat, tallow, and hides. Each <u>vaquero</u> had a specific job or field riding assignment. In the open range the cattle would mate with many of the neighbors' cattle. The <u>vaquero's</u> job was to keep his owner's herd together as best he could under the conditions.

Mexican Joe, an unmarried <u>Californio</u> from Santa Barbara, carried his one hundred sixty-five pounds well on his five-foot-five-inch frame. His dark, wavy black hair complemented the <u>vaquero</u> outfit. He liked a good show; therefore, he always dressed with a flair. Every rancho had only one majordomo. He desired to show his rank.

Mexican Joe remembered mining up north only to encounter trouble. Being Mexican, he was hanged unjustly for stealing, only to be saved by a gringo friend who cut him down within seconds before death. He carried his neck scar for life afterwards. Joe then decided to do what he liked rather than risk his life for a golden dream. He liked being a <u>vaquero</u>. He was good at that and tried out to be Sanchez's majordomo when the position came up.

Joe loved his accommodations. His small office and separate living quarters were only three miles from the ocean. This gave him comfortable weather all year long. A window gave him a view of the pasture to the south. A year-long aromatic smell of the grass, flowers, herbs, and wild mustard weed constantly came through it. Plus, there always was the marvelous breeze.

He looked outside to gather his thoughts. His old weather-beaten desk held his reports. Joe wasn't much of a writer, and the window helped. His office ashtrays were full of old cigar butts. Cigar ashes spilled over the desk and onto his chair and floor. He liked his Spanish cigars. In fact, he liked any cigar. His one fault was smoking. His cigars were like his scar -- always present.

Up early, Joe double-checked the accounts receivable versus the accounts payable on a recent trail drive. The San Francisco cattle route lost only four percent compared to the risky Sacramento run at twenty percent. He and five <u>vaqueros</u> had driven five hundred head of cattle using the coastal route. They'd arrived at their destination and lost twenty-one head. On a prior trip up central California, with a herd of five hundred and fifty, they had lost over a hundred head. Tomas would like to see the differences. They were planning a thousand-head drive.

Joe always kept one <u>vaquero</u> in the saddle around the rancho all night long. This way he had two eyes and ears patrolling the perimeter. Many Indians and rustlers looked for a free steer. He rotated the guard position from man to man. A generous reward was offered anyone who brought information that saved the rancho a loss.

Then their salary was doubled for the month.

Tomas Sanchez paid his <u>vaqueros</u> well at twenty dollars a month -- five dollars more than most of the other ninety major ranchos in the county. The men always appreciated a chance to double their salary.

Joe, in his plan for another drive, began to write his report in his normal Spanish. He plodded through it but figured it would read all right. He loved his boss and their family. His hanging incident scared him to death. He never could have a decent love affair afterward. Death came too close. The trauma ruined him for any long-term relationships. He felt he could not control his destiny. Scary.

"With greatest respect, Don Sanchez, I believe that the coastal route with a cattle drive is better financially for us because, one, less cattle loss historically, twenty-one versus one hundred and five head; two, less coastal Indians versus the fierce Tulure Indians and the San Joaquins; three, less rustlers, because they tend to assault nearer the mines; four, better dollar bottom line...“

"Ayudar! Ayudar! Tulure Indians, northwest pasture, taking our cattle!" shouted Jose Lopez, part Gabrielano Indian and top vaquero and assistant to Mexican Joe.

Jose Lopez knew his Indians. Hell, he was one.

Joe ran to the bunkhouse where the vaqueros slept and told them to arm up and hit the horses. He then ran to the cattle workers' sleeping place outside the rancho yard and told the ten young Indians practicing to be vaqueros to arm themselves and select horses out of the caballadas -- special horses best for rancho work.

Each grabbed a loaded Colt revolver and a flintlock rifle from the kitchen staff, who quickly loaded the weapons upon hearing of an emergency, as trained by Mexican Joe. Within minutes, Mexican Joe rode with fifty armed men on their way to the northwest pasture.

The Tulare Indians were moving fifty Sanchez steers down the hill toward the ocean. The vaqueros saw their cattle down the hill. Joe decided to fight. Another gang of Indians would be nearby to aid the fifteen in front of him. These central California Indians liked to split up and then regroup. Joe had to hit them now.

"Onward, vaqueros, for the rancho!" screamed Mexican Joe in Spanish as he headed down the hill in front. Drawing his revolver, he shot one Indian from his bareback horse, then another, and another.

"Watch out, Joe, to your right!" Jose Lopez yelled.

Off to his right two Indians pulled back their bows. Joe threw himself to the opposite side of the horse and came back up just as the arrows missed his saddle. Then he fired two shots from his Colt .44, still smoking from the prior three shots. He killed both his adversaries. With his first gun empty, he grabbed another out of his waistband.

"You two head off the lead Indian and turn the herd around. We don't want to end up in an ambush," Mexican Joe shouted. They kicked their Spanish horses into a fast run.

Jose Lopez shouted, "Joe, we got seven and you got five. Only three left. And they're getting away!"

"Let them go. It's not worth losing any of our men to a trap.

85

They're out there at the Santa Monica Mountains. I know these type Indians, and they're bad, real bad."

"Yes, mi amigo," Jose Lopez agreed.

"Mark your sheet double pay, Jose."

The devil rode with that kid. He'd hate to be against him.

Joe watched them regroup the herd back to the north pasture. He meditated on how to avoid these Indian clashes. He first thought about the fence he'd built down on the south pasture. Months were spent toiling on the two-mile-long, three-foot-high south adobe wall. Mexican Joe had seen several thousand dried-out steer heads on the different ranchos, so he'd brought in one load after another, finally having over ten thousand heads in their south pasture. Don Sanchez had asked if he were going mad.

Joe took each one of those old dried-out steer heads, complete with horns, and fastened them on that two-mile, white adobe fence, all at different angles, making a dangerous horned barrier for oncoming rustlers. The line of skulls reduced the south-pasture loss to nil. But the northwest terrain was different than the flat mile between the hills down south.

Joe jumped off his horse and checked that no more Indians were coming back for a counterattack. No, those Tulares respected strength. They weren't stupid. Like most criminals, they preferred to prey on the weak and unprepared. They'd probably never bother them again.

Grabbing a handful of soil, Joe noticed it was not like the clay down south but sandier and easier to dig into. Joe loved reading about old European knights, their lances, swords, and castles. The Spanish castle used moats. Yes, he recalled the castle defense — using water moats. He laughed. Tomas would think he'd gone off his rocker this time.

Back at the rancho, Joe finished his report and congratulated his <u>vaqueros</u> and Indian young men that wanted to be <u>vaqueros</u>. He promoted one cattle worker to <u>vaquero</u>, for he had saved the life of Jose Lopez by shooting quickly. Plus his horsemanship had improved dramatically when it was really needed. Joe became overgenerous and proclaimed a large fandango celebration that Saturday on his own wages. All the rancho staff cheered. They loved a party.

Tomas told him the fandango would set Joe back three months' pay. He became teary-eyed thinking that Tomas wouldn't pick up the bill.

"Joe, on second thought, with your bravery and loyalty to me and Maria, we must insist upon paying completely for the fandango."

"Whew!" Joe exclaimed quietly. He smiled, relieved. The fandango cost was equal to a year's supply in Spanish cigars. Even Cuban ones.

Tomas checked his majordomo's reports and came across an order that needed his immediate attention. He marched to Mexican Joe's office.

"Joe, what's this order for thirty shovels?" Tomas asked, checking the supply request on Joe's report.

"It will save us from losing at least a hundred to two hundred head of cattle a year."

"What do you plan to do? Bury them so the rustlers can't find them?" Tomas' face look pained.

"No, Tomas," Joe laughed. "I plan to take the shovels to the north pasture area and dig a five-foot-wide-by-five-foot-deep channel or moat-like dry area to keep out the rustler and Indian alike. And if the criminals get in to rob us, they won't be able to get the cattle over the moat because a cow or steer will never cross over something that's a deep hole. You know, the cattle are afraid. We've seen it over and over."

"I like it. Wish we could sell that idea. It would save most ranchos a fortune. But they will copy us. So be it. We're good neighbors," said Tomas, smiling broadly. "And, Joe, make sure you do this moat to protect the rancho's caballada. And make plans to be here at six tonight for supper."

"Will be done, Don Sanchez."

Chapter 13

Tomas Sanchez found his wife Maria in the master bedroom in front of the mirror by her makeup and combs. "Maria, Mr. Horace Bell and Miss Bovierre should be here in a few hours for dinner," Tomas said, standing behind her and stroking her long black silky hair.

"It will be a fine supper, my dear Tomas. I've asked Francisco Higuera and his wife to attend also."

"The Higueras?" Tomas responded. "Perfect. He was always fighting over those darn pigs grandfather used to keep. Remember how grandfather thought those pigs were his pets and therefore part of the Sanchez family? The pigs ran off toward the Higuera Rancho. When Higuera saw Grandpa step on his Rincon Rancho, he thought the Sanchezes were invading."

"And grandpa would get so mad I thought that we were going to war again, only against the Rincon instead of the Americans!" Maria laughed.

"Remember when proud grandfather pulled out his forty-year-old lance and tried to hide all the rust on it?" Sanchez said, his eyes filling with tears from laughing. "He reminded me of Don Quixote in The Man of La Mancha, only he didn't know if he was the crazy knight or the squire."

"Si, that old Cevantes book from the early 1600s. Grandpa did think he was on a spiritual quest," Maria said with her smile.

"I sure do miss him," Tomas said, wiping his eyes.

She raised her aristocratic, pointed chin slightly.

She shook her head in agreement. Well-groomed and coiffured, she dressed stylishly. Her gentle manner made her a sweet woman, easy to talk to. Spanish women visited her because she didn't gossip and had a ready ear to listen. Her habit was never to give advice unless asked. Tomas loved her to permanent distraction.

Dona Maria Sanchez's main duty, as any Dona, was to manage the rancho's living quarters: the immediate grounds, the casa, the vaqueros' bunkhouse, and the three acres on which the rancho functioned. Tomas marveled after her magical management style, her ability to make all workers into a team, yet have them feel individually important. Tomas knew that everyone considered her their patron.

Maria had under her supervision one Indian nanny for each of her children. She had two housecleaners who kept the casa tidy. She had ten Indian women who assisted in the kitchen with grinding, chopping, planning, and cooking. She had an additional ten Indian women who made and mended all the rancho's clothes. Five Indians managed the other buildings. Twelve Indian women toiled in the garden and fed the animals. They had pigs, goats, sheep, ducks, geese, and chickens. Tomas' rancho was like a city unto itself.

Tomas stopped by the kitchen. He checked with Old Maria to see what was on the menu for dinner. Old Maria was celebrating thirty years as the rancho cook. His grandfather had hired her.

"Now, now, Tomas, you git out of my kitchen!" she screamed.

He remembered when he was a small boy trying to stick his fingers in the sweet frostings, she told him the same thing. Grandpa told her to keep little Tomas in line. She never forgot. He realized that to her, he still was that small boy. No matter, dinner was soon enough, and it was always good.

Chapter 14

At five p.m. Horace stopped at the café to pick up Miss Bovierre for the dinner party. He'd rented a carriage from Thompson's. Thompson had harnessed a spirited, well-matched team. They made a huge dust trail as they trotted toward the restaurant. The horse team made Horace think of his relationship with his current lady friend. Paulette smiled as she came out. Wasn't she an attractive and seductive woman?

"You've brought a fine carriage, Horace. How's the team?"

"We'll make good time with them. Thompson's last carriage. His best team."

"Good. Should be fun tonight. I love it when someone else is doing the cooking."

"Paulette, you could have your portrait painted the way you look tonight."

"Well, thank you, Horace. I've never seen you in a suit before. My, what a handsome man you are."

He blushed. "Had to break down and buy one for the social life here. Uncle Bell said it would be a smart thing to do. Not bad, huh?" said Horace, as he took his hat off, rubbed his hair back, and bowed toward her.

"I like it, Horace. It makes you look like a young politician, or a businessman. Perhaps even a senator."

"You've got big plans for me?"

"Oui. Nothing that you can't achieve, right?" Her light French accent came through.

"Yes." Horace continued. "I like your green dress and matching hat. Is that satin?"

"Oui, it is. Came in last week from San Francisco on the steamer, the Sea Bird. I saw it in one of those San Francisco society papers."

"That's Captain Haley's ship. I came in on the same one. Guess that smashing new dress and I have something in common." Horace laughed.

"We should get going, Horace. It's getting late." He noticed she changed the subject and didn't respond to his remark. Oh, well, move forward.

Horace felt funny having his Colt .44 holstered on the floor of the carriage. It just wouldn't look right, his being dressed in a twenty-five-dollar suit and wearing a gun. He felt half-naked without it but laughed. He liked the naked part.

He slowed the horses' gait to a walk upon approaching the elegant Spanish rancho. A high Spanish arch greeted them. Horace mentioned it looked almost Roman. A four-foot white adobe wall with a red-tile capped top surrounded all the rancho buildings.

On the outside sprawled an Indian village made of crude grass huts where a hundred or so poor rancho Indian workers lived. In his travels on the Mississippi River from Indiana to New Orleans he'd seen how the poor Negroes lived. He'd also seen the beautiful mansions. The Southern plantations and the Californio ranchos had much in common.

He brought the carriage to a stop at the front door, and two Indians came and took the horses.

"What nice hospitality," Paulette said.

An Indian servant greeted them and escorted them into the casa. Paulette was led into the guests' quarters to freshen up from the trip.

Horace took a moment and looked around. The home was laid out in a large, one-story U formation. The walls facing outside were about three feet thick, and the inside walls were two feet thick. The walls made the home very cool and comfortable.

He was led into the sala, a large living room where the guests would talk before the dinner.

Soon Paulette joined him, and they commented to one another how lovely the home was. Since they'd arrived early, the servants served them a glass of wine and asked them to relax.

As they sat down in the living room, a young Indian girl, about twelve years old, entered the room, sat at the large piano, opened the top, and started playing Spanish and American tunes. Don and Dona Sanchez came in, and introductions were made.

Don Francisco Higuera and Dona Higuera entered. Tomas explained to Horace and Paulette that the Higueras owned a bordering rancho. Wine, music, and good conversation filled the room. At six p.m. sharp, Mexican Joe, dressed in a fine <u>vaquero</u> outfit, joined the group. Tomas introduced him to his guests.

"Dinner is served," an older Mexican lady said in Spanish. Tomas told Horace that lady was the best cook in California.

Tomas escorted everyone to the dining room on the other side of the casa. On the way Tomas showed them the chapel, the priest's room, the guest room, and storage room. Good grief. The place was so damn big, they even had a room for a visiting priest.

"A priest's room?" Horace asked.

"Sure, Horace. Never know when you might want to have a wedding or something," Tomas said.

Horace looked sheepishly away. A little too fast with that marriage comment for him.

Tomas continued with the tour. Outside the U-shaped home in the middle stretched a garden area over three thousand square feet. In the middle stood a Spanish fountain with its own pump. The water made a perfect romantic setting.

Tomas Sanchez thanked his guests for taking the time to come for dinner. Maria Sanchez announced the menu: the finest filleted charbroiled steaks; charbroiled chicken; white grilled corn on the cob; American baked potatoes; her special salsa; Spanish rice; Mexican salad; Spanish flan; and American chocolate cake. Horace's mouth watered at the promise of such food. Maria ordered that no one could go home hungry. All laughed.

The servants faithfully topped off the glasses. The Mexican salad had a cilantro and chili dressing. Horace found it delicious. Delightful aromas continually filtered in the room from the kitchen.

The conversation started off lightly until Horace saw Mexican Joe's neck with its terrible scar. Mexican Joe tried to cover the scar. Horace wanted to ask about it, but manners stopped him. He had a big mouth, he'd been told.

"When I was working the mines in Trinity, we never ate this fine," Joe said.

"My Uncle Billy Rubottom worked the Trinity mines. Did you ever meet him?" Horace asked.

"My God! Your Uncle? My precious Mary, Mother of God. He is my savior, my friend. We guarded each other's claims."

"My uncle likes to take care of himself."

"A gold pouch was missing. Five gringo miners tried to string me up. I was dead for sure."

The dinner table guests stared at Mexican Joe mesmerized.

Mexican Joe hesitated, remembering. "Ten seconds I'd -- Billy Rubottom knocked three of them down with an ax handle, pulled his gun on the other two, and cut me down singlehanded."

"Jes," Tomas said.

"Now I wear this neck scar. He just plain saved my life," Mexican Joe said.

"He wrote to me about a mistaken hanging. I remember -- found the sack on one gringo, who was trying to frame you -- and Billy was so damn — excuse me -- darn mad he hanged the miner by himself," Horace said.

Mexican Joe put his hand around his throat. His eyes watered. He brushed his wavy hair to cover his emotions.

"That's true. They found the marked sack hidden on one of the gringos that tried to hang me. Senor Horace -- mi brother -- any kinship to Billy is mi family." Tears then flowed from his eyes.

Horace politely changed the subject. "I understand from Uncle Alex that Billy is moving to the Monte area."

"Good. I would love to visit with him," Joe said.

"Well, how are those pigs, Poncho?" Tomas said to Francisco. Poncho laughed. His rounded hands grabbed his belly as it shook. His wife laughed at him.

"You big joker. They are fine since you gave them to me as a peace offering. Things weigh four hundred pounds each. My wife won't let me butcher them. She said 'for old times' sake.' Oh, that proud grandfather of yours. May the Lord Jesus, and Mother Mary, bless his soul."

"He loved you, especially after you lanced Captain Gillespie at San Pasqual," Tomas said.

"Well, Captain Sanchez, I recall that you were doing a little lance work on that day yourself."

"Yes, Poncho, we put many -- oh, what, twenty-two brave

Americans -- in their graves that day and sent the rest running for help. I felt that if we could keep up that momentum, we would win. But what would we win? We are better being Americans no matter what happens. There will be more choices for everyone," Tomas said, nodding. "Mexican governments changed more than we change our clothes."

"You are right," Poncho agreed, "but our ranchos would be better off if California was a slave state with our Southern brethren than with the North as a free state."

"They did what they did, Poncho. We have to believe in America. The Compromise of 1850 brought us in as a state, even before Utah," Tomas said.

"That Utah state," Poncho said, shaking his pudgy head. "Horace, I heard you were the only man to catch that Mormon fellow, heard you got him riding like a true Spanish <u>vaquero</u> with your legs only, two hands on the gun, wham! What I'd give to see that." Poncho held his hands up as if he was pointing a gun.

"Horace, you did that? You said it was just a little rough," Paulette said, feigning amazement.

"You're part of old Billy's kin for sure," Joe said.

"Got lucky, that's all."

Tomas' eyes narrowed, and he motioned to his servant to bring him a box. "It is not that easy to explain away, Mr. Bell. I was going to wait until after dinner, but I am too excited. I want you all to please listen.

"First, I have an award for Miss Paulette Bovierre straight from France with the latest hilt, a brand new thin rapier with its holder. In appreciation for teaching me English the past three years."

"Oh, I do not know what to say! It's beautiful with the golden blade guard. Thank you, Tomas -- Don and Dona Sanchez," she said with moist eyes. Horace stared at the generous gift.

Tomas grinned and rubbed his short black beard. "Horace, I can see that you are surprised. No one in the pueblo can beat her with the rapier. She's the best. She learned it in France. Horace, for you, the latest in <u>vaquero</u> wear for helping me prove to the city government who's behind the cattle rustling."

"Thanks, Don and Dona Sanchez," Horace said, taken back by their gift.

"Joe, we have a new Colt .44 for you. You can put it in your saddlebags for the next emergency. You're the best majordomo in the county," Tomas said, handing the weapon to his loyal charge.

"For the Higueras, I received notification that the Land Commission Court in San Francisco has certified your rancho deed and you now hold it fee simple. Your lands are free and clear. No more worry for you two." Tomas handed them a federal court order of proof.

"Oh gracias, Don Sanchez," they both cried.

"We want this to be happy, not an emotional mess. Come on. Maria and I are extremely happy," Tomas said. "It's time to celebrate."

Horace put his new <u>vaquero</u> outfit against his shoulders. Paulette looked at him approvingly.

Maria said, "Tomas, don't forget about the fandango." "Oh," Tomas said. "Before I forget, you are all invited to a fandango, here, Saturday night. Joe, tell Don Poncho about your moat idea. He always likes to hear your ideas because they save him from losing cattle."

"It fits, Tomas. Looking for a new majordomo?" Horace asked, kidding.

"Over mi dead body," Mexican Joe laughed.

"How about a young gringo vaquero?" Paulette asked.

"Pretty close, Paulette," Horace said.

"Maria, please tell Mrs. Higuera about the plans for the fandango. Maybe she'll help you," Tomas said.

He then turned to Horace and Paulette. "How are you two jokers doing?"

"Oh! We are getting to know each other quite well," Paulette said, glancing at Horace.

Tomas smiled broadly. "Horace, thank you for bringing in that proof of Whites, Indians, and guns from the Utah incident," Tomas said. "I can see Los Angeles soon setting up a trade route just to Salt Lake. That will reduce the profit for the outlaw and increase our export for the county. Because of your bravery, I signed your official promotion to corporal rank."

Horace's mouth opened wide, and he rubbed his hair back. "Pleased to hear that, Don Tomas. Thank you." Inside he felt warm. His move to the southern part of the state had been a wise one. God had blessed his decision over and over.

"Oui, Corporal Bell. How about a walk outside in the garden?" Paulette asked.

"Be pleased to join you, Miss Bovierre."

They walked into the moonlight not far from the dining room. Crickets made nighttime music, an owl hooted, and Horace's stomach was stuffed and content.

"Quite a night, Miss Paulette," Horace said. "Now, please tell me about this rapier -- sword thing. I'm totally amazed."

"Oui. I was with the French in Algiers as a nurse. I had learned the rapier from a friend, a French champion."

"You can — fence — rather good, then?"

"Horace, back there in North Africa I had to fight to save my dignity. I had to use a rapier. Several men, more than two... they tried to... it was..."

"Enough. I understand."

He stared at the enchantress in the soft moonlit night. She was a deadly one, yet like him, driven and purposeful. The gentle ocean breeze blew into the garden area. A scent of jasmine mixed with her perfume. Her eyes focused into the distance, unmoving as he looked at her.

"Perhaps I can teach you," she said, coming back to him. "It's fun. We'll use good protection for your handsome face." She touched his lineless cheek.

So as not to appear rude, they left the garden and rejoined the others in the dining room.

Mexican Joe was presenting the thousand-head cattle run to San Francisco to Don Tomas. Mr. and Mrs. Higuera were reading each and every word on the Federal Grant of their deed. Maria and her servants were getting the desserts ready. Horace and Paulette sat and shared coffee in the dining room. Once dessert was finished, Mexican Joe excused himself and left.

"We thank you for a wonderful dinner, your unexpected gifts, and company. We plan to be back Saturday night for the fandango. It'll be fun," Horace said, saying goodnight.

"We'll enjoy the fandango, Horace," Paulette said quietly as she grabbed Horace's arm. The servant drove up their carriage team.

"Yes, I'll get to wear my corporal uniform for the first time."

"Oui, I'll be proud of you all dressed up."

As Horace pulled out onto the road, he felt something funny, like someone watching him or hunting him. He had developed a survival sixth sense. His ranger job had taught him to be observant. He made a habit of looking around no matter where he went. Advance knowledge could protect his life.

About a half mile away from the Sanchez casa, Horace reached down to retrieve his Colt .44 and its holster. The bump they'd hit must have knocked it out of position into the back of the carriage open trunk area three feet to the rear. He was going to stop and get it when he looked to the rear first. The moon illuminated an approaching stranger -- a man by himself. He was three hundred feet back with a pistol in his right hand. His horse was closing rapidly.

"Hold on tight, Paulette. Go!" Horace yelled to Pal.

They flew. The pursuer was getting further behind. Paulette took off her hat and covered the bright golden handle of her new rapier laying on the floor.

With the man six hundred feet behind, Horace wanted to retrieve his weapon. Bringing the carriage to a stop, he jumped out and started for the trunk to open it.

"Stick your hands up, gringo. This is a holdup!" a Mexican voice said.

Horace saw two men on the side, and the one behind was galloping up. He was trapped, and in big trouble.

"Well, well, well, what do we have here?" the White man said sarcastically.

"The French looker from the café, all ready for fun," the Mexican answered. "Here's Harry comin' up."

"We could kill the big fella, have a little fun with the Frenchie and -- don't move, mister, or you're dead!" the White man said as he dismounted. The other two then dismounted, while keeping their guns trained on Horace. Horace edged

98

back. He quickly went over the options. He would be shot one or twice trying to get his gun. They wanted to rape Paulette. He could not allow that to happen no matter what.

"Merci, Gentlemen," Miss Bovierre said. "You don't have to hurt us. Horace, please stay where you are. These gentlemen want some fun, and the two thousand in gold. Right? All you want is the gold in my purse?"

The men's eyes lit up.

"T-t-t-two thousand?" the big White crook stammered.

"Wow, what a haul from a carriage," Harry said.

"Two grand — we won't hurt you, Frenchie, for that," the Mexican said with a sly smile.

All three men moved toward her to see the gold. They still kept their guns trained on Horace. Their eyes were huge in the moonlight.

"Oui, here. I'll help you get it," Paulette said while stepping down and showing as much leg as possible to distract the three men.

Horace watched the men move closer to look at her. The light from the full moon shone behind the men and onto Miss Bovierre's legs. Horace quietly went for his weapon while they were distracted. They kept moving closer to her. Horace remembered her hat was on the floor of the carriage. She lowered her dress slowly. The men's eyes fell all the way down to her ankles as she covered up. They were drooling, all three of them.

"Oui, gentlemen, you must have all this heavy gold. Here! Catch it!"

She reached down in the carriage, grabbed her purse with her left hand, and tossed the large, three-pound purse to the man in the middle. Their eyes now went to the purse. With her right hand she grabbed the rapier and did an immediate straight thrust together with a wide swiping upper C motion to slice their three throats in the same motion. It was expertly performed.

Each man was left with a six-inch incision below his jaw. The rapier severed three throats, voice boxes, and larynxes. Moonlit purple blood poured from the cuts.

A second later their nervous system closed with shock. All

their muscles were paralyzed. The men were dumbfounded and in disbelief. She had outsmarted them. Instead of being their intended victims, they became the victims. She followed the golden rule in a reversed way. Horace now had his weapon, but it was no longer needed.

The men's six eyes bugged out even more than when they were looking at her legs. Mortally wounded, they fell to the ground.

"Dirty scum of the earth. You can all go to hell!" she screamed. Then she wept hard. She didn't like being forced to take life.

Horace rushed over and held her in his arms. He let her cry it out. He rubbed her head, not saying a word except that everything was going to be okay. Minutes later, she regained her composure.

Recovering her gift from Tomas -- a gift that had just saved them from certain peril -- she wiped its blade on the Mexican's white shirt.

"Those bastards would have killed us!" she said, and turned to tears again.

"Paulette, you did the right thing."

Horace inside was at first shocked. Then quickly he saw things in her similar to him. He was glad he didn't open his mouth and say the wrong thing. He saw in her the rage he tried to hide, and he consoled her, but wondered if her tears were an act. The gal was damn good with that rapier. God she was good.

He put on his gun belt and made sure it was loaded and ready. He promised himself never to take it off again. He helped her into the carriage and dragged the men to the side of the rode. He heard more horses approaching the carriage. Not again. He quickly responded by drawing his weapon and shouted, "Who goes there?"

"Los Angeles Rangers, Company A, on patrol. Deputies Halpin, Hanniger, and Hart," one shouted back.

"Corporal Horace Bell here — Pat, Bill, George -- come here quick -- on the double!"

Horace promptly told them the story. The rangers handled

the crime scene while Horace and Paulette started a slow, consoling ride back to town.

"It's funny how much better the night air smells when you know you're going to live another day," Horace remarked to a quiet Miss Bovierre.

"Oui. Even the dirt smells good. Even the bugs look good tonight."

"You did a very brave thing back there, Paulette. Thank you. I can't tell you how frustrated I was not to be able to..."

"I know, Horace. Your gun... I knew you'd get shot. That's why I asked you <u>please</u>. A second, I needed one second to do what they chose for themselves."

"I was amazed. We're so much alike."

"I wasn't going to lose you over three villains. Oh, Horace, they wanted to hurt me — and you — real bad." She faltered and her tears came again.

"Look, you saved my life. We weren't harmed in any way. I'm relieved!"

She sighed. Horace had seen that when the chips were down, she would be there -- tough, smart, and ready. But she carried a lot of baggage -- enough to fill the carriage.

"It will be fine, Paulette. You're one fine woman," Horace said, putting his arm around her shoulder and kissing her on the forehead.

He let her fall asleep on his shoulder while riding. He cursed himself for being impotent in a serious police action. He vowed he'd never again be unarmed; he'd carry two guns. How worried he'd been when the men talked rape. He came to grips with his feelings. He'd learn from his mistakes. He really admired Miss Paulette Bovierre. He now had enormous respect for her. Yes, she was one fine woman, and one hell of a partner. However, this event had changed the way he looked at her.

Chapter 15

Peter Biggs sat in his old black leather barber chair. He bemoaned his slow business. At forty-two years old, he loved his gambling. His eager brown eyes and stocky body made him appear like a prosperous black businessman. Oh, well, he sighed. At least he knew what to wear. He dressed like a high-class river boat gambler, and the people of the pueblo enjoyed his flair for clothes and his outspoken personality. They knew they paid heavily for his barber services.

The Mexicans called him Don Pedro as an informal honor. All in all, he tried to look and act the part of a perfect black gentleman, even though he wasn't. The only barber in town, Peter had a monopoly in his chosen business. The average California barber would charge only a fourth of his prices. He wanted a dollar for a haircut, fifty cents for a shave, and seventy-five cents for a shampoo. His extra-inflated fees gave him the money he needed for gambling, his first love. And his second was sex -- Miss Lilly Brown, his one and only high-priced black whore, who provided that. For free. Oh boy -- complimentary.

Biggs traveled to California with a Southern army officer named Smith. Smith's father, the Governor Billy of Virginia, had given Biggs to his son as a manservant. Every officer in America's service deserved his own private Negro to keep up appearances. When California came into the Union as a free state, David freed Peter Biggs. Biggs, of course, didn't argue with the fortunate change as long as he could earn a living. Barbering would have to put food in his mouth. Plus, it provided gambling money. Biggs, now free, had been fortunate indeed. But the damn tables weren't so hot.

Biggs figured that the pueblo could use his talents learned while barbering three hundred Negros and Whites on the Virginia plantations. The previous pueblo barber died of the pox, so Biggs took over his small shop next to Miss Bovierre's French Café. The shop's location helped the whoring business, being across the street from the Bella Union Hotel. Biggs knew the Bella Union housed thousands of fleas, but he told Lilly "it's the best hotel in town." His shop came with a second-hand chair from San Francisco, an old, high-back chair that was so tall, the patron had to lean forward for the shearing. His floor, unlike the café's next door, was dirt, but Biggs didn't care. He cared about his appearance, not that of his shop.

As he told his customers, "I's cut hundreds of them Niggras' heads in the great outdoors that the good Lord gave me to do."

A political animal, Biggs provided much entertainment in his shop. He told them all how the Republicans were wrong -- and the Democrats were right. They called him the black Democrat. Nine-tenths of his customers were Democrats. With no other shop in town, he played the odds by keeping the majority party happy. No matter. Everyone, and that's all the fools, would pay his prices. Four times inflated. He just wished the odds at the Montgomery Gambling Saloon were as good.

He'd gotten into trouble socially the year prior at a fancy Washington Ball. Arriving early, he'd asked Mrs. Jessie Benton Fremont, the governor's wife, for the first dance. A good dancer, Bigg's loved to show off to the Mexicans and the gringos, never meaning anything derogatory, but just for fun. The Dona Bessie Ramona Fremont, always polite, had accepted the dance offer. Her famous husband encouraged her by letting his wife dance with anyone she chose.

Captain Alexander Bell had arrived with his beautiful wife and then asked the same hostess, Dona Jessie Ramona Fremont, for the first dance. Biggs laughed. Alex looked at her with narrowed eyes. Mrs. Fremont told Alex that she had already promised the first dance. When Alex requested the second dance, she honored that invitation. The Spanish and American women loved their dancing time.

Once the music started, Biggs had stepped out with Dona Fremont and started his routine. Alex Bell had downed a few too many glasses of strong whiskey, so when his friends teased him that a Negro was taking his place of being first on the dance floor, Alex's pride made him pull his Colt from his holster and charge across the dance floor at Peter Biggs. Biggs's happy dance didn't last too long. Soon his pride gave way to Alex Bell and his big .44.

Alex had gone up to Dona Fremont and asked, "Did you prefer to dance with a Negro over a White man?"

The Governor's wife had answered, "In this case, yes, because I just made Don Pedro the El Bastonero, the Master of Ceremonies, and deemed it a privilege to accompany Don Pedro in the opening waltz."

Alex grew twice as mad. He couldn't do anything to get back at Dona Fremont. So he aimed his weapon at Biggs, Biggs bowed to the Dona, and ran his pudgy body out of the dance hall. Shots rang out inside the ballroom. The men, partying as usual, shot out the lights whenever a fight started. Peter Biggs ran to the street and headed for San Pedro.

Half-drunk Alex Bell, usually a good shot, wasn't aiming that straight. His shots hit the sides of the buildings. He even fell down once or twice. Peter ran as fast as possible. Each shot took an eternity to strike something that wasn't connected to himself. He'd already peed his pants twice.

Fifteen Union soldiers stood in the pueblo that night armed with muskets and stationed at the six main corners in town, each a block apart.

"What's going on?" the soldiers yelled.

Biggs was fortunate to be dressed in formal black, and to be black. With so little light in town, he was hard to see. He was certain the whole town was out to get "that proud 'Nigga.'"

A mounted patrol of five soldiers arrived at location of all the noise. From there on horseback they chased the black shadow. They fired into the vineyards south of San Pedro and First Streets. Biggs cringed with each round. Probably the only reason the six soldiers missed was because he was black. After ten blocks, the firing stopped. Biggs started jogging.

Poor Peter Biggs said afterwards, "Da good Lord knows this child never stopped running till he got to San Pedro, twenty-five miles away!"

Many thought the soldiers had killed Don Pedro. The town grieved. Even Alex Bell apologized publicly for starting the problem because of his inebriation, pride, and chivalry.

After three days at San Pedro, Don Pedro sent a courier to the pueblo with an apology to the town in general, and to

Alexander Bell in particular that if allowed to return, he would always keep his place and never upset any of the population again. His social "mistake" was forgiven and his apology accepted. Biggs came back to town and kept his word so that he'd never have to leave Los Angeles.

Today there were no customers in sight. Biggs's bored mind turned to sex. He looked at the clock. Almost six at night. He knew his sex kitten would be in at six-thirty sharp, and he was horny as hell. But in the meantime, he needed to think about making more money. Several things came to mind, none worthwhile. Then his cat started crying. She'd just had eight kittens and she was hungry, which reminded him of something.

His last customer that afternoon had been a ship's mate who had told him about ten thousand ships piled up in San Francisco Harbor and they'd brought in a terrible rat problem. The mate said the damn rats were running through the city and scaring the hell out of the good ladies. The men were just shooting them, but the noise wasn't good for the market area where the rats found the most food. The damn pests crawled out of the world's ships, abandoned there forever, while the gold-fevered crews ran up the mountains.

Biggs had an idea from all this, but it would have to wait. Lilly Brown, his little bed tiger, was walking toward his shop. He made a good living off his twenty-five-year-old hooker from Louisiana, and he got a little free action to boot. He knew Lilly made ten times better than the hookers on Nigger Alley. Those gals were low-class whores compared to her. She was his professional. He made her charge twenty-five dollars up front. Mr. Biggs always got his forty-percent of her total business.

"What your pleasure tonight, ya old nigga?" Lilly asked.

"Evening to ya, my little kitten. Ya should be nice to ya benefactor," Biggs said, smelling her perfume.

"What's you wantin' tonight?" she asked.

"Well, let's takes this off," he said, unbuttoning her dress while locking the door, "and let's takes this off," he added while undressing himself, "and let's takes this off," he said finally, removing his underwear until he was naked.

"I's thinks that's 'bout all there is ta take off," Lilly said.

"Now, what's your little wish tonight, Mr. Biggs?"

"Here. I's found da spot," he said after turning her around and pushing her head into the barber chair and rushing her from behind.

"Oh, you dog! You's got my spot! Oh, oh, oh, baby, you's so big, Mr. Biggs. Oh, oh, baby," Lilly wailed.

Biggs got so excited he lost control and climaxed.

"I's sure hope we get more tricks this month, Mr. Biggs," Lilly said, dressing quickly. "I needs da money."

Still naked, he sat in his barber chair and watched his whore get fancy for the evening. "Tonight I's picked you up two more. You's filled from seven till midnight," he said, his eyes scanning every curve of her body and thinking to himself what a great lover he was taking care of this younger gal.

"Great, Mr. Biggs. I's be goin' then. Where's the list?"

"Rights here, my pet, all full price," he grinned, leaning forward and handing her the appointment list of names, times, and room numbers.

"That's good. Thanks. Bye, Mr. Biggs."

As she turned to leave, he caught her right hand and placed it on his wet penis. He was getting ready again. It was his way of saying he cared for her. Lilly acknowledged him, rubbed his manhood once, and then left him alone.

"Ah, I thinks I'm in love," he sighed. Now if he could forget his erection, he could clear his head and go back to his business plan.

If he went around town and bought, grabbed, stole, and borrowed every kitty cat he spotted, he could sell them in San Francisco for a fortune. He'd need a ship, cages, a broker after the first sale, and he needed to make a lot of money on this. It was perfect. He'd start that night rounding up the cats in town and hide them behind his shop in his big old chicken coup and cover it up so no one would know. Then he'd buy extra cats from anyone who'd sell them.

Within a week he'd collected a thousand cats, ten cages, and had a ship already booked. Two weeks later he'd already been to San Francisco and back. He made it a vacation. He sold each cat for two hundred dollars. The market was better than he ever imagined. He cleared nine thousand dollars in profit. Nope, Biggs was no dummy. However, his gambling habit lost him five thousand in San Francisco. He decided to stay in the pueblo, get a San Francisco agent, and ship the cats. Maybe he might clear more profit.

Now he captured the cats in new places. He'd almost picked the pueblo clean so that all the kitty cat owners wondered why they couldn't find their little kitty cats anywhere. His agent, whom he figured was a crook, grabbed fifty percent of the profit. The agent's percentage, together with his gambling losses, made it impossible for him to keep any profit, even small, from what he called his "honest idea."

He even was so depressed, he wasn't able to get it up for Lilly. This was not like him. For some reason that he couldn't understand, she wasn't complaining of his lack of attention toward her. In fact, she never mentioned anything. Maybe she was tired, or maybe she wanted to give him a break. He wished he didn't feel so lethargic. He missed her tight body, all of it, all over.

Then he lost another grand at the Montgomery Saloon and Gaming House. Ranger Billy Getman owned the Montgomery Saloon located a block south of the plaza. This place was an honest place, better than Nigger Alley's. Even so, he couldn't get ahead.

"How is ya, my sweet?" Lilly asked him one evening.

"I's down, Miss Lilly. Those crooks at the Montgomery done cleaned me out," he grumbled. She noticed he didn't even have his fine gambling suit on.

"Oh, that's too bad."

"Here's the list for tonight, just seven to eleven," Biggs said, hanging his head in despair. "Business is down, Miss Lilly. I's got ta think of something else."

"Now, Mr. Biggs, I's thought about a slogan for you ta pick up my business."

"What is it? I needs something ta make more money."

"Okay. Get this down with your pencil. Ready?"

"Yeah, okay," Biggs said.

"Here goes. 'Once ya go black, ain't never go back.' Got

108

it?" Lilly said.

Biggs thought about it for a few seconds. "Great. Goes black, never goes back. Rhymes too, Miss Lilly. I like it."

The next morning Biggs felt better seeing the fifty dollars in gold deposited in the secret hole on the side of his building. He and Lilly had arranged it that way so she'd be clear with him if she ever got robbed. After every trick, she'd walk across the street and drop off his ten-dollar share in gold via the deposit hole, which led to a small safe bolted to the inside of his bearing wall. He'd invented it himself. Crap. If he'd left the twelve grand total profit in there, he'd be set for life. "Sometimes I's a fool, but I does like those gamin' tables," he admitted out loud to himself. "Guess I's hooked!" he cried. Counting out the fifty in gold was a good day's start to rebuild his cache. He'd win a thousand today. Sure.

Chapter 16

Horace had waited too long and needed a haircut. His unruly brown hair was all over the place. He brushed it back with his hand and put on his hat.

"Morning, sir," Horace said.

"Mornin' to you, sir. Name's Biggs, Peter Biggs. The Mexicans call me Don Pedro. You can call me Mr. Biggs, son." The big, stocky man's eyes narrowed slightly. "I's talked to yous once before."

"Yes, I was in once after you closed. Nice to see you again, Mr. Biggs. Name's Horace Bell, Ranger Corporal."

"Nice to meet ya, Ranger Corporal Horace Bell, sir.

I remember your kin -- hell, he scart the shit outta me all the way ta San Pedro," said Biggs with a big belly laugh.

Peter Biggs told Horace the story of the Washington Ball. Both laughed so hard their eyes were wet and red by the time he finished talking. Peter shook when he recalled the night patrol shooting at him from horseback.

"Yeah, here I's five blocks from the party, way outta town, and these fifteen night dragoons thinks I's some kinda shootin' target. Damn bullets wissin' here, wissin' there. Knowing I's so big, I's figurin' I's gonna take one of them lead slugs in the ass for sure," Biggs said, shaking his head back and forth.

"Bet you were glad you made it without a hit," said Horace earnestly.

"Yes, sir! Now, what's your pleasure, Mr. Horace?"

Two more men came in and sat in two of the four chairs left for customers.

"Nice, rounded off, thin it out. It's always too thick. And some of your best toilet water for the dollar, okay?"

"Done deal, Mr. Horace." Then Biggs whispered in his ear, "And don't tells no one, I's hasn't laughed like dat for years. Let's make it fifty cents this time, a bargain for a friend."

Horace leaned forward in the old-fashioned barber chair to get a good haircut. When done, Biggs splattered his head with old bear grease. To keep it down, he said. Biggs offered him a soiled towel that hadn't been cleaned in a month. Every customer used the same one. Then he sprinkled on good-smelling Florida water, saying, "Your price, Mr. Horace. Come back soon, and don't forgets about my little black gal. She'd go for you like a race horse. You know, Mr. Horace, like they says, once you goes black, you ain't never go back, ta the other ones." Biggs belly-laughed. Horace wondered if he'd get a discount for a piece of Lilly Brown?

"Oh, yeah, I remember. She stepped on me coming out the door. Well, thanks, Mr. Biggs. I'll let you know." Horace wasn't into paying high prices for whores but couldn't say that to this jovial black gentleman who was scared to death of his uncle.

"Next!" was all Horace heard as he left as if Biggs had them lined up for a block. Horace laughed.

Paulette greeted Horace when he walked in the café. "Horace, how nice to see you!" Her green eyes sparkled. He grinned at her shyly and sat down.

"Paulette, please -- I'd like the special today, scrambled well."

She nodded, smiled, and walked to the kitchen.

"Horace, did you hear the news?" said Roy Bean, leaving the door open so all the dust blew in. Horace shook his head. Oh no, the bear grease would attack that dust like a magnet. Thanks, Roy.

"More dead on Nigger Alley?" guessed Horace, looking up at the nervous Roy Bean. He was more concerned with Paulette.

"Right, that's right. You live right over that infested place," Bean said. He nervously rolled his long moustache and continued to stand. "Anyway, Crooked Nose Smith got mad 'cause they killed his drinking buddy Cherokee Joe. He kills the Mex that did Crooked Nose, decided to kill more. Two Mex were trying to pick up their dead friend. These were only young Mex cattle workers, and Crooked Nose cut 'em both up for pig feed. Killed 'em both while they were having a beer at the Monte. Left 'em there to slowly bleed to death for fun. Grabbed a Mexican whore, stole her a horse, and rode hell bent for the Mexican border. Judge Burrill signed a warrant for two counts of murder, dead or alive. Better Old Crooked Nose Smith dead,

112

he said. The Monte'll pay a hundred dollars with him brought in dead because it gave 'em a bad name."

"Losing the real bad ones. All's left is Dirty Dave Boe, who'll probably break out of San Quentin before you know it," Horace said grimly.

"Don't worry, Horace. I've been doin' this work for three years now. When one's kilt, two more show up. Then the citizen's say put 'em away for good or execute 'em. No more revolvin'-door returnees. Put 'em in and throw away the key."

"Right, Roy. Got to have strong control over these vermin," Horace said, thinking about his father's favorite verse -- "There's nothing new under the sun, Horace. Book of Solomon."

"So how are my philosophers this morning? You should both be in high clover," Paulette said, coming back into the dining area to take Bean's order.

"Fine. My, you look smashin' this mornin', ma'am," Roy said.

"I just left Biggs's next door. Feel like I need a bath," Horace said, trying to change the subject. He'd forgotten to compliment her today.

"Yeah, that towel. I hear it gets cleaned every month or so. And that bear grease in your hair, it's guaranteed to ruin any wall or paint in town," Roy Bean said, laughing.

"Talkin' about the blacks," Bean continued, finally taking a chair and straddling it, "have you seen the figure on that Lilly Brown? Most women in town would die for it. Prettiest thing in the pueblo." Bean liked listening to his words.

Horace watched as Paulette's mouth dropped to the floor. Now he knew he had competition -- Bean's mouth was much bigger than his.

"Horace, and bet you didn't know that Andreas Pico and Pio Pico are half black?" Bean asked.

Paulette had already turned sharply on her heel and left. Horace was glad Roy ruined his previous compliment. Besides, Horace knew Paulette had a better figure, and she wasn't a whore. Roy Bean sure loved his whores.

"No, I didn't know that!" said Horace, ready for a good tale.

"Funny, but true, story goes like this," Bean continued.

"Andreas and Pio were drinkin' at Judge Sepulveda's Rancho down south -- ten miles north of the San Juan Capistrano Mission. Both of them are gettin' pretty polluted with the booze. One of them -- I think it was Andreas -- looked at his brother and said, 'Brother, I love you, but you sure are ugly with those huge thick lips and all.' Pio looked at his brother and said, 'Brother, I love you too, and I couldn't have asked for a better brother, but your puss is uglier than mine ever could be.'

"At that, each swore the other one looked worst. Followin' Spanish culture, a wager was made, quite large, a thousand dollars. They wanted a fair judge to make the decision who was uglier.

"There was this old witch of a gal that was so frank in her opinions that even the padres at San Juan Capistrano didn't want her around watchin' their drinkin' and carousin'. Off they go half-tanked and bringin' their manhood prides to this witch judge. They ask her opinion. She sends them off for a bolt of fancy cloth for payment. They stop at the village to buy twenty yards of the best material while she considers their dilemma.

"When they come in and hand her the cloth, she leaves quickly with the cloth and hides it. They can't stand it anymore and ask her for the third time who's uglier, Pio Pico or Andreas Pico. But, you see, she's just stallin'. "She finally tells 'em, 'You're both half black, which isn't so good. You're both half Spanish with the blood of kings, that's better.' After an hour and a half the brothers finally press their point and demand she make a decision for God, the Lord, Our Lady, Queen of Peace, and America's good.

"She looks at each one about ten more times, goes into like a trance, comes out and mumbles a few words, and now the brothers really look hopeful one will win the thousand dollars. The last words of the woman are the judgment. 'Good Spanish gentlemen, after long and hard thought, taking measurements of handsomeness, good looks and manliness, I find without a smattering of doubt that both of you are so ugly that it's impossible to choose one over the other for any beauty whatsoever. Therefore, gentlemen, I find you both too ugly for words! Good day, gentlemen!'"

"She got them both," Horace said, laughing as Paulette served his favorite breakfast. She smiled. Horace noticed his eggs had been specially seasoned with French spices.

"Just eggs and biscuits, please, Miss Bovierre," Bean said, continuing. "Yeah, the Governor and the General!" Bean shook his head back and forth. "Horace, bein' on the range these last few years taught me if we don't stop the outlaws, this Pueblo will be a pisshole. Hell, it might even be like Tia Juana Township where criminals run the place."

Horace nodded. "Solomon Pico, the Picos' brother, runs the Tia Juana Township."

"Yup," Roy Bean said, twirling his moustache. "Heard he's a fat son of a bitch."

Roy Bean continued to philosophize. "We've gotta protect this little pueblo or its reputation will be shit. Us rangers — we'll kick ass and keep it together."

Horace contemplated Roy's words. "Roy, you're right. We damn sure don't want it to be another Tia Juana."

"Yup, mi amigo, later on when we get too old for honor and glory, we can be judges. I like the sound of Judge Roy Bean, toughest judge west of the Mississipi!"

Chapter 17

Juan Flores' evil eyes looked down at the Queen of Missions. San Juan Capistrano Mission was not as dilapidated as her sister missions. Flores knew the locals supported this gem. He needed their assets to survive and prosper with his dark plan.

Juan Flores still was a striking figure on horseback or at a fandango, not tall at five-foot-eight, but slim, lithe, dark, and with calculating eyes like a hawk ready to jump on its prey. He knew his glassy and hazel-grey eyes were cruel, but to him, his revengeful, vindictive behavior was justified. Flores, after losing his wife, had come to San Juan Capistrano to meditate. Here he'd planned how he could steal gold from the Chinese. Now back to his birthplace of criminality, he'd show everyone. Maneuvering his horse around the creeks that flowed down the narrow, lush green valley, Flores felt confident as he entered the town. The general store released its aroma of hot refried beans, carnitas, and tortillas for immediate consumption while customers mingled inside among the daily mix of grocery, hardware, and soft goods. Flores' mouth watered. He was hungry.

A big German owned the store. He looked at Flores with disdain. His round belly shook as he walked up to the counter.

"Senor, may I purchase a meal? Anything will do."

"We are not a restaurant for you no-counts. I know you, your thieving. No stinking Mex in here!" the German shopkeeper yelled. Flores' neck twitched to the right.

"Jes, you old German Gringo. I will come back someday and eat on your table. For your terrible manners, you will suffer!" Flores personally pledged into the man's ear.

Humiliated, he left the store and knocked on the mission rectory office. There some Franciscan priests fed him and his horse. He was offered a hot bath and a place to rest. Flores thanked them with a gold piece.

He rode out toward the eastern hills to a secluded canyon area he designated as the meeting place. Expecting no one,

Flores was overjoyed to see Poncho Daniels waiting for him. Daniels had a hot coffee pot going. He took off his hat to wave, showing his dark Mexican features. Flores remembered the seven men that abandoned him. Nevertheless, he jumped off and hugged his loyal friend and companion. Two were twice as many as one. Flores' emotion returned to his mission. His eyes became purposeful.

"Poncho, we desperately need money, men, and horses."

"There were fifty horses at Rancho Santa Margarita, ten miles south, right by the ocean."

"Perfect. We can drive them to the border, get fifty or so apiece."

"They need good workin' horses down south."

Flores' mind quickly turned to the take. "Good. Maybe three grand total!"

That night the two stole into the large Rancho Santa Margarita. They lifted the corral log and drove the entire fifty-three head south to San Luis Rey Mission and made it before dawn.

"We're makin' good time," Daniels said.

"Yeah, but we must hurry. Only forty miles to the border," Flores said.

"I sure wish we were in Tia Juana now," Daniels said softly.

Just then an Indian <u>vaquero</u> shot by them in a gallop. By evening, Flores and Daniels looked down on Mission Valley and observed the town of San Diego.

"There's San Diego," Daniels said. "We'd better go east to avoid the town's eyes."

Riding up across the meadow appeared the sheriff of San Diego County and five of his deputies with their guns drawn. They looked pissed.

"Hold it you two!"

As the deputies slapped on the thieves' handcuffs and leg restraints for the open-aired prisoner wagon, Juan Flores decided he'd form a prison gang. He'd be the leader. He liked the name <u>Manillas</u> -- for Manacles.

The ride to San Diego left biting splinters in their butts. Each bump in the wagon reminded Juan Flores how dumb he'd been to get caught. The splinters looked like small nails.

"Why don't one of you two try to run for it?" the deputy sheriff sneered. He told them he was the jailer

and if they gave him any trouble, they wouldn't get their food. "I treat ya like a dog. Bad dog, no food."

As they rode through San Diego, citizens jeered them. A couple of the storekeepers yelled out to throw away the key and keep these riffraff out of town.

"Those gringos hate us, they are bad," Daniels said, squirming on the bench seat. Flores nodded.

"Shut up you two. No talkin'," the driver said.

They rode on quietly except for the frequently blurted "owe!" spoken over the several hundred bumps on the way to the jailhouse.

They took them to court the next day. Upon arrival, they led them into the courtroom for arraignment. The judge told them of the evidence given by the district attorney. He told them if they went to trial and lost, their sentence would be ten years in prison; if they pled guilty now, they'd only get five years. They stood in the courtroom in the same chains and handcuffs they'd been wearing for hours. Flores wanted to pee. His neck bothered him as it twitched to the right.

"Why?" Flores asked his court-ordered attorney. "Why the big difference in years if I go to trial and lose?"

"It takes time to try you, Mr. Flores, and that time in trial, with the evidence in your possession, it's dead bang, not to mention a foolish waste of court time. So they let you plea bargain," their attorney said.

"So if I plead guilty, I only get five years in prison?" Flores asked, calculating his options.

"Right. If you go to trial and lose, ten years in San Quentin instead. Got to pay for the twelve-piece band!" the attorney said matter of fact, shaking his head.

"I'll take the plea bargain," Flores said.

Daniels said, "Me too."

"Can I pee and get these splinters removed, get some alcohol to clean up the wounds?" Flores wondered out loud.

"Sure. I'll get you a set of tweezers and a small bottle of

tequila. But you have to plead first," the attorney said.

Great. Had to plead to pee.

"What's your decision, boys?" the judge asked.

"They both plead guilty, your Honor," the defense attorney said.

"The sentence of the court is five years each in state prison," the judge said. "And boys, when you get out, don't come back to my pueblo, or next time it's going to be twenty long years. Next case!" The bailiff took them in back to the outhouse where Flores and Daniels relieved themselves.

"Whew! I thought my back teeth were floating," Flores said. Daniels nodded and grumbled.

The sheriff's deputy took them to his jail wagon.

"Climb in, convicts," the processing deputy said. "We'll give you all a nice ride to the harbor. You gets first class accommodations, all the way to San Quentin." The deputy spoke with a Southern accent. Then he and his partner laughed so hard, they had to cover their mouths.

Flores looked at Daniels. Their eyes went to the floor. They were in for a hard time. The road smoothed out on the way to the harbor, but the deputy deliberately went off-road to hit major depressions when he could. Juan quickly realized the deputy was getting in extra punishment. Both lawmen laughed each time, and the second deputy kidded that the bumps weren't big enough to throw them out. Flores made another promise. The dumb deputies would be sorry someday when he came back.

With more splinters they arrived at the harbor and were taken to the Worm, a small boat that ferried out to the larger Sea Bird.

They were told not to talk, so with their chains and handcuffs, they sat down in the small Worm boat. The deputies joked that if they threw them overboard, they'd sink like a rock. Fontes knew the chains weighed too much to swim. Even more mental torture.

Quietly they transferred over to the Sea Bird under the stares of fifteen passengers. Some made fun of them. When the deputies left them for a minute, Juan Flores looked at five gossiping ladies and told them, "I'll be back in a couple of years and slit your ugly throats. Then I'm gonna pluck the eyeballs out of your tiny pink gringo babies." The women quickly moved.

Captain Haley ordered them put in a five-foot-square small storage closet with two buckets, one full of water and one for their waste. The four-hundred-mile trip up the coast with its five-foot waves would take a week.

Flores and Daniels turned green sliding on the floor, first to the right, then left, then forward, then backward. Both threw up in the waste bucket until the smell of the bucket itself made them throw up. Vomit was everywhere. They tried to stand to pee into the bucket and instead peed on each another. After a day, the bucket was full, and no one would answer their pleas to empty it. The next day the ship hit a storm. Then the storage room became a two-inch-deep rolling mixture of sea water, urine, vomit, and floating feces. They tried to stand to keep dry and upwind from the atrocious rising smell but fell into the mess with each surprise roll. With every other breath came a dry heave. Next time they swore they'd kill first and then take their own lives rather than submit to another ocean ride in this hell.

Flores' cold, glassy eyes fixed on the overflowing bucket. Poncho Daniels broke into sobs. Flores toughened and told stories to comfort his partner. He told Daniels to think about anything besides where they were. Daniels just sobbed.

The overpowering stench left the prisoners with no appetite. They daily received a bucket of water, two pieces of bread, and a half pound of green-colored beef jerky. The jerky included a buffet of flies. Flores wondered how flies got way out in the ocean. Then he realized the vermin had been with the so-called meat for days and days.

For the whole week Flores and Daniels couldn't eat anything. They barely drank the putrid water they were given. They'd be lucky to survive. Everything from their stomachs joined the mix on the floor in that hellhole of a closet. The sea air that blew in between the wood slats was their only relief. They put their mouths on the boards and tried to get fresh air. Splinters hit their lips. One was so large and sharp that it gouged deeply into Daniel's cheek when the rocking ship jammed his face into it. It left a bleeding gash.

They passed the last two days in total silence. Prison would be paradise.

Upon disembarkation, Flores told Daniels, "I'll be a leader here at the Stones." When walking on the dock to the prison, Flores acted sick and fell into the cold bay water to wash off the stench. The water was only six feet deep. The guards pulled him out quickly. The sun was out, so he walked slowly hoping to dry out.

They walked to the prison management office.

"Juan Flores, step forward. I'm Sergeant Baker. This is your home for five years' hard labor. No slackers allowed. Do you understand?"

"Yes, Senor Sergeant, I understand well," Flores said, his neck twitching.

Whack! The sergeant hit Flores with his stick. "I want no Spanish spoken here. Not one word! Only English! Any Spanish spoken will be considered mutiny. Not even a 'Senor.' Understand, compadre?" the sergeant asked.

"Yes, sir." Flores was too weak to fight, but he promised himself he'd kill this damn Sergeant Baker the first chance he got.

"Your number, prisoner, is 613. Today's date is April 27, 1854. Your release date is April 28, 1859. Count the days, Mex. Time can be added, but never subtracted. Escapes double your time. Bad behavior, fighting, insubordination, all add time. Understand, greaser Number 613?"

"Yes, sir!" Flores said. His porky ass would get fried by this greaser soon enough, the son of a bitch.

"Good. Rinse off in the outdoor showers. You smell like crap. We don't need your smell of vomited refried grease shit. Report to Deputy Halsey."

"Yes, sir." Talk about a shithead. He'd puncture his jelly belly someday.

Flores took his cold, fifty-degree, outdoor saltwater shower, shook off, and stepped into the sun for an allowed twenty minutes. The air was fifteen degrees cooler than southern California.

After he was about half dry, he reported to Deputy Halsey. Halsey was fifty-something with gray hair and a gentle manner.

"Prisoner number 613 reporting as ordered, sir," Flores said.

"Look, son, that Sergeant Baker can be a real prick. All I need from you is to follow simple orders and you'll get along fine," Halsey said.

Flores stared at Halsey. He wasn't going to be a hard ass. Good. He could use him.

"Guard Halsey, is it possible to get a letter from here to Santa Barbara?"

"Cost you ten cents, son. Five for me and five for the U.S. postal person."

"Thanks."

Halsey led him to Dorm A. Two bunks available, Flores took the bottom and Daniels took the top.

They met their inmates when they filed in for lunch.

"I'm Santos. This here's Navarro."

"What's for lunch?" Daniels asked, needing food.

"Same thing. Smells raw today. Phew!" Santos said.

"Not that tough, half-boiled sturgeon again," Navarro complained. One piece still had yesterday's roaches on it.

"Pass over our shares," Flores said. He had to eat and didn't care if it was shoe leather.

"Five times a week for lunch and dinner," Santos said.

"Yeah, and we hafta catch the damn stinky stuff ourselves!" Navarro said.

"What's served on the other days?" Flores asked, choking it down.

"More fish crap, different type," Navarro said.

"I'm Juan Flores from Capistrano. How many escapees never come back?"

"Twenty-eight tried it last year. They kilt twenty-three. Rest ain't been back," Navarro said.

"Good. We will all be leaving soon. No Yankee with restraints shall stop my Manillas."

"Excuse me," said one of the prisoners at their table. "I'm Andreas Fontes. Heard you were from the Los Angeles Pueblo. Sheriff Barton arrested me 'cause I stomped his ass. He was

123

beatin' on my sister. He arrested me for horse stealin', and the gringo sent me here." His black hair was well greased and surrounded by a hairnet.

Flores stared at Andreas Fontes. "I heard about Sheriff Barton at the missions. He deserves to die!" Flores said.

Fontes was his same size, five-foot-eight, similar build, clean-shaven, with a hate against the gringos. He'd use that to mold this group.

"If you ever want to kill Barton, count me in to be first," Fontes said.

"I'd like to start in San Juan Capistrano. It is in Los Angeles County. Barton would be target number one. Want to join the gang?" Flores asked.

"Only if I get to kill Barton," Fontes said.

"I'll fix it so you personally pull the trigger on Sheriff James Barton," Flores said.

"Sure, count me in. I have twelve men including myself proud to call us Mexicanos."

"These men shall be called the Manillas, and if I can, each one shall escape with us," Flores said.

"Your self-confidence is good. We shall join you," Fontes said.

"Then you, Fontes, shall be a lieutenant with Poncho Daniels," Flores said. "So let it be sworn to in Spanish, and so it shall be done."

"Good, mi capitan. Meet Juan Catabo, Francisco Ardillero, Jose Santos, Diego Navarro, Pedro Lopez, Juan Valenzuela, Jose Espinoza, Antonio Varelas, Encarnacion Berryessa, Santiago Silvas, and Leonardo Lopez, all loyal companions to the Manillas," Santos said.

"Gentlemen, together we shall start such a great rebellion. All of us shall be rich, out of this fish-hole, with women hanging all over us for the taking," Flores said.

Just then Halsey approached and all remained quiet. "All line up, single file, no talking, and march to the labor yard."

Flores was at the end of the line. He still weaved back and forth from the sea ride. He'd get rid of his rocky legs in one more day. He rubbed his black moustache between his fingers.

His dark eyes squinted at the prison. The prison's two stories were two hundred feet long. They formed a U with the yard in the center. On the roofs stood twenty guards with three cannon and rifles.

The prisoners were breaking stones for building more cell blocks. The guards called the place the Stones. The name made sense.

Flores counted over three hundred inmates. Forty filthy guards wore no uniforms. The prisoners wore their own clothes, the ones they'd walked in with. Most hung on them in tatters from the hard work. From a distance of eighty feet, it was difficult to distinguish the guards from the inmates. Good. A major break would have confusion for cover. He twisted his moustache and narrowed his dark eyes. They'd do it, soon.

Back at the cells, Flores looked at his new flock. Their clothing reeked and was ripped and filthy. The first thing he had to do was obtain clothing for them all, himself included. Next he looked at the bedding. The weather was much colder there, and the threadbare, simple blankets wouldn't keep a person even mildly warm. The straw mattresses needed wool or cotton coverlets to make a cushion. The filthy rags called sheets moved from the millions of lice crawling on them.

He gave Halsey ten cents and a letter to his brother in Santa Barbara. Flores addressed his concerns for his friends. Three weeks later Halsey brought him a return letter. In the letter the brother sent him money.

Flores, by working with Halsey, obtained clean, used miners' clothes, used blankets, and thirteen used bug-free mattresses. The Manillas were ecstatic.

Juan Flores sent thanks back to his brother. He saved funds for food. Halsey brought eggs and cheese to keep Flores' men healthy. Flores paid an inmate to copy the irons' key.

A month later he found a guard's dinghy left by itself. This was a chance for only three to escape. Flores was sorry he couldn't bring the rest. He called Poncho Daniels and Andreas Fontes to jump in. He undid their irons and they paddled for their lives, splashing away from the shore.

Bang! They heard the shot. A second later the boat took the

hit just an inch below the water line. The bullet tore out a whole two-inch-by-twelve-inch board. Their first escape was foiled. The boat sank. The three swam for shore and received tighter irons. They were punished by moving them upstairs.

The guard upstairs hated Mexicans. Flores missed Guard Halsey, who was more respectful toward his dorm assignees.

"You damn Mexes, stay in the back by the small window. We don't need no stinkin' greasers screwing this dorm up."

His name was Boyd. Flores promised himself that he'd assassinate Sergeant Baker and Guard Boyd someday.

Flores received double-time for his attempted breakout. Several months passed up on the second story. The time seemed like six years with their activities limited and no interplay with the Manillas. The gringos would not let them rest. All the prisoners were White, mostly from the mines. Flores was almost out of his mind.

But now he had time to plan. As he looked outside his neck twitched to the right. The view from the six-inch open-air window allowed him to see the ships come in once a week, like clockwork, to pick up the chopped rock. Boy, was somebody making money on the prisoners. The Whites kidded about how San Francisco had burned down twice already and the people with money wanted to rebuild with something more fireproof. And the prisoners' bloody hands made the warden rich, because San Quentin rock was the building material of choice. What a scam, and they got boiled fish for dinner.

Flores had to find a way out. Two years now had passed. He lay in his bunk bored. With new multi-murderers coming in, they had to clear out the lesser offenders. Especially the greasers on the second floor. "Flores, Juan, Number 613!" Guard Boyd called out.

"Yes, sir."

"Daniels, Francisco, Number 614!"

"Yes, sir."

"Fontes, Andreas, Number 569!"

"Yes, sir."

"Report to Guard Halsey below in Dorm B," Boyd

commanded. "Bring all your gear."

"Yes, sir!"

When they got downstairs, they approached Guard Halsey.

"Sir? Guard Halsey? We...." Flores asked.

"Yes. Damn. I just filled Dorm B. Don't the administration idiots know only fifty inmates to a dorm? Shit," Guard Halsey said. "Hell, Flores, go into Dorm A with all your amigos."

"Thank you, Mr. Halsey," Flores replied with a hidden smile. Flores was reunited with his friends.

Chapter 18

"All Manillas, listen up! I've got a great plan," Juan Flores said. His neck twitched to the right as he centered hid beady eyes on a map he bought from the gringos.

"Everybody here in the corner so no one else can hear," Poncho Daniels said as the Mexicans huddled together.

"Next week is Christmas week. The brick and rock ship gets here the day before Christmas, right?" Flores said.

"Yeah," said about five of them at once.

"Remember last Christmas?"

"I was with Pedro, and those two there," one said, pointing to two more.

"Damn it, we were all here," Flores said. "Remember the guards drinking?"

"Each one had a bottle. The ship brought in three cases of whiskey. Why? Can we each get a bottle too?" Antonio asked.

"Not exactly. That's why I am in charge and you follow my command," Flores said. What a stupid idiot. No wonder they caught him.

"Sure," said Antonio. "I was just a little thirsty."

"Okay. Listen up. If the guards are drunk and the ship is docked and we position ourselves near the ship," Flores said...

"Go ahead. I'm right with you," Daniels said. Around him eleven men nodded.

"Must stay away from the cannon, and the roof guards, as much as we can. Use cover, the ship, the stones, the cell block, anything that can stop a bullet. I'll take four men, rush the crew, threaten the captain, and get the anchor up. Then all the rest jump on board, across the bay for our getaway," Flores said.

"Who's gonna raise the sails?" one asked.

"The uniformed crew on board. We'd be picked off by sniper fire," Flores said.

"Will just us make it?" Antonio asked.

"A major break will have the entire prison involved.

We'll use that ruse to take over the ship. Besides us there might be another twenty to thirty men that make it.

We'll make sure only Manillas leave that ship!" Flores said as Daniels nodded in the background.

"With the liquor, the numbers, surprise, and luck, it should work," Daniels said.

"Everyone should position themselves near to the ship. Then wait for my yell in Spanish. Then we've got the element of surprise," Flores said.

The eleven Manillas agreed to the plan.

"Captain Flores, how about the guards on the ship?" Antonio asked.

"We take their rifles away, take them out with our homemade knives. Here, we made four already. Make four more," Flores said. "The crew either helps us or dies. Now is the time to practice on each other. Eight guys line up in front to block off the guards' view. Good. Begin."

They practiced night and day like a combat team getting ready to take the Mexican beachhead. The practice gave them wrestling experience too. Leonardo Lopez had Mexican Army training. He taught them unarmed, rifle, and bayonet defense. They worked together until Christmas Day arrived. They were nervous, as could be expected. Each Mexican knew where they should be to escape.

The day before Christmas, the ship arrived. The guards carried in their three cases of whiskey. Each guard had his own bottle to break up the tedium.

The next day as the bottles were being emptied, his escape ship in position, Juan Flores decided to raise the standard of revolt.

"All who dare, follow me, Juan Flores, for the ship and liberty!" he shouted in English and Spanish.

When the yell went out, most of the half-drunk guards were caught unaware. Five Manillas quickly jumped the four guards on the ship. Two guards were stabbed to death, and one they shot with his gun. The last they choked to death. They threw them all in the bay. The Manillas now had four rifles.

"Aim at those cannon!" Juan Flores shouted.

As four shots flew the seventy yards to the cannon, all guards ducked. Only one guard took a hit, but that hit slowed

130

down one cannon. The Manillas took revolvers from the dead guards. They threw Juan Flores a revolver, and another to Poncho Daniels. Andreas Fontes kept two.

Over two hundred men ran for freedom. Flores watched as several prisoners ran for the dorms. Chicken shits. Flores and Fontes jumped on the ship. The other Manillas tried to use cover to get to the ship. Thirty guards, groggy with whiskey, tried to put down the prison break. The prison alarm bell kept going gong, gong, gong. Six guards worked the cannon.

"Upward, men! Trim the sails!" the ship's captain yelled, Juan Flores' gun to his head.

Dirty Dave Boe, once a sailor in the U.S. Navy, climbed the mast and let loose with the main sail. Flores remembered him from the dorm. He always called Flores a mousy greaser. Flores would reward him for that.

The guards' single-shot rifle volleys started. It would be a bloodbath in the yard. The twenty-four guards shot down twenty-one men. Flores knew there were no doctors around. The other three might as well be dead.

The deadly cannon fire erupted. The ship was moving slowly from its dock. First a blast came from the six-pounder. A large gray smoke cloud preceded the shrapnel, a mixture of nails and scrap, and not a cannon ball. How mean, Flores thought. Shrapnel, over six pounds of flying metal, removed a half dozen criminals' heads, leaving black, reddish stumps. Twice as many arms and legs flew off on the first shot. Several men looked in shock for their missing arms. The second six-pounder went off and took out another twenty men still in the yard.

The big cannon fired. A huge fireball bellowed out its mighty throat. Twelve pounds of hot metal shrapnel flew out so fast it was invisible to the human eye. When it hit, more than fifty men were killed or wounded. Body parts piled up four feet high in the prison yard.

"Split up, you idiots!" Flores screamed.

The second and third sails hit the air. Three of the crew were still alive. One died from the guards' rifle fire. All stayed under cover while all three cannons roared again. The second blasts from the three cannon took out fifty more men. The guards fired rifles. The Manillas reloaded the rifles with the dead guards' powder and balls.

"Take your time. Aim at the big cannon," Flores shouted, afraid that they may cannon-hole the ship.

The cannon master judged the range to the ship. He stood up two hundred feet away as Big Red Horse Webster, a buffalo hunter, sighted in. The cannon master barked out elevation and windage. The cannon fired. The big round cannon ball flew over them. Webster's bullet left his rifle, striking the cannon master in the head. The next time the big cannon fired, it missed again. Flores didn't want to have the ship shot out from underneath him. Once was enough. His sentence has been extended to ten years for the last escape. This would be twenty years or death.

Sergeant Baker ran behind Guards Boyd and Halsey.

They were closing fast on the ship. Shit. He hadn't wanted to harm Halsey. Flores was in a compromising position.

Flores yelled, "Baker, you're dead meat, you porky prick!" Flores fired, hitting Baker smack in the middle of his stomach. Baker looked down and fainted. Andreas Fontes shot Boyd. Halsey took a round from Poncho Daniels. All three were mortally wounded.

Flores had a tinge of sadness for Halsey, the guard that made San Quentin bearable. He quickly dismissed the thought.

Juan Flores viewed the prison yard as they sailed slowly away. From his position at the captain's quarters, he saw over a hundred men wounded and dying. Many other prisoners had their hands in the air at the dock.   Sporadic rifle fire hit one, two, three, and four more prisoners already on the ship.

Once out of range, Flores asked his two lieutenants to tell him how many Manillas were on board. He also asked for the others on board. They reported that all Manillas, except Antonio, made it. Flores shook his head. Antonio never was too sharp. Another ten more Mexicans wanted to join up. There were five gringos, and four crew, with the ship's captain.

"Tie up all the gringos, hold them. That'll keep the ship's crew restrained," Flores said in Spanish.

The Manillas did as commanded.

"You, ship's captain, get us across the bay to here," Flores said, pointing to his map.

The ship captain and his crew quickly trimmed the sails and took their heading from Juan Flores. He told them to go due east with the strong bay wind. That would put him on the east bay only two miles from Richmond Township in Contra Costa County.

"Good job, Poncho. We pulled it off! Find us a bottle. Find bottles for all of us! We'll celebrate!" Flores said. Cheers circulated among the men as they rummaged through the captain's quarters in search of booze.

Juan Flores turned on the captain once he had a people count. "Captain, give me one good reason why I shouldn't kill you and the crew, and you'll all live."

The captain began, "Mr. Captain, sir, I, Captain Dover, can give you enough hidden money to buy horses and guns to continue your escape. That's a good reason."

"You choose wisely. That is a good reason. You've one minute to put it in my hand, and you all shall live, on my word as a man," Flores said. The excitement got his neck twitching.

The captain went to a hidden floorboard safe in the galley and retrieved the money.

"Here you are, the payroll for the prison, one thousand two hundred American dollars in cash."

"You live," he said to the captain.

To Fontes and Daniels, Flores ordered, "Strip the captain and crew naked, throw them overboard when we are three miles offshore. Give 'em life rings to float on. My word's my word."

A swim to shore in that rough bay water would take some time. Naked, they could not blow the whistle too fast. The best part was the twelve hundred dollars to boot.

Near the shore at Contra Costa and having dumped the captain and his men in the ocean, Juan Flores bade farewell to the five gringos with colorful names. The Mexicans weighted them down and threw them off one at a time. First was Red Horse. "You bastard Flores, may you burn in hell!" Dirty Dave Boe just prayed, and Stinky Bob wept, "Please, I beg of you, Mr.

Flores!" Horseface Pete was quiet, and Fat Frankie called them dumb greasers. Flores enjoyed watching his first five American victims. His dark eyes showed glee. One by one the rocks led the five aptly named men to the bottom of the bay.

He ordered the ship grounded, the sail ropes removed, and holes to be cut into the bottom of the ship. Flores then rode on the arms of his jubilant men as they ran through the three-foot water to freedom. Then under his command they pledged their loyalty to him.

They'd need horses for their trip south. They'd landed on Rancho San Pablo, per the map, a large, eighteen-thousand-acre rancho. The main rancho casa was visible. The owner, Don Luis, recently had added twenty-five horses to his stable. Flores and his gang walked the mile to see what they could buy or steal. He played the Mexican patriot to Don Luis and bought all twenty-five horses for five hundred dollars. Flores explained either five hundred for the horses or his life. Simple decision. Luis then threw in the twenty-five horse bits and reins for nothing. Probably wanted to get rid of them. They also received old horse blankets to ride on.

Bareback on their blankets, twenty-three Mexican escapees urged the horses away. In a moment they were all gone. Flores rode for half a day by the inside of San Francisco Bay, then turned his men inland away from the more-populated coastal route. By night they made it to Oakland. Just on the outskirts, Flores directed plans for a stagecoach robbery.

"Juan Catabo and Juan Valenzuela, here comes a local stage. Take Pedro and Esteban to get what you can from the passengers and the driver."

Their take was only four hundred, but it was four hundred more than they had before. The following day another stage came their way to add another five hundred dollars to the Flores Revolution Bank.

In San Jose they bought fifteen saddles and three revolvers. They needed more money for eight horses and twenty revolvers and nineteen rifles. A stagecoach leaving town with two thousand in gold provided more funds. They took the gold to weapons stores in town and bought out their stock of arms, powder, and bullets.

Now heavily armed, they roamed more slowly down the mission trail toward Los Angeles County. Juan and his followers presented a fierce front, and he needed all the men and weapons he could get. From the next victim, a three-man pack train going north, the Flores gang stole another three hundred dollars.

Flores remembered the rundown missions from his previous trip. They were all in poor financial condition and always ready to help, for money, a Catholic Mexican group. Flores wisely decided to buy from just the missions, avoiding the small towns. He covered his trail that way and left no record. Flores' dark eyes peered south. His neck twitched to the right as he congratulated himself on his major plan. So far so good.

Chapter 19

Horace remembered more than two years had passed since Paulette disposed of the three men by sword point. He now day-clerked for Judge Dimmick, a family friend. He spent his nights studying or with the rangers or at the café. Paulette and he were close friends now. The carriage incident had slowed down their relationship. Horace wanted his career plans in place before he settled down anyway. The two corporals, Bell and Bean, had their wild oats to sow. Bean still loved his whores.

His father's teachings from Indiana law hastened his current study. Horace sat in the judge's office and removed his hat. He rubbed his thick brown hair back and stretched. The judge had Horace working on the judge's relatives' land grant case. Specializing in Federal Land Grant Commission law might interest Horace down the road. He liked doing the research with its old descriptions, finding the witnesses, and proving up the deed. Horace was tired of evidence, civil law, criminal law, real property, contracts, and torts. His infatuation with the latest fad — land-grant law — swirled through his head.   He climbed on Pal to get away from the immense detail and to put things in perspective.   Riding helped him make sense of the studying. Besides, he was hungry. Perhaps, too, he needed a little female attention.

As if moved by a magnet, he found himself in front of his friend's café. He saw her through the window. Wearing a blue dress, she was playing with her light brown hair, twisting it in her slender fingers. Her long hair accentuated her perfect figure. Unfortunately, that figure was not on the menu. And it hadn't been for the last two years. She was the commitment type. He was getting to be more standoffish. Paulette joked with him that he was becoming more like Roy Bean.   Maybe she wasn't joking.

"Morning, Miss Paulette. How nice you look today."

"How kind, Mr. Law Student. How's your study?"

"Fine. How about my favorite cup of coffee to wake up my slow-thinking thoughts?"

"What are your thoughts?" she said while pouring the coffee.

"Dimmick has me researching his in-laws' rancho deed."

"That's good experience with hundreds of potential clients."

"Yes, Paulette. I need motivation, some good reason, to make law more interesting," Horace said, shaking the cobwebs from his head.

"Good money for a bright young attorney, too," she said, looking up when Roy Bean stormed into the café.

"Horace. Good. I hate to eat alone and just stare at a good-looking gal who hardly talks to me," Bean said, turning his chair and straddling it. He removed his hat. His wild hair went everywhere. "Guess I should see Biggs or get a bear tag."

Bovierre went into her kitchen.

"She's just mad we pal around too much. And Roy, don't use too much of that damn bear grease because the whores don't like it," Horace said.

"The hell with what they like and don't like. I pay 'em, don't I?"

Paulette walked back in so Horace bit his tongue.

"Yes, Roy, we were talking about the law and land grant deeds," Horace said, his eyes still seeing her blue dress reflection in the window.

"Horace, my poor murdered brother, General Joshua Bean -- may God rest 'im, and thank 'im for my saloon -- told me the story about the land grants," Bean said.

"A story. I love a story," Paulette said, handing Roy a cup of coffee and sitting down by Horace. She rubbed his leg under the table as a hidden sign of affection. Even though he knew she was teasing, Horace blushed bright pink. She smirked.

"Joshua told me that back in 1848, after the signing of the truce with America, Mexican Governor Pio Pico and friends pulled a fast one," Bean said.

Horace's light brown eyebrows shot straight up.

"Go ahead," Paulette said.

"Pico signed over fifty back-dated land grants. The peace treaty stipulated that America would honor all existing Mexican and Spanish land grants. When the army caught Pico's secret courier with the phoney deeds, the American Congress was

138

humiliated," Bean said.

"So fifty or so land grants are bogus," Horace said, slurping his coffee and spilling it on his shirt.

"No, they caught those and took them out of circulation, counselor to be," Bean said.

"Sorry. A little tired and slow," Horace said.

"Fremont's troopers chased down a Californio soldier who had some phoney land grants in his saddle. Pico's fightin' Mexican friends who'd lost the war got rewarded with land, lots of land. Get it?" Bean said.

"Sure." Horace smiled. "Fremont made his report to Congress. They were mortified and forced to create Land Grant courts to stop any possible fraud."

"Right you are. You're pickin' up rather quick now, even though I was a sloppy storyteller."

"Pico's deeds put all the land grants into question," Paulette said matter of fact, rising.

"All 517 of them. Those fake deeds forced Congress to start the Land Grant Commission Courts. There's my motivation," Horace said.

"Oui, Horace. That's why you should specialize in land grant law, especially now armed with the knowledge from Roy here," Paulette said, winking at him.

Horace winked back at her and said, "I do." That would make her think even though he didn't.

"Usual specials, men?" She rose, trying to look nonflustered.

"Yes," they both said.

Miss Bovierre left for the kitchen.

"Now all ranchos have to pay the attorneys," Bean said.

"The fees run a third, they can't have the cash, they have to use their land for payment. Roy, you sure opened my eyes," Horace said, stroking his dimpled chin. One-fifth of the whole county was up for grabs.

"Or get a gringo lawyer in the family by marriage," Bean said. Bean was right. He should be forewarned.

"Yes, that makes sense," Horace said seriously.

"Maybe you should be careful, wannabe counselor," Roy

said, teasing. "Hear about the big rodeo at Sanchez's this afternoon?"

"No. I've been in the books for months," Horace said.

"Tomas Sanchez caught me at the barracks last night and asked me to tell you to stop by. It's fun."

"Maybe I can ride Pal in a contest." He stuck his fork into his special French-spiced eggs.

"Hey, how come your eggs have got speckles all over?" Bean said with a sad frown.

"Paulette puts these things on. She knows you wouldn't like 'em," Horace said, keeping a straight face, covering his little white lie. Roy was a good friend but not too quick.

"Yeah, you're right," Bean said, as he twisted his moustache and looked down to take a bite.

Horace winked at Bovierre once again. She'd heard Bean's comment about the speckles.

"You fibbed. I heard you," she whispered and brushed his chin with her finger. He blushed again.

When Bean left, Horace asked Paulette to join him for an opening play at the theater the next week. She immediately agreed. Horace purchased the tickets, then went to the office and started his research. He asked Judge Dimmick about Bean's Pio Pico story. The judge stated that the American Army had confiscated pre-dated, signed land grants from a Mexican courier. Horace smiled. Major law fees for land appealed to him.

Horace left for Tomas Sanchez's rodeo. He pulled up at the rancho and was directed to the south pasture by Mexican Joe for the roundup and games.

"A warning, Horace," Mexican Joe said, trying to hide his scar with his hand. "If you go to our north pasture, watch out for the five-foot-deep ditches. They encourage these Indian bands you are always chasing to try elsewhere."

Horace laughed and said, "I'd love to be chasing a couple of rustlers and have them fall into that."

"Me, too," said Mexican Joe, laughing.

"See you there," Horace said.

At the roundup the <u>vaqueros</u> were separating the stock.

Horace listened as one old fellow with a fancy outfit and hat out of the Mexican-Spanish War told five Dons the rules for cattle roundup according to custom. Behind the Dons were one hundred and fifty <u>vaqueros</u> representing the five ranchos. Upon the old fellow's command, the <u>vaqueros</u> worked in different areas to search out and round up all the cattle.

Tomas Sanchez was glad to see Horace. "The old fellow is the Spanish Judge of the Plains, Juez de Campo. He makes the rules for the cattle roundup."

"He even has hanging power if we catch any rustlers or poachers out today," Mexican Joe added, staying behind to manage the large cattle stalls that were made to hold up to ten thousand head.

"Mighty big stalls," Horace said.

"These are nothing. On the Rancho Marguerita, these stalls are five times bigger," Joe said, a cigar with a two-inch ash hanging from his mouth.

Horace whistled. "Imagine one thousand <u>vaqueros</u> riding out for twenty thousand head."

"Imagine one hundred and fifty times that many cattle," Joe said, proud of the ranchos.

They waited about two to three hours when, from all sides, came thousands of cattle, hundreds from here, hundreds from there. Every corner had these <u>vaqueros</u> driving in these cattle. It became a logjam when they reached the pens. Each brand had to be checked before any rancho would allow a steer or cow into their holding stall. Within five hours the steers and cows were separated.

The Judge of the Plains moved toward an argument.

"Your Honor, we have these ten calves, too old for their mothers. They go from cow to cow and acting lost. What is your pleasure for these calves?" Don Talamentes asked.

"As the custom, all ten calves are declared orejanos, orphans, going to the Don that gave the rodeo -- Don Tomas Sanchez."

"Yes, judge," Don Talamentes said.

As the branding started, four <u>vaqueros</u> dragged four human beings behind them. When they got closer, Horace noticed they were Indians.

The <u>vaqueros</u> immediately took them to the judge, who asked the Indians questions they refused to answer. The Indian leader's response in Spanish to the judge was that he was a Chief of the Tulares, that the judge could go to the devil, and he spit in the old judge's face. Thus his fate by the Judge of the Plains appeared sealed.

The judge patiently took testimony from the <u>vaqueros</u>, who'd caught the Indians rustling cattle. One Indian testified. The other Indians told the judge the Whites were weak; if the Indians got caught, the Whites might hold them in prison, but they could break out. But they had the wrong information. Under California law, the rural judges had the power, not the pueblo courts.

"I, Judge of the Plains, with the power of the United States, State of California, given to me by their legislatures, sentence these four Indians to hang immediately on that tree over yonder," the judge said in Spanish so that the Indians could hear -- and pointing.

The <u>vaqueros</u> grabbed the four thieves and escorted them to the tree. They put all but the chief on their horses, lined them up, and secured the nooses.

Whap! went the lash upon the horse. "Screw you damn Mexicans!" the first doomed Indian yelled in Spanish before the loud snap. Then came the normal, involuntary release of defecation upon the ground. The Indians wore just a front and back waist cloth so everything fell below.

Whap! went the sound again. "Help me, Jesus! I'm sorry!" the second Indian appealed in Spanish.

Whap! "Go to hell, you Mexican greasers!" the third Indian said in Spanish. Snap!

The last Indian, the chief, had insulted the judge, the law, Spanish customs and pride. The <u>vaqueros</u> wanted to get even, so they purposely walked him through his fellow Indians' defecation and told him he smelled like shit. Then they started a game with him. They called him the Chief With No Manners, vilified him for what he'd done to his fellow braves, and scared him to death, all the while the chief not knowing when he was going to die. Finally the young chief broke down and wept earnestly for his boyhood friends and his thefts. He begged for mercy.

Not saying any more to the Indian, they took him to the hanging tree, placed him on his horse, set the noose, and said to him, "May God be with you now."

Whap! "I'm sorry, Jesus! See you in heaven, Father," the last Indian said in Spanish.

"Forevermore this place is called the tree where two went to heaven and two went to hell," the judge said to Tomas.

Some of the toughest men said a prayer for the Indian rustlers who should have stayed up north.

Horace had learned Spanish quickly from living in the pueblo and from his Aunt, Miss Bovierre, and the rangers, so he understood every word. A deep sadness gripped his soul. Logic told him had they not been punished, their life of crime would escalate; they would be taking lives, not cattle. The rangers had seen it happen over and over again.

The rodeo went on until late lunch was ready, a true Mexican barbecue, feeding all. Horace loved the open country. It gave him a sense of completeness with its delicious mixture of cattle, grass smells, and the fellowship of many men. He sat with the group and ate charbroiled beef steaks, roasted corn, tortillas, salsa, roasted rice, refried beans, and coffee hot from the fire. Everyone laughed and talked.

Some even brought their guitars and fiddles. Several groups were singing Mexican folk songs of long-ago rodeos. Soon all joined in an old favorite, clanging their cups in salute to the rodeo age. Horace sang along. Everyone hugged his fellow comrades. Mexican Joe rushed up and hugged Horace. They laughed together.

Horace had to ride back to town to report the Indians' executions. Don Tomas invited him back the next day for branding and games. The games would be a test of speed and agility, for the vaquero had to brand the cow in three spots, the fierro, senal, and venta -- the range, the earmark, and the counterbrand -- if they were to be later sold. Horace figured just from the sheer number of cattle involved that the branding and checking alone would take hours. Don Tomas told him that the vaqueros were wonderful with their lassos in rounding up the cattle for branding but that the rodeo games were more fun.

The next morning Horace arrived by himself to watch the games. He hoped to participate. He stood at one of the fences to watch the first game, a ride on a large, bucking bull. The bull weighed nearly a ton, and the various vaqueros were thrown around like popped corn on a barbecue, up and down and all around and sideways. Horace got dizzy just watching. He'd forget the bull riding game; that was for fools. They judged the best bull-riding vaquero on how long and how aggressively he rode and on his style. A young fellow from Rancho Ballona won the contest, but after the exertion, glee, and drinking, passed out.

Horace thought about entering the steer-roping contest. The first three vaqueros on their mustangs lassoed each steer and stopped in an instant, threw the steer up, and tied the legs in less than a minute. When he heard these vaqueros were beginners, he believed that the Mexicans were the world's greatest horsemen.

The better, older vaqueros came out. One with luck, skill, a quick throw and great horse pulled off the steer roping in thirty-one seconds. "Go Sanchez Rancho!" someone shouted next to Horace. He rubbed his eyes from the dust and saw the victorious vaquero was Mexican Joe. Don Tomas walked to Mexican Joe and hugged him in celebration for bringing honor to the Sanchez Casa. Mexican Joe jumped the fence and hugged Horace for bringing him luck.

The next event was cattle herding with a team of five coordinated vaqueros and twenty steers. The cattle, if not continually led, would try to escape every time. Somehow Mexican Joe and his four vaqueros outsmarted the steers and turned in the best time, per the Judge of the Plains. Nobody doubted the judge who had the power to hang.

Other ranchos won many of the roping and cattle events. The judge kept the score, and it was Ballona ten, Rincon eight, La Brea eight, Rodeo Aguas seven, and Sanchez's La Tijera seven.

Tomas shared with Horace that no one had ever beaten the

famous Rancho Ballona in the games for a long time. His grandfather, Vicente Sanchez, had pulled the chicken out of the ground right before the majordomo of Ballona did and won the games for the Sanchez Rancho, but that was thirty-five years before. Rancho Ballona was known to even hire outside <u>vaqueros</u> to win. Tomas had the backing of almost all the other ranchos in their prayers. Ballona's Don loved to snub the other Dons. They called the Ballona Don an uppity prig. Other ranchos wanted to see Sanchez, the underdog, take the victory. Tomas mentioned that with the point count as it was, anyone could win.

Tomas pointed out the semi-retired Dons that had passed their duties to their sons. Many had been there for his grandfather's upset. Tomas remarked that they were starting to bet heavy due to the current scores. Tomas pointed toward four Dons that Horace might enjoy listening to. Horace calmly walked over to be by them and hear what they said.

The four old Dons wondered if lightning could hit twice, if Sanchez could pull off a win in the relay race, get three points, and then go on to do the same thing his grandfather had done thirty-five years prior. The odds on that happening were a hundred to one, but each of the four Dons, with their special knowledge of Grandpa Sanchez's win, put down one hundred dollars with Ballona and prayed for a miracle, a ten-thousand-dollar one.

Soon the baton relay race began, an event where four obstacles were placed over a mile-long course. The race took four miles and four riders passing the baton to their teammates at mile intervals. Each rancho had only four horses it could enter. To be selected was a great honor in this highlight-of-the-day horsemanship event. Mexican Joe forewarned Horace how rough it could get.

Just then Sanchez approached him. "Horace, our fourth horse went lame. Would you do me the honor of being our fourth and final relay on this important race?"

Horace looked at his horse and asked him, "Pal, are you ready to give all you got against the best out here?" knowing that to be picked was a chance in a hundred. Pal snorted.

"Of course!" Horace cried. "We're ready!

"It will be tough, Horace," Tomas advised "But win or lose, I trust you to give your best. I expect to lead with Pal's half-brother El Capitan!"

Everyone lined up four abreast in the major event and race of the day. Nerves taut, the high-spirited participants were ready to go. After five minutes passed to get two horses to settle down, the judge started the race with a revolver fired toward the ocean.

Off they went. Tomas Sanchez on El Capitan took the lead and never let anyone see past him for the whole mile, passing each marker on cue, hitting a wonderful stride, giving the rancho a hundred-foot advantage when he passed off the baton to Mexican Joe. Joe's horse kept in front of the pack for the whole mile, and Joe passed off to the young <u>vaquero</u> Jose Lopez.

A great horseman, yet a little young, Lopez kept about even with the big ranchos running against him. The Ballona horse was fifty feet behind him. Nerves overtook Lopez, and his sweaty hands dropped the baton to the ground as he was passing it to Horace.

Horace thought fast. In less than two seconds, he jumped down, grabbed the baton, and remounted Pal on the run, all the while hanging on to his saddle horn. In front of him ran the pack of three horses. They were from twenty feet to two hundred feet away.

When he hit the saddle, he yelled, "Pal! I need this one bad! Give me everything you got, boy! Fly!" The big black horse flew by the first three horses one by one. With a half mile to go, Horace could see his competition was the best horse the Ballona Rancho owned. He was fast. Pal moved up to fifty feet from the leader, going into the last turn with a quarter mile to go. Around the last turn Pal was going flat out to catch and pass that brown horse in front.

"Go, Pal! Pass that horse!" Horace screamed.

The horse went into power overdrive, somehow he picked up ten percent, and passed the big red Ballona horse with an eighth of a mile to go.

"Go, Pal! Give me all you've got!" Horace shouted as Pal pulled away and won by twenty lengths.

The Sanchez group was ecstatic. The screaming and yelling could be heard for miles. They had beaten the best, even with an unbelievable drop by Jose Lopez. Sanchez told Horace that he was a true friend, a hero, and his brother as far as he was concerned.

Then four Dons came over and handed Sanchez eight thousand dollars and told him that thirty-five years ago, the same type of thing happened, only Vicente Sanchez had picked up the baton and beaten the Ballona horse, and that they had just taken the Ballona Don for forty thousand dollars. They wished him well on the gallo, the greased chicken grab, the last event. They had made another bet.

The final and top event, worth one point, was judged on the height of the horse and the number of tries it took to pull a rooster out of the ground. The judge would see to it that a buried rooster would stick out of the ground exactly the same height each time and be greased with tallow. The horseman would, at full gallop, bend down from the saddle and grab the rooster and pull it out of the ground. The contestant's problem was the rooster, scared from the horse, would duck its head before being plucked out.

Each rancho would enter only their best man. He had three chances to pull the chicken out. If successful, the height of the horse was measured and a judgment rendered after all had completed their runs.

The scores so far were Ballona ten, Rincon eight, La Brea eight, Rodeo Aguas seven, and La Tijera tied with Ballona at ten.

Only Ballona or La Tijera could win the games now, and the Ballona gamblers were hedging their bet of forty thousand more to lose if La Tijera won. Ballona offered every rancho except La Tijera ten thousand dollars in cash if they won the gallo contest. That would tie the score for Ballona and La Tijera and keep La Tijera from winning.

"I cannot believe we could lose forty thousand on a damned rooster," Don Talamantes of the Ballona Rancho griped.

The first contestant drawn was from the Rincon Rancho. He missed it. The rooster ducked to the left. He missed again on the second attempt but got the rooster out on his third try.

147

Everyone yelled. The <u>vaqueros</u> had heard of the huge wager involved, and the drama turned up, way up. The horse was measured and everything recorded.

The second contestant drawn was La Brea Rancho. Their <u>vaquero</u> missed the slick rooster all three times. He was hooted and booed.

The third contestant drawn was Rancho Ballona. The four old Dons were dancing. Everyone watched them doing an old Spanish folk dance meant for happiness, as does a father when he marries off his ugliest daughter.

One hundred and fifty <u>vaqueros</u> started to place their bets on La Tijera, which changed the two-to-one-hundred shot down to a two-to-one shot. Everyone was going on the older Dons' feelings. The Ballona Don sweated bullets.

Horace walked over to enjoy the old Dons' fun. The four Dons sat together and compared memories, the oldest saying, "Remember when number three was Ballona Rancho back in 1820 and they got it on the second try?"

"Yes, Jose, and then the other rancho fouled out three times, and Vicente Sanchez bumped his majordomo and plucked the little rooster out himself on the first time!" old Don Pedro said.

"And, Pedro, the place went crazy, so we better tell the Don of Ballona we will collect our money next month," old Don Manuel said.

"I'll get mine today! I'm no spring chicken, might not be here tomorrow!" Don Julian said.

"You're right, we'll all get it today," they said in unison.

Rancho Ballona's majordomo missed the first time. The crowd's attention then went to the lively guitar playing for the old, dancing Dons.

"Wish those old farts wouldn't do that damn dance. It distracts me," the Ballona Don said. "Don't miss, Pedro, or I'll have to get a new majordomo," he told his last hope.

Rancho Ballona's Pedro grabbed the rooster on his second try. The crowd went wild. His horse was measured and Pedro kept his job.

Again the four old Dons danced around like little kids playing a Spanish dancing game.

The fourth contestant was Rodeo Aguas. Their majordomo made three valiant efforts, finally falling off his horse and breaking his arm on the third and last try.

"Those damn Dons are all dancing again. What did they hear that I didn't?" the Ballona Don asked.

"Well, Don, sir, I just found out that Don Tomas has decided to run for this last event, replacing his majordomo," said Pedro.

"What? W-w-w-what the hell is going on here?" stuttered the outraged Don from Ballona yelling at the top of his lungs.

Don Tomas Sanchez asked Horace to go with him. They walked over to talk to Mexican Joe, who'd been standing by his horse and getting ready to represent the Rancho La Tijera in the last event.

Don Tomas looked at Joe's face and said, "Joe, this is hard on me. I know how important this event is for you to win. Especially when you missed twice last year and they all laughed at you. I hate to do this to you, but I have to do it for me. I am pretty good at this gallo, even as a child when my grandfather taught me how to face down the pressure and beat the other older boys."

"Don Tomas, I feel like the Lord in the garden, 'If there is any way you can take this cup from me.' You are an answer to prayer," Joe said thankfully.

"Then good! It's settled. I shall ride for the Rancho La Tijera. Win, lose, or draw, it's all on my decision."

The Judge of the Plains made the announcement for the final contestant.

"And now, gentlemen, we separate the men from the boys and the winners from the losers. Riding El Capitan in the final event is none other than our famous Californio warrior, Don Tomas A. Sanchez, taking the first run at the gallo contest. Go, Tomas, and good luck!"

Don Talamantes' mother arrived just moments before Tomas straddled El Capitan. "Mother, what brings you out here?" Don Talamantes of Ballona asked.

"Son, listen to me!" she said urgently. "Thirty-five years ago Don Vicente Sanchez won the big relay race and tied the main score with a big black named Friend. He bumped his

149

majordomo off the gallo contest. He rode it himself and pulled the chicken out first try, winning everything and costing us half our assets due to grandpa's foolish pride and wagers!"

Just as she said "grandpa's foolish pride," Don Tomas A. Sanchez reached down at a full gallop on mighty El Capitan and removed the greased rooster on his first try.

"Rancho La Tijera is this year's winner of the rodeo with a final score of eleven points!" the Judge of the Plains shouted over the cheering crowd. And nobody would dare argue with him.

"Don of Ballona, wake up! I think he fainted," Pedro said to the Don's mother.

Right then the four old Dons walked up to the passed-out Don of Ballona, said hello to his mother, the Dona, and asked for their second forty thousand dollars.

Meanwhile the other ranchos' Dons were ecstatic over the underdog winning everything. Some of the vaqueros by habit had wagered that their rancho would win. The ones that wagered from habit on the Sanchez place received a hundred dollars for each loyal dollar bet. One lucky vaquero from the Sanchez Rancho had wagered his whole salary of twenty dollars. He rode away with two thousand dollars and was telling his friends, "Now I can get married!"

Horace, Mexican Joe, and Tomas all hugged and danced to the music. Bottles of expensive wine and brandy were poured over the three by the old Dons, who were still celebrating their wisdom.

"Horace, my brother, we have all night to celebrate at our fandango," Tomas said.

"Horace, my kin, we could not have won this without you. We love you," Mexican Joe said.

Preparations for the third annual Sanchez fandango were in full swing when the victorious trio arrived. Maria Sanchez heard about the victory from a young vaquerro. She'd immediately directed the servants to make it a super big celebration. The anxious servants had already decorated the sala, the courtyard, the dining area, and the entry with vibrant colors.

The timing couldn't have been better. Three kitchen Indians were making cascarones, special colored egg shells filled with gold and silver tinsel, some with a little perfume, and some very special ones that Dons Julian and Manuel had sent over. Maria oversaw the kitchen and casa while Tomas planned.

Joe told Horace, while they were cleaning up, that they had two barrels of mescal and aguardiente, the favorite liquors of the people. Horace saw over fifty Indians working on the food alone. Horace had arranged for Roy Bean to escort Miss Bovierre to the fandango. He wanted to celebrate.

Chapter 20

Flores' first stop for food and supplies was the Mission San Jose, which had survived as only a parish church. Three wayward <u>vaqueros</u> sat slumped in front of the mission and looked across the bay. Flores ordered Daniels and two others to talk with them and see if any news of their escape had traveled south. They joined Flores' gang and told Flores he was a wanted man. Like he didn't know?

"Buenos dias, padre," Flores said. "Can I purchase some food and supplies for my little band of men?"

"Si, mi son. We are always pleased to help one who helps himself," the padre said.

Packed, refreshed, and fed, the twenty-six men left for Mission Santa Cruz on the coast.

Juan Flores had planned. First he had to gather a sense of support for the uprising and establish a following. By going from mission to mission, he found great encouragement, but he wondered was it the will of the Mexican people as a whole to follow him? If not, he'd rob and pillage on the way to safety in Baja, Mexico. With an army, he could defend himself and raid San Diego at will.

Santa Cruz Mission fed the gang, now supporting twenty-eight men. Flores heard the northern California law officers were looking in earnest for his band of rebels. He thanked the padres and left quickly. He had to keep a promise to Andreas Fontes regarding Sheriff Barton.

He cut southeast to a small village called Hollister. At the poorly kept Mission San Juan Bautista founded sixty years prior, the priests were gracious to the escaped convicts. They fed them beef brochettes and let them use the massive sleeping quarters the Spanish soldiers once called their barracks. All slept well indoors for the first time since the breakout. The mission was only an image of its prior grandeur, however, and the men still had things to grumble about.

Poncho Daniels told his leader after they left, "All the men liked sleeping indoors, Juan, but the fleas -- las pulgas -- ate us

153

alive!"

"Si, Poncho, they got me too," Flores stated and smiled as he slapped at another one.

"Still better than the Stones, right?" Poncho said, itching with both hands and scratching his matted hair.

"Poncho, before I got us the new bedstuffs, your whole bed moved from the lice just crawling around it. Like in waves!"

"It was so bad. And that steamboat ride in piss, vomit, and shit..."

"That is not funny, mi amigo. Never again will I take that ride. To the death, Lieutenant Daniels!"

Daniels saluted. "To the death, mi captain!"

"I am skipping the coastal Mission of Carmel. We'll head to Soledad Village."

The gang now grew to thirty-three. All were armed, and all swore allegiance to the cause of Mexican rebellion against the damn American Yankee.

The rundown mission at Soledad provided them with food and supplies. The warmer weather beckoned them to continue on with their trip south.

Twenty-three miles south of King City, the Mission San Antonio de Padua was like a miniature city complete with wine making; wheat crushing; making olive oil and candle and soap tallow; hide tanning; iron making with a metal furnace; and corn crushing. The padres gave them anything they needed. Like always, Juan Flores made a generous donation from his robberies to help the mission.

They spent a night at the San Antonio de Padua Mission. Though not what it once was, it still functioned, and the fleas weren't so bad.

Next they traveled to a mission near Paso Robles called San Miguel Arcangel. There they met up with ten vaqueros mad at the Americans from mining incidents. The vaqueros quickly joined Flores' mounted revolutionary army.

The mission had been in poor repair since the Spanish-Mexican War. Only the church and the priest's home remained. Juan Flores pushed the men to go south, and though tired and complaining, they agreed to move on without delay. He left a

154

fifty-dollar donation with the priest. "Come back anytime, mi son," the padre said.

They arrived at the Mission San Luis Obispo exhausted and hungry. The mission, only a shadow of its former self like so many others, consisted of the church, the priest's home, a small garden, and maybe twenty head of cattle. Juan Flores had last seen this mission with seventeen thousand head of cattle and wine, oil, fruits, vegetables, and a tile roof factory. He was sick to see how far the church had deteriorated. Relatives had been married here, and to Flores, the Yankee had wiped it out. Without Mexican government support, the missions were failing one by one. Flores was their last dream and hope.

Flores, now with fifty men, marched into the small village called San Luis Obispo. There he found a saloon where he walked in for his first public drink since leaving San Quentin. Five bearded men in dirty clothes sat inside.

"Five bottles of good whiskey for my men, bartender," Flores said.

Fifty-one men filled the place to overflowing. The bartender smiled.

Five more joined with horses and guns. "All swear allegiance to the Mexican Revolution and Captain Juan Flores?" Andreas Fontes asked. They nodded and patted their six-guns in their belts.

Flores heard the county sheriff was headed their way. They left for a mission in Santa Maria Township, a good, quiet, all-Mexican town.

Santa Maria was almost a day's ride for the Juan Flores members. The La Purisma Concepcion Mission was totally decimated when they arrived. Local Mexican people re-supplied the band for a small fee. They rested up, barbecued, and drank. Three days later they moved to the next mission.

Arriving at Santa Inez way off the main El Camino Real, or the Royal Highway, the men collapsed from the ride. The heat made the ride worse.

"Even in winter it gets up in temperature, eh, Poncho?" Andreas Fontes asked.

"Yup. In this valley off the main road, it's hot as a pistol,"

Daniels said.

"Let's find a cool creek and have a drink, amigos," Flores said, tired, his neck twitching to the right.

"Look at this place," he continued. "This old, beautiful mission fallen into hard times. Used to be huge, a jewel back in my father's time."

Flores paused, scanning the dilapidated structure. "Poncho, I vow to you this day, this mission will bloom again, be bigger than ever, if I get my way."

The one priest had four Indians collect supplies for the sixty-plus men. Another out-of-work twenty Mexican <u>vaqueros</u> lived in and around the vicinity, and they quickly joined the band. The men spent the night outside.

At sunrise they started for the Santa Barbara Mission. After an hour they hit the coast and watched the white-capped ocean breakers crash on the many rocks below the cliffs. A number of Indians dug for seafood below.

"Little naked fools," Daniels said.

"Maybe not. They dig for food while we rush to our deaths," Andreas Fontes said.

"True. They will still be here digging in a month for food, and we will be digging graves for some of us," Juan Flores said. "Look. There is the mission. I have not seen it in seven years since I was with my poor wife."

Flores made all original Manillas sergeants, and the additional ten Mexicans on the ship corporals. That gave him two lieutenants, eight sergeants, and ten corporals. The men were pleased with his administration and fairness. Picking up an additional ten <u>vaqueros</u>, they left Santa Barbara with eighty-five men.

"This army is getting too big to feed. I never thought of that before," Flores said to Daniels as they headed south. "Poncho, I want you to take care of the food from now on."

"Si, Captain," Poncho said.

Mission San Buenaventura's chief padre told Flores he was a past Mexican army officer. The padre appeared fearful of Flores' army. The padre sold them the food and supplies for a fair price, and he asked them to leave to avoid the sheriff, all this done tactfully so as not to offend the gang and cause violence against the mission or the town. Flores' men left happy with their supplies. The officers wanted to make camp toward the south anyway. They camped a mile from the ocean on the Santa Clara River. Flores planned the next jump into Los Angeles County.

At the end of their stay at the river, Flores gathered the corporals, sergeants, and lieutenants. His command troops were in a circle ready for orders. Flores walked in the center of the group and gave careful instructions.

"Two weeks from today, Sunday, we will meet at San Juan Capistrano. Each of you shall take three or four men under you. You pick them, each of you. Andreas Fontes is now my intelligence officer. He will take two men to the pueblo and watch. I want no men here to join or mix with other groups. Stay separate. It is important."

"Why?" one asked.

"You saw how scared the last priest was. We are too big. Gather more men if you can and meet in two weeks. We'll be camped outside San Juan Capistrano. From there, we will plan our attack. Agreed?" All the men nodded.

"Good. Starting now, a group leaves every hour. One takes the coast, one goes inland. These groups won't alarm the gringos. We can take our time. Gather food off the land, and in two short weeks we shall meet and start our revolution. Warn the men no shootings, no robberies, no holdups until we meet again. Vaya con Dios!"

Chapter 21

Horace stood in the guest bedroom and listened to three singers with voices of angels followed by the piano player, the harpist, the guitarist, and the violinist. All were practicing the various songs for the fandango.

Horace was proud of his dashing ranger uniform. He wore a sharp red <u>vicuna</u> hat with a broad brim and sugarloaf crown topped with gold cord wound twice with heavy tassels. His snappy blue clawhammer jacket with gilt buttons topped sky blue pants with a two-inch gold bullion stripe down the side. He carried his weapon in a patent-leather scabbard with silver mountings. It was oiled and well capped. His black boots shone to the hilt. He was mighty proud of his corporal stripes on the shoulders. He looked into a full mirror and smiled at his full-feather outfit. All told, Horace had on the perfect fandango costume. The young Spanish gals would think he was a damn general or something. God he looked good. Yup, pride came before the fall, he reminded himself as he walked into the party.

The guests started arriving just before six p.m. Tomas, as host, opened the fandango with a prayer. Within a short time there were almost five hundred in attendance. The singers sang popular tunes to guitar and violin. Everyone feasted. The food never stopped leaving the kitchen. Five serving tables accommodated seventy people at one time. The anti-dancers, as Maria Sanchez called them, gathered outside in the garden and gambled at two large monte tables. The ladies remained in the sala.

"Horace! You look so gallant in your ranger uniform!" Paulette said, meeting him in the sala with Roy Bean. Horace couldn't believe this was his third fandango at the Sanchezes' wearing his corporal's uniform.

"Well, you look rather smashing yourself, Miss Paulette, in that lavender dress. Why, no one will be able to take their eyes off you tonight," Horace replied.

"I only care that you don't take your eyes off and put them on some little senorita who would like to take a handsome lawman away from escorting me."

"As a man of honor, I shall be with you tonight and bring you back as promised."

"Horace, do you know the difference between a fandango and a baile?" she asked in fun.

"No. I think there may be, but I'm lost in the nuance."

"The fandango is a free-for-all from the lowest Indian to the Highest Don. By custom, the high ranks sneak in to get a red-carpet treatment. In a Baile, or ball, rank is invited and announced in a reception line. It is very formal."

"The dancing is better at the..." Horace asked.

"Fandango, by far, for all levels of society are there in their best clothes with all their talents," Paulette said.

"We should have a great time," Horace said.

"Yes, we will."

"They loved you today, Horace." Paulette traced the edge of her stylish hat with her slender fingers. "The whole town is alive with how you and Pal won the biggest race of the year."

He felt the heat rising in his cheeks. "I was rather pleased with Pal's performance."

"Oui. You should be with some four old Dons winning eighty-thousand dollars?" she said wide-eyed.

"Guess they got lucky."

"Thanks to you and your horse. They'll worship you tonight. Mark my words, Don Horace Bell," she teased, her red lips gleaming.

Horace looked around. Color graced the home and people were wall-to-wall. The casa was filled with music, flowers, smoke, perfumes, food, drink, and fellowship. Some guests sang along with the songs. The music of three hundred conversations filled the air.

Horace and Paulette walked into the garden area. There all the Mexican-food aromas hit their senses -- smoked pig, honey-sweet hams, barbequed chickens, sweet white corn, fried carnitas, fresh-made tortillas, refried beans, all the spices. Everything was cooked outdoors where the aroma mixed with nature smells. Horace's mouth started to water. He found a candle and placed it on the water fountain. Indian boys pumped

160

the water to make it appear to be flowing. Horace was reminded of the lake in the mountains. Miss Bovierre's eyes watched the water dance in the candlelight as they ate. Even with hundreds of people nearby, they had a romantic dinner for two.

"Smells almost as good as your café," Horace said.

Then two young Spanish ladies around twenty years of age came up from behind and cracked two cascarones on Horace's head. Horace took it as a compliment and smiled back at them. Both were petite, about five foot two inches tall, with dark black hair, thin waists, and dark, lively eyes.

"See, I told you. We haven't even finished the food, and two senoritas, not one but two, would like to take you to the barn for fun and frolic," Paulette teased.

"Terrible, isn't it?" Horace teased back as he brushed off the gold and silver tinsel. She pinched his side.

"Owe! Come to think of it, the one in blue with the twinkle in her eyes looks pretty good."

"You promised..."

They selected some desserts and heard the master of ceremonies, the tecolero, take over. Don Antonio Coronel was the treasurer for the city. As the master of ceremonies, he presided over the dances and made them fun with jokes about their origin.

The Sanchez home was one of the few rancho homes to have a wooden floor throughout. The tecolero requested the three singers and the four-piece band to start with the La Jota dance. The sala was the main dance floor, but people danced everywhere.

"Come on, Paulette. Let's dance," Horace said. "You're the prettiest gal here."

"Buenos Noches, Don Horace," an attractive Spanish lady of twenty, said. She was dressed in burgundy with a Dona's comb in her hair. Horace looked, only to be whisked away by Paulette.

"How could I ever refuse an offer like that?" Paulette replied, her green eyes looking back at the other woman.

The La Jota was the most popular dance of the Californios. Each man took a partner and placed her on his right facing another couple. The sala filled up with twenty pairs of dancers, including Horace and Paulette. As soon as the music began, the hired singers started with the lyrics, and everyone moved their hands and arms to the dance.

"Not bad," Horace said, commenting on their ability while enjoying any chance he got to encircle her waist with his long arms. They danced till the lyrics ended.

Then the singers started with the chorus, which meant that the dancers joined hands in two circles, one male and one female. These circles turned in opposite directions. They turned and turned until the partners were side by side again and took their place in the line.

The singer then sang:
"Bend your knee to the ground
Saying Jesus help me,
To the Virgin of Zaragoza
And my guardian Angel too."

And the dance continued as before with the partners turning and turning until they were side by side once more. On the last verse the dancers performed the same movements but the steps changed. They picked up one foot and then the other in time with the music, hopping as in a folk dance. The La Jota was beautiful and graceful when performed perfectly, usually by the older people. They knew it better. And the dance required a solemn dignity. The refrain was:
"Know this, my life,
How courteous I've been,
How much I've respected you,
How much I've loved.
All of the gossips
Who tried to find out
And tell lies about us
Never could begin.
Only the Court of Justice,
Powerful and great,
Put me in this prison
Where I must suffer
Where I must stay
A prisoner in irons,

162

By a women betrayed.
Never you mind me,
Ungrateful one.
Someday in your dreams,
You'll remember me.
I was your lover."

Then they had a second refrain, the same dance as before but with different words.

Next the tecolero called for the La Bamba. The music began, and one local lady expert took the floor with much drama and emotion. She was tall and young, about twenty-one, with dark black hair, a pale Spanish face, and bare feet. She made an entrance by spinning around and coming to a perfect stop in front of the master of ceremonies. There she took a large glass of water and placed it on her head. She jumped and moved her feet in impossible and complicated steps without spilling the water from her head. As she went on to singing with the instruments playing in perfect pitch, many threw their hats out to her as she stacked them neatly together.

The lyrics of the song went:
"La Bamba is tiny,
La Bamba's enormous,
The dearly beloved,
Consolation of sorrows."

Then came the money thrown on the floor as the fever picked up, then handkerchiefs stacked upon her shoulders. Finally the young woman was so stacked with pledges via the hats and handkerchiefs that she bowed out from the dance floor. As she did this, the tecolero grabbed the glass of water still on her head and yelled, "Not a drop spilled, ladies and gentlemen!"

The applause was frenzied, and even more money hit the floor. Each of the men then stopped by and redeemed his hat with a money gift according to his finances and stature.

Everyone was drinking, dancing, talking, and having a grand time. The music continued without stopping into the next dance, the Los Camotes, which was similar to the previous dance but with a different tune, words, and steps. The couples again started dancing, but this was a very slow dance. Maria and

163

Tomas gracefully worked their way on the dance floor, and Horace with Paulette. At the end of the dance, the men saluted their partners and resumed their place to continue the steps once more. The dancers, especially the women, loved to sing along.

"Ladies and gentlemen, tonight, with their approval, I present to you our gracious hosts Don and Dona Sanchez to do their rendition of the El Fandango!"

Applause shook the home as Tomas came out with a rose in his hand as Maria approached from the opposite side. They met on the dance floor. You could hear a pin drop. All heard the snapping of his fingers while he stood in place. Maria heard the castanets keeping time with the snapping of Tomas's fingers, and they both did their complicated steps to a tee. Then the music stopped.

"Bomba!" the head singer cried.

On command, Tomas had to make poetry to his beloved wife. "My wife, friend, partner, who has nine in ten years, shall be blessed with eighteen in twenty years."

The music started again and the difficult steps began again. The verses went:

"Oh! my hopeless love!
How shall I forget you?
If I tell you goodbye,
I lose the glory of loving you."
Then the refrain:
"Ay, Could it be a lie?
Ay, Could it be the truth?
These dark-haired girls,
What a poor return they give!
Ay, Could it be a lie!
Ay, Could it be the truth?"

Then for the second time the music stopped, and it was Maria's turn to ad lib some poetry.

"My gentle and loving husband, always caring, always hoping, shall see the dream of his life in the next ten."

They twisted and turned, and at the end he gave her the rose in front of a full standing ovation.

"Thank you, thank you. How about a dancing lesson, Don

164

Tomas?" the master kidded, to much laughter. "I need about a hundred years worth of lessons to dance like that!"

He continued. "The next dance is our national folk dance that now belongs to our new country America. Here it is, folks. Let our best young eight boys and girls show us how to do it right, the El Sarabe!" The tecolero did a fine job keeping the party exciting.

The young dancers came out and gave a perfect folk dance routine for twenty minutes. There was much applause, and the anti-dancers went back to monte. Young lovers found a close tree to discuss their plans, and the kitchen help started cleaning up. Music still played, but it was past midnight. They played only slow songs, sad songs of the past and lost loves.

"Horace, please come into my office. I have something for you," Tomas said as the party wound down.

"Nothing is necessary," Horace said.

"You're wrong," he said, handing Horace a receipt from a broker in Los Angeles for a shipment from San Francisco.

"Horace, you look puzzled. I'm sorry. This is a shipping receipt for a complete California Law Book set."

"What? There are only three sets in the whole pueblo. The court owns two."

"You're a true friend. I want you to have the finest tools for your profession. Lord knows I'll need a good attorney."

Horace stood with his mouth open. "I can't say anything to tell you how much I appreciate your generosity."

The books would help him in his study now and in his practice later. Gosh, what a first-class gift. He was glad the old Dons gave Sanchez the eight grand. The books cost a ton.

"You earned it today! Now go enjoy the night with Miss Paulette."

Mexican Joe walked in and hugged Horace. Horace left to look for Paulette and share his good fortune.

The Dona dressed in burgundy and the stylish hair comb stood at the door as he left Don Sanchez. Horace remembered her. Her eyes showed uncommon eagerness toward him. The hell with Paulette. She could wait until later. He wanted to talk with this outstanding beauty.

"Hello. I'm Horace Bell. And you are?"

"Jacinto Talamantes. I am pleased to finally meet you, Senor Bell. My father, the Don of Ballona, was extremely shocked with your unbelievable ride today. He has the highest respect for you."

"You are — the Dona of Ballona — wow. And you aren't mad at me?"

"Heavens no, Senor Bell, we — my whole family admires your abilities, and they will never bet against you again." She smiled.

He laughed to break his tension. This young lady was a total dish, bright and respectful.

Then Paulette walked up to both of them. "I let you go with Tomas and you're off with a beautiful Dona," she teased.

"Dona Jacinto Talamantes, please meet Miss Paulette Bovierre."

"Pleased to meet you, Dona Talamantes," Paulette said.

Horace heard the dove of a Dona say "Likewise" as Paulette pulled at him. He would definitely look her up someday soon. He remembered the judge, yes?

Jacinto reached over and cracked an egg filled with golden tinsel over Horace's uniform. He smiled back at her because that meant she was interested. She returned his smile with a welcome look in her beautiful brown eyes twinkling like the golden tinsel in the egg.

"Horace, let's get some dessert," Paulette said, leading him away. He looked back to Jacinto, who stood with a confident smile.

"Doesn't the gold tinsel mean something, Horace?"

"Nothing, Paulette, just an old custom," he said, still watching Jacinto out of the corner of his eye. My, there was an enchanting young lady. Yup.

"Horace, my dear! Who cracked their egg on you with the gold tinsel? That means they're in love," Maria Sanchez teased as she walked by. Way to go, Maria.

Horace had not seen Roy Bean all night. He looked over and saw him with two Mexican beauties going off in the night. Horace laughed. Bean loved the Spanish ladies right after his

166

two-dollar sure-thing whores.

After dessert, Horace asked, "Well, my princess of the ball, are you ready to go home?"

"Oui," she said, distant.

In the carriage on the way back to the pueblo, Horace realized he needed a companion, not a boss. He was ready for a change.

"Look, Horace. I can see the man in the moon. He gets his dreams filled too," Paulette said.

He'd read somewhere that all was fair in love and war.

Chapter 22

One hundred men in groups of three or four left every hour from the last major campsite. These twenty-three groups were assigned different directions to travel: one coastal; one toward the hot San Fernando Valley; and one taking the foothills of the valley. Each group received its share in gunpowder, bullets, and limited food supplies from Lieutenant Poncho Daniels. Flores had handed each man twenty dollars in gold before he left.

Flores developed a worse twitch in his neck which accompanied many revenge thoughts running through his mind. He covered it with his right hand as he twisted his moustache. This dual movement made him look awkward.

Flores' and Daniels' small groups each took two other men with them. Flores took the coastal route straight toward San Juan Capistrano. Andreas Fontes detoured through Los Angeles. Daniels followed Flores' path. Flores' group was the first group to leave; Daniels' was the last. They planned to meet. A full twenty-four hours had passed from the first to the last group leaving.

Flores decided to wait for his chief lieutenant Daniels and then proceed to San Juan Capistrano. Two heads were better than one, and he could make sure all the groups were on their way. He could ask Daniels about their attitudes. Flores remembered what had happened the last time he was to meet a gang at San Juan Capistrano. One day later, Flores hailed Daniels and they joined their two groups into one.

Flores with Poncho Daniels began the one-hundred-and-forty-mile trip. As Flores rode down the sandy coastline, many thoughts ran through his mind. He hadn't made the final decision to fight in a revolution against the Americans. He needed the Mexican people's feelings regarding support before he could go forward. Much would depend upon further recruiting efforts.

"El Capitan, do you think we will be successful in recruiting down south here?" Daniels asked.

"Everything depends on it. If not, we run to Mexico from San Juan," Flores answered.

"So if the people don't see it our way, we just head south and--"

"Do what we have to, mi amigo, to survive."

"Si, mi capitan."

They camped near where Malibu stuck out into the ocean. Flores sent his extra two men up into the Malibu mountains for game and asked Poncho to fish in the ocean. Gathering food was now a necessity, as supplies were gone. Flores made two sets of plans in the sand. Thinking first of a full complement of a hundred and seventy-five men, he drew plan one starting with a raid at Capistrano, a note to Sheriff Barton, an ambush, followed by a full-fledged fight. Next he drew plan two: a run to the south with only fifty loyal men robbing, raiding, raping, and stealing.

An alternate plan three came to mind. If the ambush failed to incite the Mexican people to his side, he might scatter all of his forces and run. This plan surfaced only for him to repress it. Flores kept telling himself that the people wanted the old ways back and that he needed to remove the hated gringo from California.

His two Mexican recruits in the mountains brought in a hunger-killing one-hundred-fifty-pound deer. Flores had them skin it away from camp to avoid bringing in extra fleas and mountain ticks. Poncho caught three large sea bass. A small spring running out of the mountain provided water. As Juan Flores contemplated how the spring ran from the hills to the ocean, he quietly pondered where he could run. Flores hoped his pride would not interfere with his decision.

Northwest of the pueblo, Juan Flores, Francisco Poncho Daniels, and their four men traveled by the Rancho Ballona along the coast. There they saw a beautiful woman riding a black horse from a two-hundred-foot distance. Flores thought if it were a couple of weeks later, he'd probably just take that beauty and ravage her. She looked at him and galloped off at top speed. He told his men to keep moving forward. Someday, he told himself, he might come back. She was one beauty whose eyes would haunt him. Damn, she was just as pretty as his murdered wife.

Chapter 23

Horace trotted on Pal toward the Talamantes Rancho. The judge had asked Horace to do on-sight deed research and get the Don's signature, the judge's father-in-law. Galloping up at the same time was Jacinto, as attractive as before but now with her sensuous, long black hair flying. Her red suede riding outfit highlighted her light complexion and brown eyes.

"Senor Bell, there are six villainous men there on the coast, and all our vaqueros are away," she said exasperated, pointing. "And, Senor Bell, please come back. They seem real evil to me. I think they saw me..." She was breathless and wide-eyed.

"I'll look and come right back."

Checking first that his extra Colt revolver was in the saddlebag, Horace galloped to a high hill overlooking the ocean. He pulled out a new, three-sectioned spyglass and took a look. Far below by the ocean waves, six men headed south. One looked like his old nemesis Juan Flores.

Chills went up and down Horace's spine. This could be Paul's murderer. He'd promised his lifelong ranger friend he'd avenge his death. His insides turned inside out. Frustration gripped his very soul. The pueblo had just heard the news of the San Quentin breakout a few weeks before. Northern California had served a warrant on Flores at the prison for Paul's murder. Then Flores escaped and many were killed.

Outnumbered six to one, he decided forethought was smarter than valor. His first promise must be kept to the Dona. He scribbled some notes for a later report. The day was particularly romantic with a stark blue sky highlighted by puffy white clouds and a gentle breeze. Too bad it had to be spoiled by these troublemakers.

Then he double-checked his decision. Mixed emotions ran through his head. His first job was to protect Dona Jacinto. He was compelled to capture Flores, but he was outnumbered. He also found himself smitten with Miss Jacinto Talamontes. She was simply a young raving beauty. She possessed a female magnetism that he had not experienced before. Lastly, he had his duty to the judge's errand. With his stomach turning, Horace galloped back.

"Senor Bell, did you see them?" Jacinto asked. Her face was white with fright, her black hair hanging gently over her white shoulders.

"Yes, they do appear wicked, Miss Jacinto."

"So they're not..."

"Doesn't appear they're coming this way," Horace assured her. "But one looked like Juan Flores."

"That criminal, that murderer, he would ravage me," Jacinto said.

"Um, are we alone here?"

"Yes, we are alone. The staff are building my brothers's place over that hill," she said, pointing.

"Miss Jacinto, let's not stay in the main casa. Let's move to the barracks. Bring your horse. We might have to run."

"Jes, that would be smart. Are you still studying law?" Jacinto said while they walked their horses.

"Yes. Judge Dimmick sent me to see the metes and bounds, plus get your father's signature."

"I feel much better with a big, strong ranger guarding me," Jacinto said, her vivid brown eyes staring at him. Too bad those six no-counts were around to distract him.

"We'll stay here fifteen minutes. Here, take my arm," Horace said. She was pretty strong-willed yet looked up to him. Maybe she was in love.

"Such an all-powerful arm, Senor Bell." Yup, she was in love.

"Just call me Horace." Maybe he was in love too.

"With pleasure, Mr. Horace Bell, Horace -- I mean -- I like the sound of H-o-r-a-c-e. Maybe we can become good friends," Jacinto said with a flirtatious, feminine smile.

In time Flores and he would meet again.

Chapter 24

Horace sat in Judge Dimmick's office thinking about Jacinto. He enjoyed her company. He contemplated the differences between Paulette and Jacinto. Both possessed beauty, affection, and charm. Paulette always tried to mother him and tell him what he should do in her commanding tone. He needed to explore the Jacinto opportunity. He yearned for an excuse to visit her again. When Judge Dimmick made a comment about the Talamantes Rancho, Horace's ears picked right up.

"Judge, did you mention the Talamantes place, Rancho Ballona?"

"Yes, Horace. I forgot to write down the northern boundary on their original deed. It's different than the county filing, you know."

"I know. Good," Horace said, smiling. "I'll ride out there tonight for you."

Horace rode Pal toward the Ballona Rancho. Jacinto was number one on his mind. He hadn't yet formally met the Don of Ballona, Jacinto's father. He wondered what his reception would be -- cold, warm, or hot? He pulled up to the casa. A man about twenty years older stepped out to greet him. Question number one was about to be answered. Fine.

"Si, pleased to meet, Mr. Bell. Mi Don Felipe Talamantes," he said in broken English. The Don's pleasant manner and smile told Horace that he was their hero. Gee, he was fortunate.

"Likewise. Pleased to meet you, Don Talamantes."

"Si. Hope you can... visit with Jacinto. She likes you." He was in!

"I need to see your original grant deed. I'd love to talk with Jacinto too."

Jacinto was at the front door when he entered. The grant deed was laid out on a beautiful light brown oak desk in the sala. Wine was already poured in lead crystal glasses. Horace took out his lawyer pad and took notes for the judge. He took a sip of the finest wine, his taste buds told him. Jacinto patiently watched him work. He put his pad in his coat pocket, smiled at Jacinto, and asked her for an evening walk around the main rancho buildings. They took their wine glasses outside.

"My father wants you to know that you are welcome anytime," she said when they were alone. Crickets chirped distinctive music. They reminded Horace of when he first fell in love. The sky, full of a million points of light, made this a memorable moment.

"I was expecting maybe a cold welcome, since the race. Your father, Don Felipe, gave me an extremely warm one," Horace said.

"Jes, my father thinks you are one very smart man."

"I could see he approves of me."

"Jes, more than you realize. What are your ambitions, Horace? Do you plan to stay in Los Angeles?"

"Yes, Jacinto, I do. I want a large law practice, a controversial newspaper, and a command post with the rangers."

"Good. Let's finish our wine, get back to the casa."

They walked back toward the casa, using the side garden entrance. She stopped him at the door. She placed her glass on the porch wall. She kissed him. Then she opened the door and walked in. He was surprised, yet pleased. She was one smart, feisty woman. He could see she was determined and was used to getting what she wanted.

Horace planned to come back every few nights for the next month to see if the relationship would grow. He wasn't sure, but right now he was interested. Paulette was fast falling into second place. Yes, if he were to court and spark anyone toward marriage, it might be this lovely Dona of Ballona.

Chapter 25

Juan Flores paid for his meal at the Mission San Juan Capistrano. He sat back and looked out the window toward the ocean. Nothing had changed. The German had given him a dirty look before he entered the mission. Flores' own conscience scared him; pride drove him forward. His neck twitched to the right and his beady eyes looked to see if anyone noticed.

He and his men were camped out of town. The rendezvous was only a week away.

On the second night Andreas Fontes rode in with fifteen new Mexicans. These additional men increased the revolution's manpower and encouraged Flores.

"Mi Captain, I lost Jaime and Juan in a Nigger Alley gunfight," Fontes said.

"I told the men no problems," Flores said, his eyes narrowing as he assessed the news. "Did they get any link to our gang?"

"No, we just left." Fontes fidgeted while waiting for Flores to speak.

"Those two fools' killings should stop the rest of them becoming too adventurous," Flores said. "Any word from the pueblo?"

"Si. The sheriff, Barton, has two deputies, one marshal, some constables, and sixty active rangers," Fontes said.

"Less than seventy against us. Not bad, Andreas. We'll kill them," Flores said. His reasoned half the rangers would quit when they started to fight. The Mexican people were the wild card. Would they help? But things were looking up with the extra men.

"One last thing. I bought twenty guns," Fontes said.

"Excellent," Daniels said.

"Lieutenant Daniels, store up a good supply of food. Soon we will need it," Flores said. "Sergeant Catabo, send out riders to help recruit the Mexican drifters."

The camp now grew day by day. Flores soon counted over one hundred and fifty men. The various campfires were alive with anxious Mexican patriots. He watched as more men came in. Flores discounted his own reputation as a horse thief, murderer, stealer, and prison breaker. His character would not be an issue regarding Mexican heritage and pride. He would appeal to the Mexican ranchos. They possessed the key to his American takeover. They would follow his lead.

He made his decision. That night he selected plan one. Flores singlehandedly decided to start his Mexican-American revolution. Captain Flores saw over one hundred and sixty men ready to die for him. Juan Flores wanted his Mexican dream.

Monday Flores and five officers made collections for their insurrection. They stopped at the San Juan Capistrano stores. Under the show of force, two foreign shop owners quickly made twenty-dollar donations. Flores, still humiliated by his treatment from the German, decided to keep a vow he'd made years ago.

Flores entered George Pfleugart's general store. The store was in the front of his home. Five men rudely followed behind Flores and kicked over the merchandise. The German Pfleugart immediately recognized Flores from the past. His eyes showed disgust but fright. Flores discourteously demanded a hundred dollars for his Mexican Revolution. The German politely refused. He requested they leave.

They did not.

All six men pulled out their Bowie knives and surrounded him. He begged for a chance to see what money was in his can. They told him to get on his knees and beg. He did. They made him crawl on all fours and make chicken sounds. He did. They told him to lick all their boots clean. He did.

They tired of their game. Flores told him, "You are a fat German pig who insulted me. As Mexican commander I sentence you to die on your table, where I will eat your dinner as I promised you." Four men leapt forward and plunged their long knives into his porky pink flesh. He yelped and wept as they stabbed him.

The German's kettle boiled on the stove. The six Mexicans picked up the old, bleeding shop owner and laid him on his dining table. They served themselves six large bowls of beans and carne asada. While the dying German choked on his blood, Flores and his men ate the whole kettle of beans and told the

176

German how stupid he was.

He drowned in his own blood while the gang enjoyed his dinner.

They congratulated themselves while the man died. They trashed the German's place and stole everything they could carry.

Next door, the owner left three gold fifty-dollar slugs on his front counter with a note to Flores to take it and please leave the store alone. They did. Flores saw a familiar man gallop out of town. Flores knew the man would tell the sheriff. Yes, Sheriff James Barton would be pissed off.

Chapter 26

Horace watched Sheriff Barton, cussing God, walk into the ranger barracks. Barton was indeed pissed. Sheriff Barton demanded ten rangers immediately. A German merchant was savagely killed in cold blood at San Juan Capistrano.

"Six damn Mex, demanding money, kilt German George in his San Juan Capistrano store per my special deputy," Barton said, his face red and nostrils all flared out.

"Jim, ten rangers isn't enough," Brevoort said. "I can't release just ten. You have to call up the whole damn regiment. Everyone." Brevoort stood his ground and nervously twisted and stroked his red moustache.

A ranger detective spoke up. "Luie, I've been by the mission. There's way over a hundred no-good Mex camped in the hills. We have good reason to think Juan Flores is there too."

Other rangers told the Luie what they knew. Horace mentioned maybe it was the Juan Flores gang that stormed San Quentin Prison. Roy Bean told the lieutenant to stand tall. Barton steamed. He took a drink from the whiskey bottle he was holding and belched. He rubbed his five-day-old black stubble.

"Damn it, you bunch of chicken-shits. Are you with me or against me?" Barton said. Horace watched as Barton rocked on his heels back and forth. Booze clouded Barton's judgment.

"Sheriff, the area is too explosive. You'll need the full ranger complement to fight those numbers," Brevoort reiterated.

"Explosive my ass! It's just six damn Mex murdering storekeepers down there. Brevoort, you're a measly red-headed horse's ass," Barton said as he stormed out the door.

Horace remembered the six Mexicans riding toward Capistrano. Damn. They were probably the same gang. Jacinto had been in real danger. Lovely Jacinto. He wanted to be with her.

"Bell, wake up! Stop your damn daydreamin'," Brevoort yelled, agitated by Barton.

Brevoort told his corporals to sound the alarm and activate all fifty reserves. Horace was assigned to alarm and cover the

179

north and western ranchos. Horace decided to cover the ones on the north first and the western ones the next day. He'd spend the night at Sanchez's. They packed their gear and got ready to ride.

Horace asked Roy Bean, "Where's the ranger captain -- Dr. Hope?"

"He's been dryin' out at the San Fernando Mission. An alcoholic, you know -- an alky. Brevoort's stuck with the whole damn show," Bean answered.

"This looks serious, Roy. What do you think?"

"Partner, Barton's pride is takin' a blind flyin' leap into a Mexican Hades. Brevoort is right."

If Horace were in command, he would have made the same conditions to Barton. Barton's whiskey ego put a burr up his ass that no one could reason with.

Outside, they all watched as Sheriff James Barton left with five men. Barton demanded all the town's constables become his posse. Horace noticed that Barton and his drinking friend, Charles Daily, a blacksmith, left side by side with their bottles in hand.

"See you chicken-shits later!" Barton and Daily yelled, waving their bottles as they galloped out of town.

Horace hoped they'd pass out and fall off their horses before they got into real trouble.

The constables -- Little, Baker, Hardy, and Alexander -- looked godforsaken and trapped as they followed Barton. Horace felt sorry for them. He saddled and rode out as ordered to the northern ranchos. He planned to be at Sanchez's rancho that afternoon. He'd have to wait to the following day to see Jacinto. He was trapped too.

Chapter 27

Flores sent Fontes two miles down the rode to bait Sheriff Barton. Fontes' girlfriend promised to unload the posse's guns when they stopped for lunch at Don Sepulveda's Rancho. Flores felt like a huge Cheshire cat ready to spring on the rat. He'd kept his promise to Fontes. Soon guns would be blazing.

Six miles from the rancho, Flores waited impatiently.

To watch, and for cover, Flores and Daniels waited behind a small hill.

Fontes galloped toward the gang. Behind them came the sheriff's posse -- Barton was first, followed by three more. Two of the posse had stopped way back. Flores licked his chops. Now the Mexican-American war would start anew. The gauntlet was thrown.

Flores signaled his men to start the ambush. His men fired at will. First to fall was a big-bellied fellow shot in the stomach. Next were the other two following Barton.

Daniels shot Barton in the arm. Barton fell off his horse like a wounded fish. He flopped around and tried to keep his shotgun and his revolver. Now it was Fontes' turn for revenge.

Fontes dismounted and walked back slowly to confront the sheriff.

"Goddamn you, Barton, I got you now!" Fontes sneered, out of breath from the excitement of the chase.

"I reckon I got you too, Fontes," Barton said, shaking from the gunshot.

Barton lined up his revolver sights and pulled the trigger at twenty feet. The hammer fell on an unloaded chamber. Barton, frustrated, tried again and again. He realized that somehow his enemy had unloaded his six-gun. His face and eyes turned to shock.

"You don't even give a fellow a fair chance!" Barton cried out. Barton quickly rolled over and fired both barrels of his double-barreled shotgun. Fontes hit the ground, but Barton missed.

Fontes grinned and walked slowly to where his opponent lay. Barton's arm wound poured out blood and stained his long-sleeve white shirt. Barton's right hand held his wounded arm in pain. His eyes showed complete mortal fear.

"Barton, you never gave me or my sister a fair chance, did you, you miserable drunken son of a bitch?" Fontes said.

Barton looked up, wept, and pleaded for mercy. Fontes' eyes beaded up. He calmly pulled the trigger. The bullet shattered Barton's right eye. Flores grabbed his mouth in excitement as the bullet took out the rear of Barton's head. A big glob of red blood and brains lay in the dirt of Sand Canyon Road. Fontes fired three more times, each shot striking Barton's heart. That heart had ceased to beat a moment before.

Flores walked up and slapped Fontes on the back. He congratulated Fontes on ending Barton's life. Fontes walked over to the side of the road and threw up. He didn't say a word to Flores. Andreas Fontes mounted his horse and headed south.

The two deputies that stayed back had watched the action and quickly galloped away. Flores gave orders to kill them both. Flores' fifteen Mexican soldiers chased the two men back toward Sepulveda's San Joaquin Rancho. Flores smiled; the revolution was under way.

Daniels went from body to body to grab the spoils. Flores joined him. In glee they found money, watches, guns, and personal items. Flores ordered the Mexicans who remained there to take care of the posse's bodies. They completely disrobed and cut up the cadavers. They dismembered and decapitated the men. They stuffed their private parts in their now dead, separated heads. This was done as a deliberate insult to the Americans.

As Flores rode to the top of the hill overlooking the first battlefield, he shouted back, "Now, my Manillas, we have made a statement showing how fierce we are! The posse is dead!"

Late that afternoon Horace pulled up as planned at Tomas Sanchez's rancho. General Andreas Pico was already there with thirty fully armed <u>vacqueros</u> and fifty extra horses.

Inside, Tomas rubbed his short beard. Pico and Sanchez were yelling at one another. Tomas motioned Horace inside the room and told Mexican Joe to shut the damn door.

"Horace, here's the facts," General Pico began. "Four men

were killed hours ago. Constables Frank Alexander and Frank Hardy witnessed the ambush. This is what happened. Barton called Don Juan Sepulveda a fool for being afraid of a few Mexicans during his lunch there. Four miles away from San Joaquin Rancho, the Barton posse spied a fellow off in the grass. They didn't realize he was a decoy. But since the fellow ran, they took up the chase.

"Frank Alexander and Frank Hardy stayed back a half mile. It seemed strange to them that one man would be out alone. They sensed a trap. First they checked their guns for bullets. When they found them unloaded, instant panic went through them, and they halted. We suspect a girlfriend of the ambush perpetrators."

Pico continued. "Hardy and Alexander stopped just in time to see the slaughter. They watched as each man was shot off his horse, one by one, as they'd been led into an ambush.

"First Daily hit the ground, then Little, then Baker, and lastly Sheriff Barton. The only gun fired by the sheriff's party was Barton's double-barreled shotgun. Barton missed, both barrels full. Their own pistols -- they were empty so they wouldn't have been of any use.

"At least fifteen gang members fired their bullets at Hardy and Alexander. They fled. They both recognized Andreas Fontes, the Sheriff's girlfriend's brother. He was the decoy whom the rest chased. Barton probably saw Fontes and went livid, his pride getting him killed. "Hardy and Alexander rode like hell to escape the Mexicans shooting at them. With bullets kicking up the dust around them, they made for the Sepulveda Rancho. Don Sepulveda lent them two rested horses. They raced out the back gate. Even with the fresh horses, the fifteen Mexicans gave them a race for their lives.

"Their entire fifteen-mile escape ended when Hardy and Alexander crossed the Santa Ana River. The Mexicans stopped at the edge of the river and let them go. Both deputies were scared, and outraged.

"Alexander headed to my town home. The pueblo must be going crazy. Tomas and I request your professional opinion."

Horace quickly responded, "You and Tomas must ride out

immediately and put down this insurrection."

"And if we do not?" Tomas asked.

"Tomas, each and every gringo in Los Angeles will use it against every person of Spanish or Mexican descent, period!" Horace pressed.

"Calm down, Horace, I see it. Let's go, mi general. You too, Horace. Mexican Joe, you stay here and guard my family. Don't leave. It's too dangerous," Tomas said.

General Andreas Pico had his big black, Captain Tomas Sanchez had El Capitan, and Horace rode Pal. Behind them were sixty of both ranchos' finest vaqueros and the fifty extra horses for the rangers. Pico told all vaqueros, "We are riding to protect Mexican honor in America. We cannot fail. We have to stop the revolution."

Each rider had a rifle and two revolvers. Sanchez and Pico left the fifty horses at the barracks. The rangers would need the extra mounts. Three rangers quietly fed the animals and watched the Pico-Sanchez army leave for a bloody war.

Pico ordered no prisoners taken, no quarter given. The gringo population would only trust a total elimination of Flores' gang. Each of these conspirators had to die as soon as possible. If not, no Mexican would be able to hold his head up or walk down the street in the Pueblo de Los Angeles. If they eliminated the criminals, they'd be respected as the first-in, first-to-fight, and first-to-win corps.

Next to Sanchez rode his assistant majordomo, an expert with the gun -- Jose Lopez. Horace smiled remembering Lopez's drop of the horse race baton. Lopez's hunting ability was second-to-none.

Lopez looked at Don Tomas Sanchez and said, "Mi Capitan, I will personally shoot down twenty-five of these banditos for you."

Horace noticed Jose's five revolvers. Just like David and Goliath in the Bible. David had picked up five stones, not for a miss, but in case Goliath's four brothers came after him. One stone to kill each of the five family giants. Jose Lopez was going out with twenty shots in five revolvers and two more in his rifles. He'd promised twenty-five kills.

Sanchez told Horace, "With this young man's skill, I assume Jose will have thirty dead before the army catches up with him."

"Vaya con Dios, brave soul," Horace said as he saw Lopez getting smaller and smaller on the horizon.

Flores watched through his spyglass. He saw his large group of men way in the distance. One man rode behind the main body. The lone horseman seemed to fly as he galloped. The group turned to see the horseman approach. They waved at him. Flores thought something wasn't right. The horseman rode between them. The horseman shot all six men, at once. Their horses stopped. Six Mexicans fell onto the dirt road. Flores was sick.

The horseman paused to reload. Then he rode hard again. Flores saw four more of his men approach the horseman. The man passed through the four, and at the last second, drew two revolvers and fired four times. All Flores' men fell on the dusty road. God. He'd just lost ten men.

Flores observed the horseman approach the first campsite, his first guard post. His men walked toward the horseman. Flores saw the horseman talk to three men. Quick as lightning, the horseman drew two revolvers and shot all three. Flores looked through the spyglass to see his men fall.

The lone horseman rode out of view. One man was wiping out half his army. Flores panicked. He had to warn Daniels. He rode quickly to his main camp.

"Poncho, I just saw one man kill thirteen of ours," Flores said. His neck nervously twitched to the right.

"I got a report that twelve more were killed, seconds ago, by one man!" Daniels said.

"Twenty-five men? Poncho, many men will come from the pueblo. This was their point man," Flores said. "We're in bad trouble."

Daniels' mouth dropped to the dirt. They heard more gunfire. Flores and Daniels hurried to look. Down below at the first guard post were five more dead men all shot in the chest. The horseman galloped away. Juan Flores saw firsthand the leftovers of the horseman's killing.

"He's gone," a Flores soldier said. "We're doomed, Poncho.

185

Too many too fast."

Flores realized he'd made a tremendous error in judgment. The wealthy southern California Mexicans were against him and his cause. They would not support him. The upcoming battle would decimate his entire army. Sad, he realized his chance for Mexican glory had faded, much like the Spanish-Mexican heritage he treasured. His romantic revolution was blowing up right in front of his face.

He gave his last command to the camp. "Heros and patriots, we are in retreat. Run for your life! Go in different directions. If you don't run, you will be dead. Run!" He shouted to them at the top of his lungs.

Over one hundred men broke up into smaller groups heading in separate directions. Each man was now scared to death of the one-man killing machine.

Juan Flores and Poncho Daniels took flight. First they rode up the Santa Ana Mountains. As the brush thickened, they dismounted and walked on an old Indian path. Snow, turned to ice, made the trail slippery. The steepness of the jagged purple peak had them crawling over the rocks as they led their precious escape horses around the icy obstacles. Finally they reached the peak and looked back.

Far distant popping sounds rose up from below. Flores imagined all his men eliminated. Sadness crept over his spirit. The rangers thwarted his plan. A lousy hundred men made him a failure. Now his men died on California soil that he wanted to reclaim for Mexico.

The Santa Ana Mountains would offer him respite. The next day they would be around Murrieta Hot Springs. They would defeat the trackers and double back to hide by the Canyon Christianitos with its creek. There, five miles from the ocean, he could decide how to avoid the enemy.

"Where did Andreas Fontes ride after he kilt Barton?" Flores asked Daniels as he shivered in the cold and covered his neck twitch.

"He left for Mexico and told me we'd all be dead in a week," Daniels said, holding his blanket around him.

"Not if we can outsmart them damn gringos," Flores said.

Chapter 28

Horace heard the gunshots ahead. Jose Lopez was alone out at point. What a brave <u>vaquero</u> he was. Someday Jose would step into Mexican Joe's shoes if he came out of this battle alive.

Horace was a little jealous of Jose for he seemed to be involved in all the action. Must be glory and honor mixed in his soul. Horace wished to join in the battle to win, but he couldn't be impatient. Soon he'd be in the thick of it. He would see danger blended with glory and possible reward.

Tomas Sanchez rode next to him. Behind them the <u>vaqueros</u> made ready for battle against the numerous Juan Flores gang. Horace realized they were outnumbered three to one, but they had right on their side. He quickly perceived that being right would not stop any bullets. He had to be prepared.

Up front Pico halted the small army to have a quick meeting with Sanchez and Horace.

"Flores' men look to be in retreat or worse, a guerilla warfare posture. We'll need to split up to conquer them," he said to Sanchez and Horace.

"Mi general, how would you like it done — the breakup?" Sanchez asked.

"First I'll address the men, Tomas."

Pico turned to his men. "Brave <u>vaqueros</u>, you must shoot to kill anyone that runs. We can't trust them, and we don't need any damn survivors. The American court system is too weak," he shouted. All nodded.

Pico reached back, put his right hand on the saddle, and spoke to Sanchez and Horace. "Horace, take ten men and support Tomas' flank. Tomas, take twenty of your <u>vaqueros</u> and flush the wide canyon there."

Tomas took his men and saw twenty men fleeing west toward the ocean. Tomas gave chase. Horace followed. The Mexican posse had to kill the revolutionaries or forfeit their American future. The only way Sanchez and Pico could ensure the Americans' trust was to be absolutely brutal toward the Mexican criminals. Pico knew the gringo population would always think any free, lone Mexican was a Flores revolutionary. Any prisoners he captured would be later released by the court system if not hanged. The prejudiced American opinion forced Pico to command immediate field justice. All Flores' gang had to be eliminated.

These criminals caused a sorry state of affairs.

Horace empathized that so many were to die. He told Tomas that Barton's pride over his squaw started the deaths. Ironically, Sheriff James Barton was the first to die. Horace saw Barton as the shameful grim reaper who had harvested the hate he'd planted in Fontes.

Horace led his ten vacqueros and engaged the sixteen men who now charged. They fired a volley at fifty feet aimed at these aggressive sixteen. Five fell. The other eleven gang mambers were shot by crossfire and a determined charge by Horace and his ten men. He was now in it heart and soul. Damn he loved the bittersweet chase.

Horace saw Tomas, unhorsed, under fire across the narrow valley. He spurred Pal and rushed to back up his friend. Tomas remounted and formed a calvary charge. Horace was almost there as Tomas led his men. He heard Tomas yell, "Charge!" Five of the gang were run through by Sanchez's cavalry, which carried their old, ten-foot Spanish lances. They had a one-foot pointed blade that widened to three inches at the bottom. The cavalry called it the sticking of the pigs. Horace wondered if the Juan Flores gang would be the last to feel the stick of the steel blades in battle.

Soon General Pico and his men joined forces with Sanchez at Flores' San Juan Capistrano campground a few miles north of the mission on San Juan Creek. Pico and Sanchez wanted Flores found now. Horace was pleased to see Jose Lopez fall in behind Sanchez. He was still alive. Gosh he was a hell of a fighter.

"Tomas, we must get Flores and Daniels -- take care of the Mexicans' dirty laundry -- before the ex-Texas Rangers show," Pico said, continuing. "Captain Sanchez and Lieutenant Lopez, you and your men cover the run toward San Gabriel. Corporal Bell, come with me and Manuelito. Him and his braves are the best trackers around."

188

Horace rode with Chief Manuelito, who kept an eye on his braves. The chief shared with Horace that his fifty braves loved their freedom and autonomy on Rancho Santa Margarita Las Flores. Both Andreas and Pio Pico owned the immense rancho down the San Diego coast. Governor Pico had helped out the Portrero Indians as a friend and benefactor.

The trackers found a trail made by twelve or more men going over the Santa Ana Mountains. Pico made an educated guess and went in pursuit. Dense, tangled cacti poked the men with painful thorns as they led the pursuers onward. They dismounted and led their horses up the steep trail. The Indians were used to their mountains. Horace found them intolerable. Soon they'd be in the higher cold, dark purple, cragged rocks that peaked the mountain range. Crap. Why couldn't Flores have made this easy? Guess it wouldn't be any fun if it weren't a pain in the butt.

Horace took off his hat and rubbed his hair back. He felt the January chill coming from the top of the five-thousand-foot mountains. Snow lines trickled down the slopes like white frosting on a chocolate cake. From a distance the pine trees grew up like a tall cornfield ready for harvest. The serrated, violet peaks beckoned them forward.

They watched for their prey which should be nearby. Pico felt certain they'd find the Mexican prince of murderers soon. The trackers told the Indian chief the pursued were a few hours ahead. Pico and the others still weren't positive who they were tracking. They just hoped it was Flores and his gang.

By three in the morning their hopes were satisfied. The Portrero Indians reported they had located Juan Flores, Poncho Daniels, and ten more Manillas. Pico, the Indian chief, and Horace woke their men and pulled out immediately toward Flores' high mountain camp.

Horace told Pico, "I promised my dead partner I'd get this son of a bitch, General. I want him tonight."

The general nodded. His frame, though small, exuded leadership. His dark moustache held the nighttime mountain frost. Horace discerned they both wished to close the book on the bandits, especially on Juan Flores.

The Indian chief ordered his braves to throw rocks, make animal sounds, and rustle the brush to keep the Flores gang from getting a good night's sleep. Horace smiled, thinking that he would have his chance to capture Flores once and for all.

Juan Flores had a fitful sleep. He was nervous, his neck twitch woke him up, rocks fell, animals called out, and he felt like someone was watching him. By early morning he heard many men screaming and yelling right on top of them. Down they came from nowhere. Suddenly dust, dirt, rocks, Mexicans and Indians spilled onto the camp. Juan Flores and Poncho Daniels jumped on their horses and fled, leaving the rest to fight.

They wouldn't make it, Juan Flores thought, as he rode flying. He told Daniels to break off and split up. Two relentless men chased Flores over the hills. He looked back and pushed his loyal horse to the maximum. They followed him through the dark, deep canyons.

He found a trail up over another purple peak. As he looked behind, he saw them there like a shadow he couldn't shake, sticky honey he couldn't throw off his fingers. The two strangers stayed on his heels for miles and miles in the dark. They paced him, ready to trap him. He felt cornered; there was no way out. He'd be caught like a caged animal and go back to the Stones. Hell no. He'd die first. But would he?

Finally Flores came to a steep cliff. He didn't like the risk. He sent his loyal horse first. Its new silver trappings throwing light slivers in the moonlight, it dashed deathward. As it flipped, the horse moaned, its frightened eyes bidding a sad goodbye to his keeper.

Flores was sickened to lose his companion, the one he'd purchased after the prison break. He watched as it fell several hundred yards way down beneath.

The two pursuers pulled up behind him. Flores heard their footsteps. He had to face it; he was caught. He turned slowly and said, "I guess you got me."

Andreas Pico and Horace whacked him in the head, and all went black.

Chapter 29

General Andreas Pico and Horace bound Juan Flores while he was unconscious and put him on a horse. They took him back to Flores' campground, which Pico made his new <u>vaquero</u> headquarters. Tomas Sanchez brought in Poncho Daniels. Now they had both of them. They would hang them in the pueblo within the week.

Horace asked Tomas how he'd captured Daniels. Tomas and three men had watched a canyon Indian trail leading up the Santa Anas. They were camped half asleep when a man came down hellbent with fright. He was afraid, for he made no effort to be quiet. He tried to ride right past them, but a <u>vaquero</u> took his ten-foot lance and swung it at his head. Daniels' head missed the blade but hit the shaft hard enough to dismount him.

"I doubled the <u>vaquero's</u> salary and tied up Daniels," Tomas said with a laugh.

"One hundred and ten men are dead," Pico said. "The ranchos lost fifteen good men."

"Tough times, tough men," Horace said.

"Sorry times, sorry men," Tomas replied.

"Both," Horace said.

Horace and Tomas walked over to see Flores and Daniels. Tomas handed Horace Barton's personal items. Flores had carried Barton's gold watch and shotgun. Daniels had stolen a Navy revolver with "Barton" carved in the handle.

Two hours later, Flores awoke and looked around. Still groggy, he saw Daniels next to him. The dark, damp night ushered in a dense cloud that became a thick fog. The smell of wild wet plants passed his nostrils. A lone hoot owl made his call -- "Wh-o-o-t, wh-o-o-t." Everyone around was sound asleep, secure in their capture of the worst bandit in the Los Angeles Pueblo's history.

The dampness made him shiver. Flores, bound back to back with Daniels, moved his right foot back and carefully fingered for his right boot. Sweet Mary! They hadn't searched his boot! He pulled out a small knife and cut Poncho Daniels' bindings.

Then Daniels did his. In the dark fog, they crept slowly toward the horses while their exhausted captors slept.

Flores went to the main horse rope securing the camp's horses and cut it. Daniels stole two guns and held back two horses. They leapt on them and fired two shots from their guns. The untied horses stampeded. Flores and Daniels galloped away.

Shots rang out behind them with cussing and swearing. More shots were fired. Flores yelled back, "We beat you damn turncoat <u>vaqueros</u> and rangers!" He laughed with Daniels until they cried. Their pursuers would be hard-pressed to chase them on foot. Damn it all, they were both free again!

Now, where should they go? Most likely they'd look for them to escape toward Mexico. They had to hide in the mountains, travel by night, and go where the rangers and <u>vaqueros</u> wouldn't be able to find them. Freedom and victory was theirs.

"Juan, they talked when you were out. They killed over a hundred of us!" Daniels said.

"Then they don't need to make it two more, mi amigo," Flores said. "I've got a plan. My other ones failed. This one must not."

They'd have to confuse their trackers and cross over to the Laguna hills, live from the land, and stay there for a few months. He and Daniels would split up after the Laguna hills and go north. In the hills they would shave off all their head hair. They needed new identities to survive.

Chapter 30

Tomas and Horace were frustrated by Flores' and Daniels' escape. Hours later when they regained their horses, they and their men tracked them but lost their trail at the San Juan Creek. The criminals used the clear crystal water of the creek bed to cover their tracks. Tomas speculated perhaps they'd hidden in the Laguna hills, Horace thinking they'd doubled-back to the Santa Anas. No matter. They'd vanished.

Tomas watched immense dust clouds coming toward the camp. One full day had passed since he and Pico rode out. Now the dust clouds from two ranger armies were converging on San Juan Capistrano. These men would continue the mop-up operation. Tomas was pleased that he and Pico put down the Flores revolt quickly.

Tomas and Horace talked over coffee. "Horace, my men captured twenty of Flores' gang and put them in a box canyon with Pico's majordomo. He's that gruesome one -- big, ugly, and mean. The ex-Texas Rangers came and asked him for my prisoners. I think they didn't trust us. The large suntanned <u>vacquero</u> rode back into the canyon and brought out forty bloody ears on a crude, vulgar rawhide necklace and told the ex-Texas rangers, 'Senor, they confessed to their sins and were punished!'" Tomas saw Horace smile.

Horace's entire ranger troupe pulled up. Bean told Horace the pueblo was in chaos, the army had dragoons stationed at the pueblo, the home guard was posted at the major mountain passes, and the citizens slept with their guns.

"No Mexican is safe there alone, then," Tomas said.

"Like you said, my friend, sorry times, sorry men," Horace said.

Tomas was chagrined at the reality of the battle. He told Horace, "Many of Flores' gang were seduced by the promise of wealth and status. Now they are a footnote in history."

Tomas hoped the putdown of the revolution would return the Los Angeles Pueblo back to its semi-gringo status quo for a long time. He and Pico had made their civil defense statement for the citizens.

Tomas recognized Lieutenant David Brevoort from Los Angeles and counted sixty rangers. Another group of rangers from El Monte under acting Sheriff Burns joined with the L.A. men. These were the same ex-Texas Rangers that demanded Sanchez's Mexican prisoners and saw their ears. Now they'd clean up the Mexican battlefield that he and Pico had already won.

The rangers broke into squads and started search parties. Tomas and Horace joined in with a small squad of seven more. They found a party of four Mexicans who surrendered and were bound. Horace's men then found another three. Soon the total captured numbered fifty-five.

These prisoners would be moved to the city jail yard and chained to jail logs for trial. Tomas had no faith in the American court system. They'd hang maybe ten and the rest would go free to rape and rob again. His grandfather's system had been better. Grandfather would have hung them all, for all had crossed the line. Once they were gone, the citizens would never have to worry.

After four days, Tomas decided to go home. His rancho needed him, and they had accomplished what they had set out to do -- quash the rebellion.

"Goodbye, Horace," he said. "With your help, we saved the pueblo. I hope now we have peace and have preserved our Spanish heritage."

"Vaya con Dios, mi amigo," Horace said.

Chapter 31

Mexican Joe remembered Don Tomas' words not to leave the rancho, but he thought it was foolish advice. Besides, the youngest Sanchez boy, a one-year old, needed medicine. Four days had passed since Don Tomas had left. A ride into town, to save the boy, wouldn't hurt. Tomas would do the same for him if he had a son.

Mexican Joe's cigar ash fell on his lap. He brushed it to the office floor. Someday he should sweep the office out.

There were no fighting sounds anywhere around the rancho. Perhaps he was being stubborn too, for he wanted to go into town and escape the quiet. Dona Maria had told him to stay put until Tomas came home, but he assured her he'd be back. He saddled up and rode toward the pueblo.

He trusted that Don Tomas and Horace were safe. He prayed for them, the rancho, and his <u>vaqueros</u>. He prayed for all his friends and the sick child.

Joe noticed the army's roadblock up ahead. He didn't recognize the three soldiers. He stopped, as he was told. He took a good look around. The army men had three-day-old stubble and drank from whiskey bottles. They seemed gruff and hateful. Mexican Joe prayed again. He was close to town and could see the old Sanchez two-story adobe.

The army dragoons yelled at him and told him to dismount. He did.

"You Mex! That's a mighty fine horse. Where did you steal him from?" the sergeant in uniform said.

"He's mine," Mexican Joe said.

"Call me 'sir.' Damn Mex. Where are you runnin' from?"

"Sir, I'm the majordomo for the Sanchez Rancho. Don Tomas Sanchez employs me. He's the Democratic boss for the pueblo, and a councilman."

"Look, Mex, we don't need any trumped-up two-bit tellin' us how important he is. Look over there. We's already hung two like you." The sergeant pointed.

Mexican Joe gasped. Two men hung limply from dead tree

branches. These soldiers were drunk and determined.

"And we don't like no stinkin' Democrats neither," the sergeant said, weaving back and forth.

"Senor, wait a minute. Please hold on..."

"Shut up, Mex. You look like a Flores ganger to me. And you didn't call me 'sir'!"

"Sir, please... I'm trying to get medicine for the child," Mexican Joe explained.

"Shut up, Mex. Your horse is too fine, and your clothes look stole to me."

"Please, sergeant. I know all the men from the drum barracks, you know, Captain Goode, Lieutenant Johnson..."

Mexican Joe looked toward the pueblo, his eyes hoping to see someone he knew.

"We don't know them sons-a-bitches, and don't care. We're stationed at Fort Tejon. Who's the commander there, wise-ass Mex?"

"I don't know, sir. They do not visit my rancho."

"I got a damn new rancho for you, Mex, down below where you all belong," the rude sergeant said.

"No, no... not again." Mexican Joe pulled his shirt collar up toward his neck.

"What you doin' there, greaser? 'Again,' huh? Git off that horse," the sergeant commanded.

Mexican Joe started to dismount but felt the sergeant's impatient, dirty hands already pulling him down. The other two men tied his hands to restrain him.

"Look at your neck, you dirty Mex. Start sayin' your Hail Marys."

"It's a mistake!" Joe pleaded with the men.

"String 'im up, soldiers. He's escaped before. Ain't gonna this time. Nope. Time we make it right," the sergeant said, grabbing a swig from his whiskey bottle.

"Yeah, sergeant. Looks like a Flores bandit to us too," the corporal said.

"Bring me another bottle after you hang the Mex,"

the sergeant said, walking away. "Damn tough job being judge and jury." He laughed.

Mexican Joe felt the rope graze his scar and he started to weep. Ever since the last time, he'd felt doomed, like living a deathlike life. In silent fear he'd been waiting for this moment. For this reason he'd never had a wife, nor any children. Where was his savior this time?

He prayed. Tears flowed in prayer to Jesus and Mary. He prayed for the hangmen. He asked God to take his unfairly sentenced soul into His kingdom. Would the next life bring eternal happiness? He felt the rope tighten. He choked, "Here I come, Lord." He took his last breath of pueblo air.

Chapter 32

Horace returned to the pueblo the next day. He needed to be tested by Judge Dimmick and two other judges. He faced three grueling days to write his answers on seven specific law questions covering all four points of law. After his last day of testing, he felt good but tired. He walked toward the ranger barracks and saw Andreas Pico.

"Horace, Andreas Fontes made it to Baja."

"Too bad. Maybe we can go over and bring him back for trial," Horace said.

"Fontes was bragging how he beat me, 'old General Pico,' at a local Tia Juana bar. A fat old Mex rose, pulled his Bowie, and cut Fontes from ear to ear," Pico said.

"Is that right? Good. Something he said pissed off the big Mexican?"

"Yup. As he fell, the old Mex said, 'Name's Solomon, Solomon Pico, and you pissed me off messin' with my brother Andreas.'"

"Huh. Your brother stood up for family pride -- like a code of honor," Horace said. He wondered if Solomon would have won the ugly contest.

"He's still my brother, murdering... he can't come back here, but blood still runs thick in the Pico family."

"Somebody should tell Barton's woman her brother is dead."

"Lost 'em both, didn't she?"

"Yes. Sad about Mexican Joe too. We all loved him."

"That was the worst tragedy in the whole Flores mess. Sure devastated poor Tomas."

"I'll ride out tomorrow and give my respects."

"Please give mine too. How did your attorney testing go?"

"Good, think I'll pass. Should be able to represent the ranchos soon."

"We need you, Horace. I'll send you some business." At the barracks Horace saw a list of promotions. His name was on top. Wow. That was the good news he needed. He now was a brand new ranger lieutenant! The Flores campaign brought him the promotion. He wondered what Tomas and Andreas Pico would receive.

"Hey, counselor-to-be, you made it, Luie Bell," Roy Bean said.

"Frankly, Bean, it's been a great day today. Finished up the Bar test too." He had to help out Bean the next time he got a chance.

"Looks like you take command of C Troop next week," Bean said, twirling his moustache and hitching his pants.

"How about you let a new Luie treat you to pie and coffee at the café?" Horace said.

"Sure, Luie Bell, you son of ... I'd love a piece of apple pie and a piece of that Miss..." Bean said.

Horace rubbed his hair and put his hat back on.

At the café, Bean twirled a chair and straddled it.

"Horace, you look all beat up. That damn test, huh?"

"Yup, Bean, that and all those deaths Barton caused. Let's cheer up! I should really celebrate and cut loose!"

Paulette came to the table and said, "Congratulations, Horace, on the ranger promotion. How about the Bar? Oui or no?"

"Thanks. Probably..."

"Go ahead. Please, please go ahead," she pressed.

"A big oui!" Horace grabbed Paulette and hugged her.

"An attorney and a lieutenant! Well, my little Horace, things are going well for you now," Paulette said. Her eyes scanned him. Jacinto was sure a better match. Hands down, Jacinto was a winner.

"Yup, soon he's gonna have a license to steal all the land he ever thought about," Bean said, half kidding. "He can even git hitched to the lady of his dreams!"

Yes, Bean was right. Gosh, a few months ago he'd only thought about Paulette.

Judge Dimmick opened the door and slapped Horace on the back. "You did it, my boy! We all agree, Horace Bell, Los Angeles Pueblo's newest Attorney at Law," the judge said, gesturing with his hands as if he were hanging up a shingle.

"Thank you, judge, for your help," Horace said.

"Well, boy, for your first case I am giving you the Ballona Rancho grant. I'm just too darn busy, and Pico has the common council conned to have you to represent the Los Angeles Pueblo grant!" the judge said.

"That's grand!" Horace said. He had two big clients the first day. Ballona meant Jacinto too. The judge's wife had to be in on it; the family wanted him involved.

"Your Ballona clients want to see you tomorrow at the rancho. Plus, the city council meets tonight. It needs to make the selection formal," the judge said.

"Thank you again, Judge Dimmick, for all your assistance. Be confident I won't let your relatives down," Horace said.

"Nice old judge. I'd be just like him," Bean said as the judge left.

"Well, counselor, what is your desire?" Paulette said.

"Two pieces of your delicious apple pie, two cups of coffee - - hot," Horace replied.

"Good." She left for the kitchen.

"Okay, partner, what's on your mind?" Bean asked.

"When I get a handle on this, I want us to chase down Flores and Daniels and put an end to them," Horace said.

"They'll be in Mexico," Bean said, frustrated.

"Nope. Sanchez and I followed their trail by the Capistrano Mission. He felt they'd doubled back and headed into the Laguna hills to the north, not to the south."

"You think they'll hide out for a month or two, then go north to San Luis Opisbo or somewhere like that?"

"Exactly. They'll change their looks but not their lifestyle," Horace said, confident.

"We can follow the state sheriff's reports and see if similar crimes come poppin' up," Bean said.

"Sure enough, Corporal Bean. I'm recommending you for the next sergeant's job," Horace said with a smile.

"Pie time," Paulette said in her lightly accented voice, brushing her long brown hair back with her slender fingers. "Did you hear that the Democratic city fathers drafted Tomas Sanchez to run for sheriff and Don Andreas Pico for California State Assembly?"

201

"My God, Miss Bovierre, you know everything!" Bean said.

"Two fine men, two great heros. They'll make it," Horace said. Now he knew their reward.

"I've got my heros right here," Paulette flirted, circling them with her outstretched arms. The men smiled. She walked to the kitchen and said softly so they could hear, "And one is a brand new real estate attorney -- my attorney." She smiled. Horace saw her reflection in the window as she waved back to him.

Chapter 33

Horace rode out to congratulate Tomas on his candidacy for county sheriff. He couldn't ditch his deep feeling of loss for Mexican Joe. Something big and tender was missing, something whole was gone, and he knew what it was. Horace missed the spirit of Mexican Joe. He trusted it had broken free to heaven.

Tomas met Horace at the door and hugged him like a brother. Tomas, who'd heard from an eye witness, told Horace how the army had harassed Mexican Joe. They'd hanged him because he was a finely dressed Mexican on a first-rate horse. Horace heard how he'd been going to town for the baby's medicine.

They realized not a thing could be done, nor proved. They knew the truth. They looked at each other frustrated. Horace vowed to get both Daniels and Flores brought to justice. That was all he could do to somehow make it right. Flores had made himself only easier to hate.

Horace was glad to leave the rancho because the Sanchez family needed time to grieve. He looked forward to the familiar ride to the Ballona Rancho. He'd made at least ten visits to Jacinto, but nothing since the Flores incident. He had a lot to share with her.

Don Talamantes and Jacinto greeted him. The young Dona was elegantly dressed in the latest fashion, a long green dress with a slight show of her ample bosom. Mighty flattering. They sat down and discussed what was needed for proving up the land grant. The young Dona interpreted for her father, who spoke fluent Spanish and little English. Legal words were better for Horace in English. Horace noticed that Jacinto's Spanish word choice conveyed the complete legal burden. He appreciated her talent and saw how well it could work for him in the future.

After the discussion, the Don requested Horace stay for dinner. He accepted. Jacinto offered to walk him to the nearby specific metes and bounds listed on the original land grant for the Mexican government. She changed into a flattering walking outfit and led the way.

She stopped at the rancho's main water storage pond, a beautiful, secluded spot surrounded by green healthy trees. She took off her hat, opened her blouse a bit, and ran cool water over the top of her breasts. Her long, vibrant black hair caught the sun's rays. She tossed it back over her shoulders. Her brown eyes were bright with life.

"Horace, when I was young, I thought this was the most romantic spot on the earth. I dreamed someday to show it to a very handsome man. Now that is fulfilled," she said.

"Why thank you, Miss Jacinto. You too are one handsome lady."

"Gracias. You don't have to call me Miss. May I be so forward and ask, are you attached to anyone, Mr. Bell, I mean seriously?"

" I -- have a friend, might I not say -- I'm not promised yet. You caught me totally off-guard, Jacinto."

Horace weighed the possibilities. Paulette was comfortable, though a few years older than he. She was mature in her outlook on life and had looks and property. He was fond of her. Jacinto Talamantes held promise in many ways. Most of all, he thought he loved her. She had charmed him the first moment they'd spoken at the fandango. She would own a large piece of the Ballona Rancho as her dowry and inheritance. Many Americans would love to marry a Dona. The Dons encouraged their daughters to marry American attorneys. With the American legal system already in place, the Mexican culture appreciated having a lawyer in the family. Jacinto had looks too. She was young and innocent, yet refreshing. She was obviously interested in him.

Paulette and he had never made promises to one another. The quandary he faced was his own. Now that he was an attorney, didn't he want to move up in society? Were his prior relationships helpful or were they a hindrance? Did law make his ethics based more on the material? He knew it was a personal dilemma. Right now he wanted to kiss the available young lady in front of him.

"Now that you've thought about it for a few minutes, Mr. Bell, I'd like to look into your eyes," Jacinto said, provoking him.

She put her light-complected Spanish face next to his. Her perfume fused with the wild smells around the pond. Her eyes glistened in the sun's rays.

Her bosom was still wet when he grabbed her. Her two arms flew around him. Again he smelled the aroma of her Jasmine-flowered perfume. He kissed her, she kissed him. They kissed one another. He fondled her. He wondered if she would be his lover. He was ready...

Horace heard the thundering hooves of a galloping horse. The sound stopped at the edge of the trees.

"Lieutenant Bell!" someone yelled.

"Yes -- here I am," Horace said, annoyed and impatient. Her lips and perfume left their trace on his mouth. He still tasted them, and wished to resume.

"Horace, it's me, Roy. I found Poncho Daniels in Santa Maria," Bean yelled. Damn Bean. He'd screw up the perfect date.

"Sorry, Jacinto, duty calls. This is the bandit who rode with Flores. Promise. I'll be back and we'll finish this. Sooner the better," Horace said, flashing his lady-killer eyes at her. She got it!

"Si -- I know, my handsome knight. Just come back. Soon."

"I will. I promise," Horace said.

Now he'd promised. He wondered if he'd promise more. He was torn. Conflict raged in him. He had to sort it out -- Miss Paulette Bovierre and Dona Jacinto Talamantes. Thank God Daniels would now get all the conflict.

Chapter 34

Horace learned from Bean that the sheriff at San Luis Obispo had seen a Mexican troublemaker in Santa Maria who was causing problems for the Santa Barbara sheriff.

"Horace, the man in Santa Maria has a scar just like Daniels."

"Okay. And we know Santa Maria is a total Mexican town."

"Yup, and the one kinda damn place that son of a bitch would look for to hide out," Bean said.

"We gotta go, sergeant. That'll be him," Horace said.

They covered the many miles to the Mission La Purisima. Bean mentioned that Santa Maria was only ten miles away. Bean remembered the parish priest from San Gabriel's mission. He told Horace Father Jose was five feet tall and five feet around.

Father Jose greeted Roy with a bear hug. Horace saw his beer belly go up and down. They laughed and joked about Roy's Headquarters Bar that had kept Jose's parishioners intoxicated.

"That's so they could stand your sermons, pastor."

"Roy, you had them so drunk they snored and made me lose my place."

"No, Father, you couldn't keep your place because of all the sacred wine I kept givin' you for free. Buckets of it," Bean said.

Father Jose gave out a big belch, and a bigger belly laugh. Then they all laughed together.

Roy Bean asked Jose if any strangers were making trouble. Jose told them that a tyrant, Francisco Robles, had taken over Santa Maria. He had gold and was terrorizing the women after his drunken parties. Horace asked what he looked like. His general description fit Francisco Poncho Daniels -- his manner, his build, and his facial scar. Evidence of that scar pushed them onward.

Since Bell and Bean obtained special county deputy status, they left at first light. Santa Maria was a small Mexican village. Horace knew the married women would not like a tyrant. They asked two of them for the whereabouts of Francisco Robles.

They gladly pointed to a rundown shack with many whiskey bottles outside. Horace smiled. Some things never changed.

Guns drawn, they stormed in the front door. Two surprised nude Mexican women jumped up and tried to cover themselves. Roy Bean became distracted. He couldn't take his eyes off the one with huge breasts and large nipples. Horace saw the other one with smaller tits hit Bean on the head. Bean loved his damn whores.

Horace glimpsed Poncho Daniels, blocked by these naked women, laughing and running away. Horace watched as Daniels disappeared out the back. Then something hit him on the back of his head, and he went black.

They woke to find Daniels gone. They both had head lumps and headaches. They washed quickly for the pursuit. The married women pointed to the south.

They flew after Daniels down the coast. He was an hour ahead. Bean and Horace were tired. They rested an hour at Santa Barbara and resumed the chase.

The coastline soon made a half-moon shape. Horace yelled and pointed. They had just caught sight of him. Daniels was close.

Horace let Pal full out. Horace could feel the horse's power, his hooves flying across the sand flat out over beach water that sprayed as waves rolled in. Horace felt exhilarated. He loved the chase, the excitement, the ocean splash, the breeze, the wild aromas, and the glory. He could almost taste the honor.

Pal pulled way ahead of Bean's horse. He was closing the gap. Daniels now was only a few hundred yards away. Horace's body flowed smoothly to his horse's galloping beat. Soon it would be a gunfight, then perhaps hand-to-hand combat.

Horace readied. His head started to sweat. He told himself to be calm.

Horace saw the whites of Daniels' eyes at about a hundred feet. Daniels fired two rounds at him to no avail. Having the bullets whiz by made Horace sweat more. The third bullet pierced Horace's shirt. Damn. This was getting too close.

Horace got mad. "Get 'im, Pal!"

"Goddam ranger, I'm gonna kill you!" Daniels yelled as he

looked back. Not if Horace could get him first. Just then Daniels' horse tripped on a beach dry wood log. Head over heels, Daniels flew over the wet sand. His head hit another log. He splashed down unconscious.

Bean reined up a minute later. Horace pulled out his shirt, looking sad.

Roy Bean started to laugh. "Almost shot your sorry ass off that damn champion of yours."

"Yup, this one got mighty close. Tie 'im up, Sergeant Bean."

"How about we just do a little target practice and save the county court costs?"

"Love to, but this treasonous no-good would be better brought to court and made a public spectacle, don't you think?"

"Damn it. Guess you're right. If we try 'im in court and quickly hang 'im in judgment, that gits a message to 'em."

"Roy, we need to make the citizens feel good and end this thing right. They'll think we can handle anything."

Bean saluted. "Sometimes I feel you're bigger than life, Lieutenant Horace Bell, sir."

Chapter 35

Horace and Roy Bean rode into the Los Angeles Pueblo with Daniels. The whole town came out to watch. He'd been right to bring him in for trial.

The town vigilance committee was called immediately to meet. They brought Poncho Daniels to the Bella Union Hotel and held court. They took ten different witnesses. Each one testified to some specific felony they'd witnessed. The committee quickly decided Francisco Poncho Daniels' fate. Horace listened as they read the verdict. Poncho Daniels would be hanged until dead the following day. The vigilance committee wanted the entire town to see the infamous criminal go to meet his maker.

The members of the committee were also the city fathers and councilmen. They called a city meeting to order after the trial. Mayor Coronel called Horace Bell at the meeting to come forward. They passed a motion making him the pueblo's attorney to the Land Grant Commission Court. He now would represent both the city and the Ballona Rancho.

Horace packed his best suit and left the next day for San Franscisco. He rode to the San Pedro Harbor and boarded the steamship. He remembered arriving four years before, an excited, hopeful young pup. Now many of his dreams were realized -- he was an attorney, a ranger lieutenant, and city hero. He didn't want pride to get ahold of him. He still had much to do and think about, particularly his love life, his personal dilemmas.

Horace enjoyed talking to the ship's captain, Captain Haley's brother, and the passengers. When he saw Biggs, he said "good" out loud. He could get a haircut when the ocean settled down. Horace tolerated the swell, but it made his stomach weak.

"Hello, Mr. Biggs. What brings you on board?" Horace asked, noticing Biggs was dressed to the hilt.

"Well, Lieutenant Bell, how you doin'? Just bringin' in fifty house cats for San Francisco. They gots a terrible rat problem.

Mighty helpful for 'em."

"Hope you sell them right off and can enjoy the town a little."

"Thanks, my friend. I gots rid of my agent. He was ascalpin' me," Biggs volunteered.

"That way you get all the profit, and maybe a game or two," Horace said, winking.

"Yes, Lieutenant Bell, I do gets to enjoy a game or two. These cats will only bring fifty apiece, with the recession, you know."

In San Francisco, Horace saw the two-story elaborate Federal Courthouse. What an impressive building. The clerk calendared his cases. They called his cases two days later. Horace was well prepared with proof of both clients' deeds' authenticity. He brought evidence to a sufficient degree that satisfied the federal three-judge court. He received confirmation for both clients.

He was elated. He'd just earned over ten thousand dollars, a good five years' salary! Now he could set up an office and be a shingled and honored member of the Bar. Professionally, he felt great. He waited two days for the court writs, packed them for the trip, and caught the next steamship south.

Horace leased a small, furnished office at Second and Main Streets. Even a few pictures hung on the walls. His law books looked impressive on their shelves. Stylish Spanish red curtains hung from the windows. He smiled at the substantial, dark Spanish furniture -- brutal, hard, caustic ambience for his human frame.

Sitting at his massive desk, he worried about obtaining new clients. He planned to wait for the city council meeting the following day to present the confirmed land grant deed to the city.

Then his mind turned to love. He thought about Jacinto. He must deliver their deed. He rubbed his hair back. He thought about Paulette Bovierre. He remembered he always shared every achievement with her. Now he hesitated to tell her about his life's most portentous success. He could see his first pueblo love changing into friendship. Now the biggest thing was how could

212

he get this accomplished, move from love into friendship, without making an enemy. This was still a small town. And Paulette was loyal. Paulette he'd known for years, while Jacinto was the new Dona on his block.

His thoughtful daydream was soon interrupted. Jacinto burst into Horace's office. She was dressed in a bright red satin dress with black trim and bonnet to match. Her brown eyes danced all over the room. She took off her bonnet and swirled her hair around. Horace's eyes followed the swirling motion, and he smelled her lavish Jasmine perfume.

She boldly came right up to him. "Horace, I was in the pueblo and heard you've opened a new office. Jes -- how grand it is," she said, her eyes inviting him to kiss her.

He grabbed her hands, separated them, and took a step back. "Gosh, you look splendid, Miss Jacinto. I was just thinking of you."

"Now, aren't you the one. Always there with a pleasant compliment."

"I mean it. You're absolutely smashing. Also, I have something for you from San Francisco."

"Is it personal or business?"

"Business first."

Her eyes went to the floor. She looked sad. Horace could see her heart was more important than her rancho. My, what a woman.

He opened his desk drawer and pulled out an official-looking deed with a four-inch embossed gold United States Land Court seal on it.

Her eyes opened wide. She understood quickly what he was handing her. She changed in an instant from sadness to extreme happiness. He was impressed. Nothing would really get her down long.

"Oh, Horace, I do love you," Jacinto said.

She laid the deed on the desk and rushed him. Her arms flew around him. He kissed her. She kissed him with ardor. He couldn't help himself. A beautiful woman in a red dress, with her body pressed hard next to his, made him respond back. They kissed and kissed again.

Paulette Bovierre came in. She looked straight at them. Her hand rushed to her mouth. Her green eyes showed shock and they blazed at Horace. Then she turned on her heels and rushed out. Guess his decision-making process was relegated to history.

He kept kissing Jacinto. He was ready to make love to her on his desk. He stopped himself. Enough harm had been done to his friend Paulette. Perhaps she might even come back. Horace couldn't be sure.

"Mr. Horace Bell, could you do the Talamantes family the honor of joining us tonight for dinner?" Jacinto asked.

"Of course," Horace said. He needed to settle the payment for services, and even more important, see how serious he was about the romance.

"Five o'clock, then," Jacinto said with an assured smile.

Jacinto left. He combed his messed hair and went to the café for a late lunch, and judgment. Horace didn't like to leave unfinished business, or unhappy friends.   He wasn't overjoyed with his reception as he entered the café. Paulette glared at him over the other two businessmen. He speculated she might drop a pot of coffee on him.

"Lover boy, how can I help you today?" Paulette asked loudly and cooly.

The businessmen both looked over and smiled. One quietly mentioned to the other -- a lover's spat. They nodded.

"The special, please, Miss Paulette," Horace said sheepishly. He felt like a caught-in-the-act love convict.

He was glad when the men left. She had embarrassed him, as she meant to. She served him and walked away. Her eyes showed hurt and distrust. He rubbed his hair back and finished his meal. Tomorrow was another day. That night Jacinto would be waiting at the rancho to meet with him. Dinner would definitely be more fun than lunch.

Chapter 36

Horace left early for his dinner date at Jacinto's and arrived on time. Jacinto volunteered that dinner would be served in an hour. Horace asked her for a walk in the cool night air. Walking around the rancho buildings for the second time, Horace noticed how well it was laid out.

"Horace, I want you to know that I first saw you the day you came to town," Jacinto said.

"You saw me on the stage, four years ago?" Horace asked, his eyes wide.

"Jes. I was with my father at Don Wilson's store. I watched you go into the café."

"You did? Why tell me now after three months of courting?"

"I walked up and saw you through the window. I thought you were the most handsome man I've ever seen, and I want to hold no secrets from you," Jacinto confessed.

"Do you still feel the same?" Horace asked.

"Jes. Even more. But I saw the way you looked that day and today when the café woman came in."

"How's that?"

"Back then you were smitten with her. Today I do not think she's that important to you. Am I right?" Jacinto was going straight to the point. Horace had to make his decision right then or harm this fragile relationship. Above all, he had to be truthful.

"I went to the café for lunch. I did not talk to her -- she isn't that important, you are right."

"Good. Then what do you think about us?"

"You'd make a good partner, friend -- lover -- my, aren't we being candid."

"Jes, my dear Horace. I want to be forthright from now on. That way you know how I feel about you."

"Yes, I do, my sensuous Jacinto. And I love the way you are. I really do."

She almost jumped into his arms. They held each other

215

tightly. They kissed as if for the first time.   Horace felt more than smitten. He might actually be in love. Yes, he was in love, and she was too.

She stole him back to her special spot by the pond. On a large flat boulder she became very hot sexually. Soon they were past kissing into serious petting.

Her mouth was delicious. She was perfect to kiss, even better than Paulette. He wondered what she would be like to make love to.

"That's our dinner bell, Horace, my love," Jacinto said, reacting to the loud clang. "Now you get to see the whole family again."

Horace felt a little uncomfortable, but when she grabbed his hand and led him back to the casa, he knew where he belonged.

Chapter 37

Horace smiled at his land grant case board on the office wall. Two cases won, he'd brought in five new ones that week.

Paulette told him she still loved her Frenchman and that she could never trust Horace again. Sadly, he realized that old flames never made good friends. He vowed he'd stay civil to her regardless.

Roy Bean burst into the office. He was excited.

"We got 'im, Horace -- Juan Flores -- on the Simi Rancho, just north!"

"Before I change clothes, Sergeant, who's the informant?"

"One of his old gang got liquored up at my Headquarter's Bar last night..."

"Go ahead, tell me." Horace was impatient. He could only go if this was a good lead. The law office was much too busy for a vacation.

"I says, 'How do you know it was him?' to the dirty Mex," Bean said. "He said, 'Remember Big Red and David Boe on our ship? Flores made me tie 'em up with dem rocks and throw 'em overboard. He kilt 'em. Flores calls himself Juan Robles now, he does.'"

"Deduction on four points, Roy. One, only a handful know about the escape ship. Two, few were on it. Three, Robles is the same name Daniels took. And four, liquor frees the tongue! Let's ride, Sergeant!"

"Luie, spoken just like a damn attorney!"

They rode the fifty miles to the Simi Rancho and talked to the majordomo. Horace had researched the Gaudalasca property previously, a neighbor which bordered the Simi, his client. The rancho was enormous and included one hundred thousand acres.

"Tomas Sanchez, my wife's relative, has fondly talked about you, Lieutenant Bell. How can I help you?" asked the majordomo.

"We need to quietly find a Mexican named Juan Robles, possible new hire this year," Horace said.

The majordomo had three hundred men employed, plus five

hundred Indians for room and board. Bean's eyes bugged the size of a twenty-dollar gold piece as he watched the man look for the name. He twisted his moustache while Horace rubbed his hair back.

Then the majordomo cried out and covered his mouth.

"I found him."

"Where is he?" Horace asked.

"Ya, where is the damn Mex?" Bean interrupted.

"Hold on. Is he a renegade?" the majordomo asked.

"Yes, maybe he is, and Don Tomas Sanchez will always be indebted to you for the assistance," Horace said respectfully.

"Juan Robles works the lone area in a cabin by Mount Pinos. Few miles from Fort Tejon. He's on loan to my brother on the San Francisco Rancho up north."

Fort Tejon was thirty miles from the Simi Rancho. White trails of snow snaked down Mount Pinos on all sides. Horace and Roy rode briskly and watched their horses' nostrils flare as they sent out whiffs of hot steam into the freezing night air. Each hoof step crunched the harsh ground. Sweat froze on the men's foreheads. Their eyebrows were white with frost. They looked expectantly ahead for the warmth of the fort.

The soldiers would be helpful. They were the same ones that worked the Juan Flores uprising. They had guarded the pueblo's roads. "Unfortunately, probably the same ones that hung Mexican Joe," Horace said grimly to Bean.

Snow was still on the ground at the fort. Horace and Bean left their horses for tending and warmed their hands at the pot-bellied stove. Horace was acquainted with the major from a city function. The major listened and explained to his three soldiers the importance of their mission. He then directed Horace, by map and words, to the specific cabin on Mount Pinos. They left at first light.

"Damn, must be ten degrees," Bean said.

"Yup, just like when I almost got this bandit back at Calavaras County," Horace said.

Still hating the cold, Horace led them forward. They rode five miles in snow as high as the horses' knees.

They found the suspect's log cabin. Ice was everywhere.

218

The five men secured their horses outside. It was near three in the morning when they burst into the cabin door with guns drawn. They'd all been asleep -- five guns on five surprised men. Bean was right. The infamous Juan Flores stared through the darkness.

Chapter 38

Flores had his hand next to his gun. The damn Indians had scared the shit out of him in the Santa Anas. Since then, he'd kept his gun in the sleeping bag. Someone yelled in the cabin. Flores shook his head to wake up. Dreamed, did he? No. Still groggy, he saw a blue-coated soldier with a revolver in the cabin. The door was open. A cold wind bit into his face.

Oh shit! Through the moonlit window he saw the same Ranger -- Daniels called him Bell, maybe? -- the same one that whacked him before. Some other goddamn ranger yelled again. Now Flores heard him.

"Put your hands up, Flores!"

"Hey, no comprende. What? I'm half asleep, man." He played dumb. He needed time to escape again.

"Put your hands up, Mex!"

A soldier sprang in front of him. Good, dumbshit. Flores whipped out his gun. Bang! Someone left at the sound of his gunfire. Two soldiers jumped toward him. He shot both in the head. One soldier fell, then the other two. Maybe with luck he could get out of this shit trap alive.

Flores saw a shadow hurling toward the door. Bang! His bullet hit flesh. Flores narrowed his eyes to see his well-aimed chest shot. He heard the man groan as he hit the icy ground outside.

"Bean, I'm hit! Cover the door!"

"Horace, I'm comin'. I'll cover you."

Flores saw his four Mexican roommates run out the door. The shots scared them. The room smelled like a big Mexican bean fart mixed with gun powder.

Flores made an evil grin. Completely dressed, he grabbed his jacket and cut in front of the last Mexican. He boldly sprang on an army horse, looked at the men on the ground, grinned, and said nothing. Swiftly kicking the horse, he escaped. One minute later he vanished over the mountains.

Flores figured the ranger would help the other one, giving him twenty seconds. Damn he was good and lucky. Twice he'd tricked the devil and gotten away. He wasn't going to give them a third chance.

He planned for a warmer climate. God, he hated the damn mountains. He only stayed there to lay low for a few months. He wondered how they found him. Damn rangers. They always crept right up his ass. He'd push to the west, follow the coast, and be drinking mescal down in Tia Juana before the week was up.

He remembered the damn pine trees from Calaveras County. God, they were even worse now. He needed never to see snow or pine trees again.

He pulled his jacket collar over his ears. Jesus, the night air was cold. These mountains chilled his bones. He was tired, dirt tired. A warm woman would be nice, one with class, a high-bred Spanish beauty, one still young. Maybe a virgin? He needed to violate her, get it in deep so that he fired his rocks off. He'd show them once and for all how easily he could desecrate their territory. He'd get even with the high-and-mighty Mexes and the damn Yankees too. He'd scare them all to death.

He remembered a beautiful woman galloping by the ocean just below Malibu -- her red riding outfit, the red scarf, her jet black hair blowing back -- and that face, so like his wife's. What a face it was -- so fair, so Spanish, like a goddess. He could never have a woman like that again. He'd have to take her, force her, and have fun.

Maybe he'd find her. She was perfect. And she was on the way to Mexico.

Chapter 39

Flores led the horse down the mountains to the Santa Clara River. A day later he was on the coast going south. That would trick them. They'd think he'd gone through San Francisquito Pass toward the pueblo. He took the long way, but it had water and damn warmer air.

He was sure the rangers were pissed. Flores laughed. He'd picked off three dumb eager-beaver dragoons. Damn -- he hoped that never-give-up ranger died there. He was becoming Flores' worst nightmare. He'd found Flores twice. He'd escaped twice too. Good. Taught his ass not to mess with Juan Flores. That ranger was dead meat, bought and paid for, if he ever saw him again.

Flores found the mesa where he'd first seen the high-Spanish beauty on horseback. He made camp on the beach. A few hours later, a <u>vaquero</u> approached and dressed him down. Flores acted scared. The <u>vaquero</u> dismounted. He took Flores' actions for weakness. Flores sprang up, turned on him, and held a knife against the <u>vaquero's</u> neck. With specific questions, Flores grilled him about the young Dona. The <u>vaquero</u> told him about Jacinto and the rancho casa. Flores severed his head, picked it up, and threw it down the beach. The blood poured out across the sand. Flores watched as finger waves lapped at the decapitated head, then larger swells grabbed it and rolled it in and out with each set.

The Indians had a game they played with a ball and sticks. Back and forth they went, just like the waves.

"Idiot! Never mess with Juan Flores!" he sneered, grinning. "I'm invincible!"

Her name was Jacinto Talamantes.

He stopped far enough away to watch the casa. At late afternoon, he couldn't believe his eyes. There she was -- young, beautiful. Jacinto Talamantes would soon be his to ravage and take. He could choose his time. He was the hunter, she was the prey.

She rode alone toward a large circle of trees. He waited for a minute and trailed her.

She sat by a large pond profuse with water lilies. The setting was a perfect romantic place for her violation. He tied his horse and sneaked up on her like a coyote after a rabbit. She didn't even turn as he knocked her out.

He put her on the large flat boulder. He took off her clothes -- first her blouse, then her underclothes. What a great set of tits. He just played with them and watched for her to awaken. He pulled off her riding pants. Boy, what a good set of legs and...

She lay before him entirely naked. He took in the sight of her white body. He was sexually excited. His manhood stood out.

He tied her hands together, then poured pond water on her face. She woke up and tried to scream. He stuffed a piece of her blouse in her mouth. It cut the noise. She kicked. She fought like a damn tiger. He tied her legs down. Her eyes glared with fear. He told her to get ready.

He mounted her, took her three times. She moaned, she cried; she was going crazy. She mercifully passed out. He splashed her face with water again to bring her back. She moaned. She avoided looking at him but finally did with her pleading brown eyes.

His knife was already out. "They never gave my wife no mercy, so you don't get none," Flores said.

She started to choke from the cloth. He pulled it out and told her if she screamed, she was dead.

"I won't -- just let me go. Anything you want..."

"I wanted my wife, that's all."

His eyes turned to a gray, glassy look. His face held no conscience. He took his one-foot Bowie knife and cut her throat from ear to ear. Her life blood poured out on the garden pond rock. "Bitch!" he said.

Chapter 40

Tomas Sanchez was the newly elected sheriff. He was called to investigate Jacinto's murder. The sight of the young woman, his rancho neighbor, once full of life, made him throw up his dinner. He was simply outraged. He had seen death his whole life, but this was vile, brutal murder. He had selected Roy Bean to accompany him to save Horace the knowledge and pain. First Mexican Joe for Sanchez, and now Jacinto for Horace. Horace had told Sanchez he loved her.

"Sheriff, over here," Bean called.

"What have you found, Roy?" Tomas asked.

"The horseshoe print in the damp earth here. God damn it, look," Bean said.

"Good God. They're all stamped USA."

"That means the murderin' son of a bitch was in the U.S. Army. Or was Flores on that stolen horse?"

The majordomo walked up. He had a sack with a vaquero's head in it. He told them that the horseshoe markings were exactly the same he'd seen. Now there were two murders. Damn. The majordomo had tracked the prints ten miles south. The killer had to be headed toward Mexico.

"Horace'll be ready to ride in a few days," Bean said, his eyes piercing, watery and angry. "This makes more vengeance for him," Tomas said, his eyes cast to the ground. "Sergeant Bean, you track him as good as you can. I'll tell Horace and send a squad to back you up. Get going, my friend, and for God's sake, be careful."

Chapter 41

Horace was in his office. He planned to have dinner at the Ballona Rancho the following night and ask for Jacinto's hand in marriage. His body ached. The pueblo doctor had yanked out Flores' bullet from between two broken ribs. A huge black-and-blue bruise surrounded the wound. Wrapped in bandages, he felt confined. After tomorrow, he'd try to locate that damn Flores. Gosh, it hurt just to move.

He looked at his ticking clock. Seven o'clock at night.

Tomas walked in. Tomas' eyes greeted the floor. Something was wrong. He looked like death warmed over.

"Hi, Tomas. Gosh you look perplexed. Anything wrong?"

"Yes, my friend. I've just come from the Ballona Rancho." Tomas broke, then he wept.

Horace grabbed him. God, it really hurt to move.

"Tomas, it's me -- Horace. Is Jacinto all right?"

"It's so hard --" Tomas sobbed.

"Just tell me, please?"

"Jacinto, my neighbor for twenty years, that lovely, beautiful young woman, was murdered! Horace, she's dead!"

Horace drained of strength. Shock turned to dizzy tears. Not Jacinto! He forgot his wound pain. His heart agonized. He felt a forever scar upon him, like Mexican Joe's scar. Damn, this was a rough life.

Tomas held him and wept. Horace had lost his wife to be. His whole life would change. Jacinto was perfect for him. Now she was no longer.

"Tell me how, Tomas. How..."

"We know Flores stripped her, tied her up, raped her several times... slit her ear to ear with his knife."

Horace gasped.

"Roy and I saw the U.S.A. horseshoe prints. He killed a vaquero too. We know it's Flores. The tracks led to Mexico."

Horace's eyes opened wide enough to cover his whole face. He drained to a deeper white, then flushed bright pink with anger, building to brilliant red revenge. He brushed his hair back and wiped his eyes.

"Don't say one more word, Tomas. Please go home and comfort Maria. She needs you now."

Horace put his closed sign in the window. He went to his supply room, struggled into his riding clothes, and came out dressed.

"Horace, you can't... you aren't well enough," Tomas said.

"Honestly, Tomas, this isn't about the pueblo. It's not about the one hundred and sixty dead. No, my sheriff, mi amigo, ranger partner, this damn thing is now <u>personal</u>. He killed my future wife, and that <u>son of a bitch</u> is going to die. I'll get him no matter how long it takes. I swear it on Paul's and Jacinto's graves!" he said, his eyes wet with determination. Tomas walked with him and Pal to Thompson's corral.

"Bean's on Flores' trail. Do you want your squad to follow?" Tomas asked, looking up at Horace in the carriage. Pal was tied alongside it.

"Roy is as pissed as I am, Tomas. Our passion would only be hampered by my squad. Months might pass until we find that <u>despicable</u> coward."

"Maria and I will pray for you and Roy. Please, Horace, if you can bring Juan Flores back for yourself first, and me second."

Chapter 42

Flores quickly left San Diego. A stranger, who looked like a ranger, had arrived. Flores made sure he didn't see him or his new companion in town. Esteban Contreres was his new sidekick. Contreres rode with him at the mission. Flores told him that he, Contreres, must be blessed because Los Angeles let him go. Stupid gringos. They captured the criminals for felonies, then they had to prove up their crimes.

They rode for the Rancho Tia Juana. He still kept his army horse. The damn animal was strong, and he liked the payback. The border was twenty miles.

Flores liked having Contreres for a companion. Contreres once tried to escape from the pueblo jail. Barton caught him and almost beat him to death, and it took him months to mend.

"Loved it when Barton got his," Contreres said.

"This is where Pico killed Fontes," Flores said.

"We'll stay away from that fat greaser Pico," Contreres said.

Rancho Tia Juana seemed different than the Mexican-American ranchos. They moved spider webs when they entered the office. Flores saw old newspapers on the floor. The kitchen sink moved with roaches by the hundreds. The adobe walls were lined with thin ant stripes that ran up, down, and sideways. The dirt floor was a huge ashtray. Old cans of half-eaten beans lay deserted on the floor. Flores now felt comfortable; he felt at home.

Flores grinned. He recognized the majordomo from San Quentin. Damned if he wasn't released months before his breakout. The majordomo hugged Flores as an old friend. They'd shared the unspeakable.

"I'm Pedro. We slept in the same dorm."

They laughed about the raw fish and the lice, their rags crawling with vermin. The rocks... oh, those damn rocks. They broke and carried those rocks until their hands bled. The two commiserated about the duly-departed. Flores told him about all the dead in the revolution. Flores felt good about his new home and friend.

Pedro told Flores and Contreres that he was in command and that the owner stayed in San Diego. He offered Flores a foreman's job on the east side away from everyone. Contreres and he would stay at the line shack. These positions had become available last week when two got drunk and dead in Tia Juana.

Flores glanced at Contreres. Contreres' eyes were wide. Flores got the clear warning.

The shack was three miles out. Together they pushed open the ramshackle door. The shack was worse than the main casa. The door moved the trash two feet deep on the floor. The window had been used as the ingress and egress. Months-old food stuck to old pans. The week-old vacancy had encouraged a half-dozen scorpions and thousands of red stinging ants. Dirty rags served as mattresses for the four rickety wooden beds. The place stunk of dog shit mixed with trash.

"My, Contreres, looks like home," Flores said.

Contreres laughed. "Better than nothin', but not much. I'll clean it up."

"I'll find us something to eat."

"Too bad the dog ain't here or he'd be dinner."

Flores shook his head and left. He came back with rabbit for dinner and rattlesnake dessert. Contreres fired up the outdoor Spanish oven.

Flores looked at Contreres. "You smell like dog shit and piss."

"I'm gonna splash in the river. Thank God it flows to the ocean."

"You'd smell even worse if we camped on the ocean with all the turds floating west."

"I'd probably drown in shit."

"Aren't you hungry?"

"No, amigo. Just need a bath and a good night's sleep. Damn scorpions almost got me," Contreres said, slapping his pants. He tore off his clothes and ran for the river.

Flores looked inside the shack. Contreres had cleared most of it out. The fifteen-foot-square hovel was home. They had a roof, two beds, an oven... what more did they need? In time the stink would dissipate.

Flores felt insulated. The rangers would be hard-pressed to find him, and Pedro would be quiet. The best part, they were in Mexico, an unfamiliar, foreign country to the gringo.

Chapter 43

Horace ached from more than one source in his body. His ribs killed him, but his whole being missed his lovely Jacinto. He longed to touch her, wished to talk to her, to no avail. She was in another dimension, a spiritual one on which his father had preached countless sermons. Memories of his boyhood days and of Jacinto's eyes full of life juxtaposed like hot and cold rods into his soul. One day he'd face his mortality. He hoped to put Flores there soon.

By the time Horace arrived in San Diego, his overworked emotions stopped close to logic. The carriage springs had failed to dull each bump and bang in the hundred-mile trip. The pain from it all made him tough. Pain and purpose dulled his mind to the loss.

Horace pulled up at the hotel. He needed a drink and sleep. Tomorrow they'd be on Flores' trail.

Horace wasn't surprised to see Bean waiting for him at the bar.

"Horace, this must be a real tough one on you."

"Real bad, Roy. How can we find this cowardly bastard?"

"The bartender told me a Mex fitting Flores' description left yesterday with a local named Esteban Contreres," Bean said, twisting his moustache.

"Bartender check out?"

"Sorry, Horace. He's a special sheriff's deputy, one of ten."

"Good. Which way, if I couldn't guess?" Horace asked with a forced grin.

"Yup, down to old Mexico. I was waitin' for backup."

"It's here. Let's leave tomorrow."

"Rangers got any friends down there?"

"Maybe, but I don't think we could call him a friend. More like a problematic relative."

Bean eyebrows came down. "How's that?"

"Let's see tomorrow."

The next day they arrived at a hole-in-the-wall they called a cantina in Tia Juana. They ordered a beer. The water was even more putrid than the Zanja Madre in L.A. A gruesome Mexican near three hundred pounds, his skin lined and aged like old leather, approached with a scowl on his face. Horace saw hands like bear paws. "I think this is our relative. If all fails, we shoot it out here," Horace said.

"Some friend! I'd rather have an enemy!" Bean choked.

"What are you two stinkin' gringos doin' in my town?" the big Mexican said.

"Andreas Pico sent us to bring back the killer of his young and precious Goddaughter," Horace said.

Horace couldn't appear intimidated. He was going on pure blood feelings and family pride.

Bean twisted his moustache with both hands. Horace took off his hat, laid it on the table, turned the other way, and winked at Bean. Bean's eyeballs almost popped out.

"Keep your damn badges hidden. I'll help out my brother Andreas Pico any way I can. You name it," Pico said.

"Good," Horace said, turning back.

"Name's Solomon Pico. These five banditos are my gang here."

"Name's Bell, Horace Bell. My partner is Roy Bean."

"Jacinto Talamantes' murder, real sad. Heard about it," Pico said.

"Yes, it is," Bean said. Horace tried to act unaffected but had to wipe his eyes.

"Solomon, have any strangers, one or two, passed by going south?" Horace asked.

"Not here. Jorge, ride south and check with Roberto in El Descanso. Pronto!" Jorge jumped on his horse and galloped south.

"Is there anyplace they could hide around here?" Bean asked.

"Not really. They have to come out to eat or work, right?" Pico asked.

"Any old San Quentin discharges living around here?" Horace asked.

"Me and my five men. We killed the rest. Let's see," Pico said.

234

"Great question, you dumbshit!" Bean whispered to Horace.

"Oh, jes! The majordomo at the Rancho Tia Juana was there too," Pico said.

"How many places, barracks, casas on the Tia Juana Rancho for the <u>vaqueros</u>?" Horace pressed.

"Main casa, a real pigsty, shit everywhere, not much more. It's a huge rancho, Senor," Pico said.

A gang member whispered in Solomon Pico's ear.

"Wait. Pedro said the two bastards we killed last week lived at the rancho line shack six kilometers east," Pico said, continuing. "The two assholes called me a fat prick, so we cut theirs off and made 'em eat 'em."

"Fine," Horace said. He tried to keep his composure.

"Could one or two of you show the way there? It's best to go tonight, real late."

"For Andreas, my blood brother, and my blood Goddaughter, we will all go past darkness," Pico said.

The rider came back from El Descanso. No one had passed there in a week. Roberto had killed the last couple.

"Great place you've found us," Bean whispered.

"Calm down. Your pecker's still attached," Horace said.

Bean looked down and fright went over his face. He covered his private area with his hand. Horace smiled.

Probably more afraid losing his whores than anything else.

Pico came to the hotel around midnight. All seven men rode to the line shack in the dark. The full moon gave light. Animals, small and large, moved from the men breaking the overgrowth. They left their horses with one man and crept in slowly. They surrounded the shack.

Horace and Pico entered the shack first. Each one knocked a man out with his gun butt. The rest entered and carried the men outside. The moonlight told the truth. Horace felt peace. Flores was in custody.

Contreres woke before he was tied and grabbed for his boot knife. Solomon Pico saved Bean's life by shooting the man five times. The bullets started at the head and went down, hitting the man's bones from head to waist. He fell dead.

Horace thanked Pico. Bean almost kissed Pico, but thought

again.

Pico asked Horace if he wanted Flores dead too. Horace said he'd promised Solomon's brothers, Andreas and Pio, that they could hang him. Solomon Pico, with family honor, said, "Vaya con Dios, mi amigo." Solomon and his gang left.

Horace now had to face his hate and pain. He could kill the son of a bitch right then and there. He wanted revenge. Paul and Jacinto were gone from this life forever. To move from hate to logic... the conflict was overwhelming. If he killed Flores, hate won. If he brought in the despicable demon, Horace would save himself -- he wouldn't become like Flores.

Right was right. Tomas Sanchez had begged him to do the right thing. The good part was knowing that the Pueblo de Los Angeles would use the law and hang Flores.

Horace decided. He shared with Roy Bean what they had to do. Bean agreed.

"Just glad we didn't end up like those guys who lost their peckers in wonderful downtown Tia Juana," Bean said. Flores woke the next morning. He was on his stolen army horse riding belly down. Ropes secured his hands and feet. He moaned and groaned with each step. Horace held him by the hair and gave him a drink.

"Well, you bastard, you'll get a fine welcome in Los Angeles."

Flores' eyes glared back at him. He did not say a word. Horace let go. Flores fell back in the stomach position over the saddle.

They entered the pueblo. People were everywhere. Shouting occurred. Men fired their guns in the air. People screamed with joy. Shopkeepers closed their shops and walked along. Everyone wanted to be part of bringing the worst criminal in Los Angeles' history to justice.

Horace looked back and saw four hundred citizens walking lock-step behind. He smiled, seeing his decision confirmed.

"Horace, I was just going to mention..." Bean said.

"No, Roy, not that damn glory thing. Let's just enjoy this for what it is, a final finish of the Juan Flores gang!"

"Yup, he ain't gonna get away, even if I put him in irons

with me."

"Mark my words, Roy, they'll hang this murderer today."

"Or we will, right?"

"Right."

Chapter 44

Horace pushed Flores off the horse into the street in front of the Bella Union. Horace saw the city fathers forming a vigilance committee right on the spot. He took off his hat and rubbed his hair back.

Paulette ran up and kissed him on the cheek. "Oui, you are some man, Horace Bell," Paulette said. She'd missed him.

Bean undid Flores' leg bindings. Bean pushed and kicked him into the committee hearing. Sanchez grabbed Flores at the door and led him to the table in front of the committee. Horace watched as the witnesses took a few minutes each. The evidence against Flores mounted: the German shopkeeper's horrible death; the insurrection against the American government; the murder and mutilation of Sheriff Barton and his deputies; other murders, including Horace's loved ones.

Soon the mayor and fellow rangers decided a judgment of conviction. The Committee of Vigilance unanimously concurred. The penalty was to be decided in a minute. All agreed.

The mayor stood up and addressed the crowded makeshift courtroom. "The defendant, Juan Flores, the convicted murderer and bandit, will be hanged by Sheriff Sanchez until dead in four hours, at five o'clock sharp." Everyone cheered. Pandemonium broke out. Guns fired. Drinks were on the house, and it became a huge party.

Horace listened as the mayor told Tomas, "We'll hang him on John Gollier's Wagon Shop entrance. No need to spend money building a gallows. Scoundrel needs to be hanged quick!"

Horace agreed. Sanchez congratulated him for bringing Flores in alive.

Paulette walked up to his side. He wondered if he should try again. No, he'd grown away from her. An outstanding, shapely woman, she deserved more, someone just a little older. Her five to six years on him would always work against him. His ego needed a better match. She still loved the Frenchman anyway.

239

The whole thing was moot. Why even think about it.

"Horace, how about a cup of coffee and a piece of pie?" Paulette asked.

"Sure." Horace motioned Bean to stay away.

The two sat at the café table. The place was empty. She looked at him with her green, blazing eyes. Horace read those eyes. She played with her long hair, twisting it in her fingers, waiting.

Horace thought for a long time before he talked. He wanted no more emotional problems, for himself or anyone. He lost his young love and didn't want to restart an old love. Horace still cared for Paulette. He just didn't feel the urge to reignite the relationship. The feelings were still there, though.

"Paulette, how have you been?"

"Fine, Horace. A little bored. Not much fun here."

"Any news here?"

"Not good. A number of bankruptcies. You know the rest. Money is real short. Still no bank in town. I think we're in a depression, Horace. But the good news is you -- and Flores."

"They'll hang him in a few hours, and then the whole Juan Flores gang is finished."

"Your law business will grow, Horace. People will remember you as a hero for years. You'll have a fine career."

Horace looked at her wanting eyes, beautiful, sparkling green eyes. He almost felt like... Gosh it was hard to stay composed.

The door opened and Roy Bean walked in. He took a chair, turned it around and straddled it. Thank God.

"Hi you two," Bean said.

"Hello, Roy, my other hero," Paulette said. Roy smiled.

Horace was lost again in thoughts of Jacinto -- her wonderful brown inviting eyes, her kiss, her aroma, her trim body, her youth lost – her death. His was a death of love's innocence.

Chapter 45

Flores looked out the jail yard toward where they would hang him. He looked back at his life and felt the finality. Soon he would not listen to anyone on earth. The priest had arrived two hours before, and he made his peace with God. He asked forgiveness for all his many sins. He and the padre discussed his future spiritual life. Flores felt some peace.

At 4:45 p.m., Sheriff Sanchez walked a shackled Juan Flores toward the gallows post at the Wagon Works entrance. Dressed in white pants, a light vest, and black merino sack coat, Flores was somber. His neck twitched to the right every few seconds. He faced his death knowing he deserved the penalty. He prayed each step with the priest.

Around Flores three hundred citizens jeered. The dragoons with the cavalry stood by when Flores was allowed to climb the three wooden boxes. The spiritual guide let him climb on his own. The citizens became quiet. They wanted to hear what he would say, if anything. When the sheriff tied his arms and placed the noose over his head, he expressed a wish to say a few words. The committee leader granted his wish. Horace walked out from the café to hear him speak.

"I am ready to die. I have committed many crimes against you. I hold no ill-will against any of you, and I hope you hold no ill-will against me. I now ask for a blindfold and to leave my body to anyone who wishes to give me an honest burial. I am ready to die."

Tomas Sanchez covered Flores' head with a handkerchief, pulled the boxes away by horse, and Flores fell. His neck broke and he was dead. No more cheers, no more party. The end had come to a vicious criminal and the end of a major gang.

Horace felt no hate or remorse for Flores. He didn't feel anything at all for Flores. Though his loved ones were in another world, he would grow from this because he still belonged in this world. Somewhere, someplace he'd find another love. But he'd never forget the love he had for Jacinto Talamantes and how her life was cut short, way too short for him.

Chapter 46

Horace and the others nearby were quiet afterward. He felt the winds of change blowing into the pueblo. Yes, it had grown. The small town had almost tripled to five thousand mankind now. His practice would grow too. He had grown wiser.

He looked next to him and watched Paulette, her lovely smile, her strong backbone. She needed someone more mature than he. Yes, she was also part of history, his past history. Horace needed a future.

He wished he hadn't been such a young idealist, but he was in love with the conquest -- something higher, more moral, more noble, and with more honor. He loved his town, his state, and his country. What next? Yes, he asked, what was next?

"Horace, how about we take a ride tonight?" Paulette asked.

"Paulette, maybe some other night. Right now I'd like to go home and collapse."

"Oui, some other time. I'd like that, Horace."

Horace could see that she was still interested. He felt like a ball she could play with from time to time.

She loved someone, and he was across the ocean and in love with someone else. She couldn't have him. That was why she'd come to the pueblo. Horace loved someone he couldn't have in heaven. He understood.

Horace walked Pal toward home, his head down.

Tomas Sanchez ran up to him. "Horace, have you heard about Andreas Pico?"

"No. I hope it's not bad?"

"Good news. He's been elected to the State Assembly to represent the pueblo, and they made him the General for the entire State of California Civil Defense."

The news revived Horace's spirit. He had reason to believe in the future.

"Horace, what are your plans now that Flores is dead?"

"The ranchos still need a good attorney to protect them. I haven't lost a case yet before the Land Grant Court."

"I just received a land grant summons, Horace. I wondered

if you could represent the Rancho La Cienega O'Paso de la Tijera?"

THE END

About The Author

Born and raised in the Los Angeles area, I was a policeman, a sheriff, and a marshal. I graduated from the Los Angeles Police Academy in 1967. Back in 1974, I was allowed unlimited admission into the private A.B. Perkins Historical California Scholar Library at the main L.A. County Depository in Valencia, CA. Then and there I found a lifelong passion for California's historical past.

I hold a Masters Degree in Business Management from the University of Redlands, and taught Police Science Classes at Long Beach City College. . I have written The Los Angeles County Sheriff's Badge History. Also, I was contributing author of Centurion's Shield - The History of the Los Angeles Police Department. My memberships include International Police Historical Society, and I sell an internet book called Badge Hallmarks for Police Collectors. I have owned and managed two court reporting corporations for twelve years. I am now researching and writing the sequel novel.

My immediate family has accumulated 100 years as Los Angeles peace officers. My father and my uncle (our neighbor) were Los Angeles policemen. My grandfather joined the Los Angeles Sheriff's Office in 1929 after service with the Huntington Park Police Department.